SHY GIRL

WARNING

Despite its deceptively cute cover, this book is not a lighthearted romp. This is a story with quite disturbing content, including explicit depictions of gore, psychological manipulation, physical abuse, kidnapping, and body horror. If you picked this up thinking it is a quirky, feel-good horror read, consider this your warning: it's not. This book dives deep into the visceral, the raw, and the unsettling, and while it might keep you turning the pages, it will also leave you squirming and linger in your mind for days. Proceed with caution.

SHY GIRL

Mia Ballard

Copyright © Mia Ballard 2025

The right of Mia Ballard to be identified as the Author of
the Work has been asserted in accordance with the
Copyright, Designs and Patents Act 1988.

First published in 2025 by Wildfire
An imprint of Headline Publishing Group Limited

1

Apart from any use permitted under UK copyright law, this publication may
only be reproduced, stored, or transmitted, in any form, or by any means, with
prior permission in writing of the publishers or, in the case of reprographic production,
in accordance with the terms of licences issued by the Copyright Licensing Agency.

All characters in this publication are fictitious and any resemblance
to real persons, living or dead, is purely coincidental.

Cataloguing in Publication Data is available from the British Library

Trade Paperback ISBN 978 1 0354 3792 4

Lines from Sylvia Plath poem 'Elm', published in the collection *Ariel* © Faber & Faber

Collar illustrations © FreePik/Kalyanchesnokov

Typeset in Bembo by CC Book Production

Printed and bound in Great Britain by Clays Ltd, Elcograf S.p.A.

Headline's policy is to use papers that are natural, renewable and recyclable products
and made from wood grown in well-managed forests and other controlled sources.
The logging and manufacturing processes are expected to conform to
the environmental regulations of the country of origin.

HEADLINE PUBLISHING GROUP
an Hachette UK Company
Carmelite House
50 Victoria Embankment
London EC4Y 0DZ

The authorised representative in the EEA is Hachette Ireland,
8 Castlecourt Centre, Dublin 15, D15 XTP3, Ireland
(email: info@hbgi.ie)

www.headline.co.uk
www.hachette.co.uk

To the girls who bite back

> "*I am terrified by this dark thing*
> *That sleeps in me;*
> *All day I feel its soft, feathery turnings, its malignity.*"
>
> —'Elm' by Sylvia Plath

PROLOGUE

I wear a pink dress, the kind that promises softness and delivers none. Its tulle is brittle and sharp, brushing against my fur like a thousand tiny teeth, a cruel lover that bites with every move. Every scratch keeps me in place, a reminder of what I am: a pet, a thing shaped for looking, for praise, for command. The bows on my pigtails pull too tight, yanking the skin and stretching my head into something neat, into something pleasing, a quiet violence made beautiful. White socks climb my legs, their frills delicate, a whisper of innocence over the bruises beneath, the ones he says shouldn't happen if the socks are there—but they always do.

The ache is low and rhythmic, a second heartbeat in my ribs, steady and insistent, the kind of pain you get used to until it becomes part of you. Then the door bursts open, and he enters like a storm, dragging the sour stink of liquor behind him, his presence filling the room and turning the pastel air brittle. In his hands is a cake, gleaming, its pink frosting too smooth, like plastic dipped in sugar, like something that belongs on a screen, too perfect to hold.

White piping curls at the edges in tight loops, crafted for someone better, someone not me. Across the top, in delicate cursive, it says: *Happy Birthday, Shy Girl.* He crouches low, sets the cake on the floor, his grin stretching too wide, his teeth sharp, a predator in party clothes.

"Surprise," he says, his voice cracking the silence like glass. A birthday. Mine. Time here doesn't have edges; it drips and folds, days bleeding into years, into nothing at all. Birthdays don't make sense to me anymore. But the cake is real, and it's in front of me.

I lower myself, fur brushing against the stiff fabric of the dress, and crawl forward. My snout dips into the frosting, the sweetness rolling over my tongue, thick and sticky, a flood that chokes but insists on being swallowed. Beneath the pink gloss, the cake falls apart, crumbling into ash that coats my teeth, hollow sweetness that fills me with its nothing. Still, I keep going. Lick. Swallow. Lick. Swallow. His laughter cuts the air, sharp and jagged, a sound too big for the room.

"Good, isn't it?" he says, his voice slick with liquor, his amusement curling like smoke. "You're welcome, girl. Do you love me?"

I lift my head slowly, frosting clinging to my fur, sticky and pink, streaked like a brand. I meet his eyes and shape the only answer I've been taught to give.

"Woof."

It comes out low, a blade cutting through the sweetness. He laughs again, fuller this time, his delight spilling out and smothering the air, the kind of laughter that doesn't leave room for anything else.

"That's my girl," he says, his hand heavy on my head, stroking the fur like he's soothing a loyal animal. But his touch binds more than it soothes. His voice dips, soft but sharp, a knife wrapped in velvet. "Happy birthday," he says.

I lower my head again, back to the cake. The frosting clogs my throat, its sweetness sticking, refusing to let go.

Lick. Swallow. Lick. Swallow. The dress scrapes. The bows pull. The bruises pulse beneath my fur, matching the rhythm of the breaths I take without control. This is who I am now. A pet. A shape carved by someone else's hands, a thing devoured piece by piece, until there is nothing left but obedience, the quiet, and the hurt. Until hurt is all that remains.

ONE

I never thought I'd end up here, standing on the edge of a decision that feels both ridiculous and inevitable. It's like staring at a box with DO NOT OPEN: *Bad Decisions Inside* stamped across the front, already knowing my hands will tear at the lid. Already knowing I'll pry it open just to see how bad it can get.

I'm broke—not the latte-skipping, tightening-the-belt kind of broke, but the hollow, all-consuming kind. The kind of broke that eats away at your insides, makes you question the shape of your morals, smooths out the edges of what most people call acceptable. Desperation doesn't crash down all at once; it seeps in, quiet and steady, until you're choking on it, gulping for air. It tastes like shame. It tastes like I'm letting down not just myself but everyone who came before me, all those ancestors who clawed through history just to get me here, just to watch me drown in a mess of my own making.

But it didn't start with money. The cracks in my life began long before that, a slow fracture widening over time. It started years ago, when my mother left. I was six. I still remember her—her hair, black and glossy like a crow's wing, the smell of lilacs and cigarette smoke that lingered even after she was gone. She used to braid my hair, her hands quick and firm, pulling tight enough to make my scalp hum. Tight enough to feel like permanence, like something solid that wouldn't come undone. But permanence wasn't her thing.

One day, she packed a suitcase big enough to hold forever and walked out the door.

I sat on the steps, knees tucked to my chest, waiting for her to come back. I don't know how long I waited. Long enough for the sky to darken, long enough to learn she never would.

My dad stayed, but in pieces, in fragments that didn't add up to enough. He worked double shifts at the factory, his hands calloused and streaked with grease, his breath sour with whiskey. He wasn't mean, just absent in ways that mattered. By ten, I was walking to the corner store to buy groceries because he wasn't sober enough to do it. He'd shove a crumpled twenty into my hand and mutter, "Knock yourself out, kid."

By twelve, I knew how to keep the lights on. I'd call the electric company myself, the numbers on the back of my dad's credit card memorized and rolling off my tongue like a prayer. They never asked why a kid was calling, never questioned the small but mighty voice on the other end of the line. They didn't care. As long as they got their money, the lights stayed on.

Numbers became my refuge. Clean, sharp, dependable. Numbers didn't leave. They didn't get drunk. They didn't walk out with a suitcase or come home reeking of liquor. I was good at math—better than good. I built my life on it, a fortress made of equations, algorithms, sharp corners and clean lines. It was a promise: if I could just be precise enough, exact enough, maybe I could keep the chaos at bay.

Accounting seemed like the logical path. Safe. Boring, but safe. I built my life around spreadsheets and formulas, around the certainty that numbers didn't lie. Until they did. The mistakes started small—a decimal in the wrong place, a column misaligned. But they grew. Missed deadlines. Angry clients. I'd stay late, rechecking, triple-checking, running my fingers over the same rows and cells as if the answers might change. My boss didn't care about my rituals, only the results. The pressure built, and my precision cracked under its weight.

Eventually, I was fired. Unemployment is its own kind of hell. Rent. Bills. A parade of due dates I couldn't outrun. My brain gnawed at the problem as if it could chew its way to a solution, turning it over and over until every angle was frayed. Borrowing money felt like begging. Job applications felt like flinging darts in the dark, the targets moving further away with every throw. What I needed wasn't politically correct—I needed something that was immediate. Radical.

That's when I remembered the TV segment, the woman with her flawless hair and a life draped in silk, funded by men old enough to be her father. Sugar daddies. At the time, I'd laughed at the absurdity of it, the glossy fiction of her ease. But now? Now it felt like a possibility.

Could I do it? Should I do it? The questions spiraled into

equations: risks divided by rewards, costs subtracted from benefits. My brain, desperate for a foothold, clung to the math.

I didn't look the part. Long legs, sure, but paired with a flat chest and hips that refused to curve, a body that felt like a compromise. My hair, wild and black like my mother's, defied every effort to tame it, springing back no matter how much I pulled. My face was "quirky," which is what people say when they mean not beautiful, but just interesting enough. Still, surely someone out there had a niche for girls like me.

I researched obsessively, the way I always do. Forums, reviews, spreadsheets comparing platforms. I settled on SDForMe.com—just reputable enough to feel safe, just sleazy enough to feel possible.

Signing up felt like undressing for an audience, each question pulling at my seams. *Describe yourself.* I stared at the empty box, the truth hovering like a weight: broke, anxious, spiraling.

Instead, I typed: *Ambitious. Curious. Open to new experiences.*

A lie, but a convincing one.

Next came the stats: height, weight, ethnicity. I hesitated before selecting "mixed race." It was true, because my mother was half White, though I thought of myself as just Black. Still, I had just enough lightness in my skin, just the right type of hair, the right type of hobbies, the right type of demeanor that people in college used to call me "Oreo." I hated it, resented it, but ignored it all the same. What could I say to that anyway? *Thank you? Fuck you?*

Then came the preferences: age range, income level,

generosity. I adjusted the sliders like I was tuning a machine, trying to manufacture the perfect equation, one that balanced survival with dignity.

Finally, the photos. My awkward selfies glared back at me like evidence of failure. I analyzed them until I hated every angle, every shadow, until even the ones I could tolerate felt like betrayals. I chose a few that didn't make me wince and uploaded them anyway.

When I hit submit, my chest tightened. I slammed the laptop shut and stared at the wall, the enormity of what I'd just done pressing down on me like the weight of a stranger's gaze. My brain, relentless, looped through its litany of questions: *What if no one responds? What if someone does? What if this spirals out of control? What if it works?*

The questions clawed at me, but the numbers were louder. Rent. Bills. The unrelenting weight of what I owed and couldn't pay.

I'd opened the box. All I could do now was wait to see what spilled out.

TWO

The next day, I dress with purpose. A white turtleneck, pressed slacks, and a leather jacket that hugs my shoulders just right. Small gold hoops slide into my ears, neat and forgettable, the kind of thing no one second-guesses, on which no one will focus. My hair is pulled into a high bun, tight against my scalp, clean and contained. In the mirror, I see someone who might pass for important, for brave.

Kennedy will lose it when I tell her. I'm the responsible one, the rule-follower. The one who color-coded the grocery list, who double-checked the tip at dinner, who carried an umbrella on a sunny day just in case. My life has always been defined by borders, neat lines I never crossed.

I've known Kennedy since college. Kennedy lives without borders. She's messy, vivid, radiant. Her phone was always missing, her lipstick always smudged, her nights long and full of strangers for whom she never felt the need to apologize. Somehow, it's always worked for her. She has a husband now, a garden overflowing with basil and kale, a dog that barks at everything, and a two-year-old named Liam, who laughs so hard his whole body shakes. She exists in sharp, bright colors.

Me? I exist in grayscale. I am thirty, alone, and unraveling quietly enough that no one's noticed. Yet.

The bistro smells like roasted garlic and fresh bread. The windows are wide, the kind that let the whole street watch you eat, and the tables are small enough for it to feel like the people next to you are in your conversation. Kennedy is already there when I arrive, her dyed platinum-blonde bob freshly cut, slicing clean across her cheekbones. Her lipstick is red—not just red, but *vivid*, the kind of color that demands attention and gets it. She waves when she sees me, her movements large and confident, like she's pulling me into her orbit.

One time, Kennedy and I sat in this same spot and watched a man get tackled by two officers for flashing some women walking by. He was wearing nothing but a long coat and looked like he was on meth. He clumsily ran from the cops only to be caught right away and when they tackled him to the ground, his trench coat had ridden up and you could see his flat white ass. Kennedy laughed so hard she spilled her drink, a gin and tonic that soaked the useless little cloth napkin they always put in front of you, the lime wedge sliding off the table and onto the floor.

"This place is never boring," she'd said, her voice loud enough for the horrified couple next to us to stop mid-sentence and look over.

We sit. The menus are comically oversized and it smells faintly of citrus polish in here. A glass of white wine appears in front of her, golden and shimmering, while I stick to water. Kennedy orders a salad; I say I want nothing to our waiter who is so alien-like handsome he takes my breath away. Kennedy doesn't ask what I want to drink. She already knows I'll stick to water.

She leans forward, her elbows on the table, her energy pressing into the space between us. She's waiting, her smile soft but expectant, the way someone smiles when they know there's a secret and it's only a matter of time before you spill. Her voice is light, casual.

"What's new, Gia?" she says, the question landing heavy despite its ease.

I trace the edge of the menu, feeling the ridges beneath my fingers. The words sit in my throat for a moment before I let them out. I tell her. Not all of it, not the depth or weight, but enough for her to understand. Enough to shock her.

Her expression shifts, quick and electric. Surprise, amusement, something else I can't place. Her glass of wine hovers near her lips, her head tilting slightly as she watches me like I'm an equation she hasn't solved yet.

"Seriously, Gia?" she says, incredulous. "You?"

Her laugh breaks the space between us, warm and loud, a sound that should make me feel lighter but doesn't. I straighten the glass of water in front of me, aligning it perfectly with the edge of the table. The reflection ripples, the surface broken by a tremor I don't want her to notice.

I speak again, quieter this time. I tell her about the research, the precautions. How I've read every review, how I've weighed every risk. "I've thought this through," I say, defensively. "I've even made a list of potential risks and how to mitigate them."

Kennedy blinks, her mouth curving into a half-smile. "Of course you have," she says, her voice softer now, almost fond.

The space between us feels heavier, filled with something unnamed. She leans back in her chair, studying me from a new angle, her glass clicking against the table as she sets it down. When she speaks again, her tone surprises me. There's no judgment, no sharp edge. "Just . . . be careful," she says. "I don't want to have to come rescuing you."

The words loosen something in my chest, enough for a laugh to slip out. It spreads through me like warmth, faint but steady.

The bistro hums around us—clinking silverware, murmured conversations, the dull thrum of ordinary life. The moment folds into itself, settling between us. When we part, I don't feel lighter, not exactly. But I feel less alone in the weight of it, and for now, that's enough.

THREE

Back home, my life folds itself neatly into the borders of its routine. The front door locks first: one turn to the right, a pause, then back left to check, and right again. A ritual, a trinity of assurances that no one will enter without permission.

My shoes come off next. They align themselves precisely by the door, their heels touching and toes angled just so, forming a triangle of calm. The symmetry pulls me back to myself. I exhale, a long, slow release of air, as though I've been holding my breath all day.

In the kitchen, I retrieve the meal I've assigned to Tuesdays: a roasted chicken breast, a half-cup of steamed broccoli, and a neat, compact mound of white rice. The microwave is set for one minute and forty-five seconds—never more, never less. The seconds tick down with an unbearable slowness, each beep of the timer reminding me that even the smallest things follow rules.

I eat standing at the counter. My feet are planted shoulder-width apart, grounding me. Each bite is chewed with purpose, a steady rhythm—ten presses of my teeth before swallowing.

My jaw moves like a metronome, keeping time in the stillness of the kitchen.

When I finish, the plate is rinsed immediately. I slide it into place among others in the dishwasher, the fork and knife laid parallel, each slot in the silverware rack an invitation for order.

Then, the couch. The remote feels cool and solid in my hand as I press power. *The Golden Girls* theme song hums through the living room, warm and familiar. This is when my brain finally quiets. The canned laughter is impersonal and safe, cushioning my thoughts like a pillow pressed gently against my face. Two episodes—exactly two, no more no less—before I rise, like clockwork.

The workout comes next. Thirty minutes with resistance bands, the motions as repetitive as dinner: pull, release, pull, release. My body works mechanically, but my thoughts continue their relentless loops. The overdue rent. The follow-up email for a potential job I sent two days ago that hasn't been answered. The job applications scatter across cyberspace like confetti thrown into the void.

Afterward, a shower. The water is nearly scalding. My skin blooms pink under the spray, and for a moment, I feel real. It reddens my skin, burns the surface, makes me feel tangible in a way I need. The soap I use smells of lavender, but it's the heat that matters, the way it makes the world shrink to just this—just skin, water, and the steam that curls like a second body around me. The towel is folded when I finish, its edges even as I drape it back over the rack. Lavender lingers faintly in the air.

This is when I usually crawl into bed for my nightly cry. It is not the dramatic kind. There are no sobs, no gasping for air. It's quieter than that: measured, like a leaking faucet. The tears come slowly, silently, rationed as though I fear one day they'll run out. I wipe them away with the edge of the pillowcase, careful to keep my breathing even, the act as much a part of my routine as brushing my teeth.

But tonight, instead of reaching for the tissue box, I reach for my phone.

The red icon of SDForMe.com lights up the screen, a small glowing symbol of the choice I made. My thumb hovers for a moment before I press it, the app opening to reveal two messages. My first messages.

The first is from Nathan. He is forty-eight years old. I like that number, the roundness and evenness of it. His profile picture is a curated kindness: salt-and-pepper hair, a smile that suggests he is safe, dependable, boring.

His message is polite, almost clinical:

`Hi, Gia. I'd love to meet you for coffee sometime. Let me know if you're interested.`

I reply quickly, my fingers moving before I've had a chance to second-guess:

`Hi. Thank you for the message. I'd love to meet for coffee sometime. :)`

The smiley face is purposeful. Flirty, but not desperate. I press send. My chest tightens immediately, the weight of crossing a line I can't uncross settling heavily in my ribcage.

The second message waits, its subject line deceptively casual: **Hey, beautiful.**

I hesitate, then tap it open. My stomach drops. The profile picture loads slowly, and when it does, I see a man older than Nathan, with thinning hair and round glasses. He looks like my father. My actual father.

I close the message without reading further, my hands trembling. The delete button feels like a lifeline, but even after I press it, the image stays burned into my brain.

I used to think about killing myself as if it was something I might get around to eventually, like folding laundry or cleaning out the fridge. Not in a big, dramatic way—not the kind that you dangle in front of a therapist to see if they'll flinch. It was quieter than that, more practical. A passing thought, casual and constant, like a low hum in the background, like a draft slipping under a door.

One time, I lined up a bottle of my prescription Xanax on the bathroom counter. Popped off the childproof cap, tipped the pills out into a neat, glinting row. The little white tablets gleamed under the light, each one a promise of nothingness. I thought about swallowing all them, one by one. I imagined the ritual of it, the finality. But even then, I hesitated. It felt messy, unpredictable. What if it didn't work? What if I just ended up in the hospital, hooked up to tubes, everyone looking at me like I was a failed experiment?

I couldn't bear that—being alive, but worse.

That thought was worse than dying, so I put the pills back in the bottle, screwed the cap on tight, and tucked it back into the medicine cabinet. Left it there like a secret, something I might revisit later.

That was years ago, before I got fired. Having my job helped with those thoughts. It gave me rules to follow. People relied on me. Deadlines, spreadsheets, a reason to set my alarm. It gave my life the illusion of structure, and I clung to it like a raft in open water. It held me up like scaffolding.

But the job was a mask, not a cure. It hid the cracks, but didn't fix them. I've been depressed far longer than I've been unemployed. The firing just stripped away the pretense, left me raw and exposed, with no one for whom to perform. Now, the pills are still in the cabinet. I know exactly where they are, tucked behind the expired cough syrup and half-empty bottle of Advil. I don't think about overdosing on them as much anymore. Not because I don't want to disappear, but because I don't trust myself to do it right.

I set the phone face down on the nightstand, its glow extinguished, but the tightness in my chest doesn't ease. I lie back and stare at the ceiling. The tears come, hot and slow, carving tracks down my temples. They pool in the hollow beneath my jaw, heavier than usual, but quieter, somehow.

Tonight, the tears feel different. They are not despair, not hopelessness. They feel like something else entirely—something sharp and terrifying, carving space for whatever comes next.

FOUR

The next morning, my fingers reach for my phone before my eyes fully open, before my lungs expand completely with their first breath. The screen wakes with a small vibration, casting a faint glow in the dim room. Ten new messages.

I sit up abruptly, spine snapping straight as though this is an announcement I must honor. *Ten.* My heart flutters, light and quick, as I swipe through the notifications. I read the names first, letting each one settle in my mind, savoring the anticipation like peeling back the layers of a perfect fruit.

Each message is proof: that I exist, that someone sees me, that I am more than my diminishing bank balance or the lack of job offers in my inbox. For a brief moment, I allow the warmth of it to flood through me, but it doesn't last.

Reality creeps back in, messy and unwelcome. The mental list reassembles itself. Today, I need to apply for more jobs. Again. My cover letters have become mechanical, tweaked and polished until the words feel as if they belong to someone else. Five months of unemployment, and my savings account is a wasteland, the numbers dwindling as the days stretch forward with no relief. My rent is now three days overdue.

I exhale slowly, setting the phone down, its screen facing up, the messages lingering on the edge of my vision. In the kitchen, I begin my breakfast routine. The oatmeal is measured: one-third of a cup of oats, water poured to the exact line on the measuring cup. No milk. Eight blueberries are added one at a time, pressed gently into place with the back of my spoon, forming a perfect circle around the edge of the bowl. Symmetry makes it taste better. I've convinced myself of this.

The ritual grounds me, the steps calming in their predictability. The world outside may be chaos, but my blueberries are always symmetrical.

After eating, I return to the phone. My thumb hovers for a moment before scrolling, rereading the messages, prolonging the moment of being wanted. At the bottom, Nathan's name stands out, his reply almost instant after mine last night.

Are you available tomorrow afternoon for a quick meet by any chance? I know it's last minute, so feel free to say no, I understand. lol.

I read it three times. Four. Each pass sends a small jolt through me, a pulse of something unfamiliar—excitement, or maybe panic. The tone is careful, considerate. The "lol" softens the words, makes them feel less like a request and more like an invitation.

My fingers move faster than my thoughts. **YESD** I type, hitting send without hesitation.

The screen confirms it, the message sliding into the thread, and I see my mistake. The caps. The garbled letters. Wrong. Imperfect.

"Fuck!" The word escapes me, sharp and loud in the quiet of the apartment. My chest tightens, a familiar knot forming beneath my ribs as I type again, this time steadying my fingers with sheer will.

Sorry, dropped my phone and accidentally hit send. I meant to say yes, I'm available this afternoon to have a cup of coffee with you.

I hit send and stare at the screen, watching the words leave me again, hoping this time they are enough.

The phone buzzes again almost immediately, a tiny pulse of life on the kitchen counter. It's my father, and the screen lights up with the same flat, gray attempt at connection he's been sending for years.

Hey, Gia. Hope you're doing okay. Let me know if you need anything.

His words are antiseptic, sanitized, like wiping a bloody wound with a dry rag. I swipe the notification away without reading it twice. His name disappears, but the weight of it lingers, settling somewhere deep. He's been doing this forever, these little empty gestures dropped like crumbs on a trail he never plans to follow. And I used to eat them, thinking if I just gathered enough, they'd lead me somewhere that felt whole.

The last time I contacted him I was in the hospital four years ago, barely holding myself together. I don't mean that figuratively. I mean my body was shutting down, my insides clawing at me, fever rolling through me like waves in a storm. It started with this guy I met in college. His name doesn't matter because I hate him. He was the kind of guy who loved telling esoteric jokes and thought that made him deep. He loved pretentious films and dropping big words when not needed. He was extremely smart, and he was extremely dumb. He had a tongue ring, cheap and shiny, a prop in his performance of being different.

He went down on me often, said it made him feel "generous," like that was some kind of personality trait. The metal felt cold and strange, but I let him do it because it made him easy to deal with afterward. I didn't know the ring was flaking, tiny shards embedding themselves in me like splinters in wood, until my body rebelled. The fever came first, then the pain, deep and sharp, like something was trying to carve its way out of me. I dragged myself to the ER, sweat slicking my back, my head light and buzzing. The nurse took one look at me and called for a wheelchair. Inside, they hooked me up to fluids, poked and prodded, the air around me full of whispers and sharp questions that were embarrassing to answer. I was too far gone to care about dignity. When they asked if there was someone they could call, my brain went blank for a moment before his name tumbled out, unbidden.

Even as I said my father's name, I felt stupid. But there was this tiny, trembling part of me that still believed in him. I pictured him bursting through the hospital doors, his face flushed with panic, his arms ready to hold me, his only child. I imagined him sober for once, smelling of aftershave and worry, his voice cracking as he said, *I'm here, Gia. I'm here.*

Instead, he didn't even answer the phone. I lay there, hooked up to machines that beeped softly in the dark, while the nurse adjusted my IV and asked if there was anyone else she could call. It was two days later, after they'd scraped the infection out of me and left my vagina raw, when, finally, his voicemail came. His voice was thick, sluggish, dripping with whiskey.

"Sorry, kiddo," he slurred. "Got caught up. Hope you're feeling better."

That was the moment I stopped trying. I stopped waiting for him to be someone who cared enough to show up. Stopped hoping he'd be more than a drunk with a half-dead conscience. I didn't cry. I just stared at the wall until the nurse came back with discharge papers and a bottle of antibiotics and face that said, *You poor miserable girl. Alone in the hospital with an infected pussy and no family to visit. Tragic.*

Now, every so often, his messages come through, fragile little offerings that crumble as soon as I touch them. I don't delete them anymore. It's easier to let them pile up in my phone, like junk mail.

In my bedroom, I undress methodically. Each article of clothing is folded into a neat square, stacked neatly on the dresser. I sit cross-legged in front of the full-length mirror, adjusting the angle until it feels correct.

I stare at myself, my body, the hollowness of the space between who I am and who I'm trying to become.

I whisper to the reflection, a chant as steady as my breath. *"Nathan will respond to me soon."*

Again. *"Nathan will respond to me soon."*

The words are an anchor, holding me in place, keeping me afloat.

FIVE

My hobbies include cleaning, watching *The Golden Girls*, reading, and crocheting. That's what I write on my profile. It sounds safe, almost aggressively so, like a porch light left on to welcome someone home. I know it reads like a placeholder for a real person, like the kind of woman who blends neatly into the edges of your life without asking for more. On a regular dating site, it's probably tragic—one more soft blur in a sea of sharper, shinier options. But on a sugar-dating site? It feels like strategy.

It says: I'm simple. I'm boring. I won't cause drama. I'm the girl you pick when you want the luxury of forgetting someone exists between arrangements. I imagine a man reading it, scrolling past profiles full of curated cleavage and sunlit vacations, landing on mine like a sigh of relief. No neon signs. No fireworks. Just someone who'll hand him a sandwich and maybe crochet him a scarf before vanishing into the quiet corners of his life.

It's not that I don't have more to say. It's not that I don't have sharper edges. It's that I know how to package myself in ways men find manageable. I've learned to press myself into neat, soft shapes, to smooth over the parts that snag or bite. I'm the woman who remembers your mother's birthday, who folds your shirts just the way you like, who leaves before the silence turns heavy.

When I picture Nathan reading my profile, I imagine his eyes skimming over the words with the same kind of ease he'd bring to ordering lunch. Something light, something familiar, something that won't linger. I imagine him nodding slightly, satisfied. *This one,* he thinks. *She won't ask for too much.*

Right now, I'm working on a sweater for the man who lives in the park. He says his name is Turtle. Turtle has a permanent tan, the kind you get from existing too long under the sun without permission. His hair hangs in dark brown matted ropes down his back, and he almost never wears a shirt. He's thin but not fragile, with muscles that don't come from gyms but from the kind of uncalculated labor that keeps you alive. When he plays hacky sack, he moves like gravity doesn't stick to him the way it sticks to everyone else. I can't tell if it's grace or just indifference.

I haven't seen him for weeks. I figure he's moved on to another park, another city, the way people like him seem to move without leaving footprints. But today, there he is, right in the middle of the park. The sky is soft and overcast, the kind of weather that makes colors sharper, and he's barefoot in the grass, tossing the hacky sack into the air like it's a balloon, his silver arrowhead necklace that hangs off a piece of worn leather bouncing off his glistening muscled chest.

I sit on the park bench a few feet away, the unfinished sweater bunched in my lap, my hook working faster than usual. I am trying not to think of Nathan and what he'll say to me when he responds—if he even does—so I distract myself with Turtle. I watch him kick the hacky sack into the air, his movements languid and swift, and I crochet faster. The sweater isn't anything fancy—just a simple pullover in a shade of muted green that reminds me of a Christmas tree. I have no idea if Turtle will even wear it. I can't picture him in anything that doesn't expose his ribs to the sun. But it's something to do. Something to finish.

When the sweater is done, I slip it into a fancy black velvet drawstring bag and walk toward him. My legs feel stupid and mechanical. Turtle kicks the hacky sack with the side of his foot and catches it with his hand as I approach. His eyes are clearer than normal, the color of old pennies, and they scan me without judgment.

"Hey," I say, my voice too loud, the way it always gets when I'm nervous. "I made you something."

He tilts his head, his hair swaying like vines. "For me?" he asks, his voice slow, the words spread out like honey.

I nod and hand him the bag. He opens it, pulling the sweater out with long, dirty fingers, holding it up to the light.

"Whoa," he says, a grin breaking across his face. "This is . . . wow."

"It's nothing," I say quickly. "Just, you know, in case it gets cold."

He holds it up to his chest, the green fabric looking almost luminous against his tanned skin. "This is dope," he says, his voice warm. "I haven't worn a sweater in years. I didn't think I'd need one, but . . . yeah, this is cool. Thanks."

I shrug, trying to look like it isn't a big deal, but something about his gratitude feels bigger than the moment. He slips the sweater over his head, and it fits almost perfectly, the sleeves just a little too long, the way I like them. He stretches his arms out, letting the fabric settle.

"Fits like a dream," he says, spinning in a slow circle. "You should sell these or something. Make a fortune."

I laugh. "Yeah, I don't think the world's ready."

Turtle grins, his teeth beige and uneven. "The world's never ready for anything good," he says, kicking the hacky sack back into the air. I turn around to head back to my apartment.

Before Turtle disappeared, I would bring him sandwiches, ham and cheese or peanut butter and jelly wrapped in plastic, little baggies of chips, sometimes cans of Coke. I'd slip them out of my tote, trying not to look like I cared too much, and hand them over like it was nothing. Turtle always smiles, always says thanks, his voice loud and booming like sunshine. He sits cross-legged in the grass, pulling the sandwich out and taking slow, deliberate bites, like he's stretching the moment, savoring it.

"What's your name, girl?" he'd ask, crumbs clinging to his lips.

I'd tell him, and every time, he'd nod like it's the first time he's heard it even though I've told him several times. "Gia. Cool name," he'd say, and I laugh. My name sounds different when he holds it in his mouth. Like something exotic; like art.

He doesn't care about names, not in the way most people do. Names don't mean anything to Turtle; it's the presence that matters, the body in front of him, the food in his hands, the hacky sack bouncing in the air.

Turtle talks like a man who's seen the end of the world and decided it wasn't worth reporting. He stretches out his words, rolls them around like he's savoring the weight of them before he lets them go. His sentences twist in ways that don't always make sense, but I follow them anyway, like a dog chasing a scent it doesn't recognize.

Sometimes I'll say something ordinary—"The weather's been weird lately"—and he'll look at me like I've just handed him a riddle. "Weird is good," he says, kicking his hacky sack into the air, his bare foot arcing up like it's part of some slow, sacred dance. "Weird means the world hasn't gotten too comfortable. Comfortable is dangerous. Comfortable keeps you asleep when the house is on fire."

I never know how to respond to him. He speaks in riddles, and I don't always have the patience to solve them. But his voice is warm, laced with something quiet and knowing, like he's peeling back a layer of the universe and letting me see inside.

"Why do you keep bringing me food?" he asks one day, tilting his head as I hand him a sandwich wrapped in wax paper.

"I figured you could use it," I say, shrugging.

He nods, his dreads swaying like a curtain, and takes a bite.

"You're feeding the wrong part of me," he says, his words muffled by peanut butter and jelly.

"What does that even mean?" I ask, laughing despite myself.

He points to his head, then his chest. "This part's starving," he says, tapping his temple. "And this part's drowning." His hand lingers over his heart for a moment, his eyes clouding with something dark and distant.

I want to ask him what he means, but the moment slips away before I can grab it. He's back to his hacky sack, his body moving like the laws of physics bend for him, and I know he won't answer me if I push.

"Why do you call yourself Turtle?"

"'Cause everything I need I got on me. Everything I need is here." He pats his worn army-green backpack next to him, and then points to his heart.

Turtle doesn't believe in small talk. Every question he asks is a thread, and he tugs until he unravels something raw. *Why do you read so much? Why don't you have kids? What's the worst thing you've ever done?*

Sometimes I try to flip the questions back on him, but he dodges them effortlessly, as if he's been running from himself for years. I'll ask him about his family, and he'll respond with something like, "Do you think trees feel lonely in winter, when all their leaves abandon them?"

He makes me laugh more than I expect. I laugh not because he's funny, but because he's so thoroughly himself that it borders on absurdity. One time, he asked if I'd ever cried over a tomato.

"The heirloom kind," he explained, holding an imaginary fruit in his hands. "The kind that looks like it fought its way out of the dirt. It's beautiful because it's bruised, you know?"

I didn't know what to say to that, but later that night, I thought about it while I crocheted. About the way Turtle talks as if he's trying to explain the world in a language only he understands. About how his eyes get glassy when he stares at the sky, as if he's looking for something he lost up there.

He's smart, sharper than his appearance suggests. There's a darkness to him, though, something frayed and restless at the edges. I can see it in the way his jaw tightens when he thinks no one's watching, in the way his laughter sometimes catches, breaking apart before it fully lands.

"You ever feel like you're too heavy for your own life?" he asked me once, lying back in the grass, his hacky sack forgotten.

"Yeah," I said.

He nodded, closing his eyes against the sun. "Sometimes I think I'm carrying someone else's weight," he murmured. "Like I stole it by accident, and now I can't give it back."

I didn't know what to say to that, so I said nothing. We sat in silence, the wind brushing through the trees, and for once, it didn't feel uncomfortable. It felt like something we were sharing, something fragile and unspoken, like a secret the world wasn't ready to hear.

I watch him for a while longer, the sweater billowing slightly as he moves. Though Turtle isn't attractive—not in any conventional way—there is something about him that pulls me in. Maybe it's the way his long, chunky dreads hang down like roots seeking ground, or the sharp gaps in his teeth that make his smile feel lived-in, as if it's survived something.

Sometimes, late at night, I'd find myself thinking about him in ways that unsettled me. What would he be like in bed? The thought repulsed me, twisted my stomach into knots, but it also lit something low and smoldering, something I didn't know how to name.

Turtle could be a project, I told myself. Someone I could make better. I could clean him up, straighten his teeth, pull his life out of the dirt and make it bloom. But secretly, I think it was the other way around. Turtle, with his effortless grin and his sun-worn skin, his easy way of breathing through a world that hadn't been kind to him—he could make *me* better. He carried nothing but a backpack and the hacky sack in his pocket, and he radiated light. Turtle didn't need a home because he *was* home, in that loose, easy way I envied.

Maybe, I thought in my lonelier moments, I could be his home. The thought was ridiculous and fleeting, but it was mine. A selfish little fantasy I'd let run wild, just to feel its edges.

"Hey!"

I freeze, turning back around. His voice always had a way of stopping me in my tracks.

"Do you think this'll be acceptable to wear in California?" he asks, grinning, holding out his arms like he's modeling for a catalog. "I think I'm gonna make my way there tomorrow. Warmer outside, you know? Better for sleeping at night."

The words land heavy, like stones in my chest. My smile drops, but I force it back into place, flimsy and hollow.

"I'm sure you can wear it there," I say, my voice thin, barely mine.

His honey-colored eyes glint in the sun, bright and warm, as if the idea of leaving doesn't faze him at all. "Sweet. Thanks again, lady," he says, giving me a quick thumbs-up before tossing the hacky sack back into the air.

I stand there, my heart tangled in something I don't understand, something I don't want to name. The tears press hot behind my eyes, sudden and sharp, threatening to spill.

"Yeah. You're welcome," I say, the words trembling as I back away, my feet dragging, the space between us stretching like a thread about to snap.

Turtle turns back to his game, his body moving with that effortless grace, his dreads catching the light, the sweater I made for him hugging his skinny frame like it belongs there. I stand frozen, watching him, memorizing the way he exists, the way he fills the space around him without even trying.

I know that it would be the last time I would ever see Turtle, and the fantasy of us quickly falls away.

An hour later, his message comes through, the vibration rattling the coffee table like a pulse pulling me out of myself. My hand moves faster than my mind, snatching up the phone with a kind of reflexive hunger, the kind I'd stopped admitting but which I still felt. The screen glows, and there it is:

`Great! How far are you from downtown? We can meet for coffee there.`

I read it twice, three times, as though it's more profound than what it is. I tap his profile again, his main picture coming into focus: a placeholder white man with neatly cropped hair and a smile engineered to communicate effortlessness. The kind of man you pass in a park or a grocery store and immediately forget.

Except now, I don't forget. I notice the slight sag of his eyelids, the tension in his jaw, the tightness of his smile. The way his face looks as if it's been worked on, chipped away, sculpted into something just palatable enough to not scare away women. It's nothing extraordinary, but I let myself linger anyway, replaying the vague softness of his words in my head.

I type quickly, clumsily: `I'm not far at all . . . just an hour. I guess that's kind of far for most people, but I like driving.`

The lie comes out smooth, natural. I hate driving. I hate the way the road demands so much of you. I hate the lights, the traffic, the inevitability of being lost somewhere unfamiliar if you take a wrong turn. But I'm not about to say that. I hit send and watch the message dissolve into the thread.

Immediately, my stomach tightens. I refresh the chat, compulsive and frantic, as though my eagerness might force his response into being. Nothing. I refresh again. Still nothing. The silence stretches, unbearable and personal, until my brain conjures the worst: that I've said something wrong, that my eagerness has slipped through and left him cold.

And then, finally, the phone lights up again. His reply is short, almost dismissive:

`Haha ok then. Well, how about two o'clock at O'Malley's?`

I don't know O'Malley's. I've never been. But admitting that feels like a small failure, so I type back with urgency, my fingers moving too quickly: `I'll see you there at two!`

When the message sends, I toss the phone onto the couch like it's scorched, my chest fluttering with a dissonant mix of relief and panic. The room feels too small, too still. My body itches for release. I drop to the floor and start doing crunches, fast and hard, each movement biting into the muscles of my stomach. My skin feels tight, my breaths shallow, but I keep going until the ache becomes a steady rhythm.

When I stop, I'm shaking. My shirt clings to my back, damp

with sweat. I peel it off and step into the bathroom, the steam rising before I even turn the water on. I crank the heat up as far as it will go, the first scalding spray hitting my shoulders and making me gasp. The sensation burns, sharp and grounding.

I close my eyes and let the water batter my skin. But it doesn't wash him away. Nathan lingers—his face, his words, the careful restraint in his messages. I try to remind myself of the rules, the lines I've drawn in my head. This isn't about him. It's about money. About rent. About survival.

If he doesn't offer anything substantial, I will walk away. I say it to myself like a mantra. *I'll walk away.* But then the questions creep in, unbidden. What will it feel like to sit across from him, to watch him move in real time, to hear his voice? Will he be like the image I've built in my head, or something different? I have only known of his existence for one day and I already feel a strange obsession creeping in, settling deep in my bones.

I have a problem with men. I am either obsessed with them, or I want nothing to do with them at all, depending on the state of my life at that moment. Nathan goes into the obsessed pile.

Not so long ago it was Thomas. Thomas from work, Thomas with the long eyelashes and the clear baby-smooth skin, with the tiny Jewish 'fro that sat on his head like a crown. He reminded me of Michael Cera, or that other less famous guy that looks like Michael Cera. He wore messenger bags slung across his chest and sweater vests over collared shirts. He had brown eyes that looked too soft for someone in accounting and a voice that cracked sometimes when he got nervous.

We worked together for five and a half years, exchanging polite hellos and little else. He was the kind of guy who never said anything unless he was asked directly, and even then, his answers were short, just enough to keep the spotlight moving past him.

The text message came out of nowhere. It startled me because I hadn't given him my number. Then I remembered—the employee group chat where all of our numbers were listed, laid bare for everyone to see whether we liked it or not.

Hey, this is Thomas. I'm sorry you got fired. I was wondering why I hadn't seen you in a few days. Are you okay?

I stared at the message for a long time. Thomas had never shown any interest in me before. We'd exchanged maybe five sentences in all the time we worked together, and now, suddenly, he cared about my well-being? It felt suspicious, but also nice.

Oh. Hi. Yes, I'm fine. I sent it, then immediately regretted how stiff it sounded, like I was brushing him off when, in reality, I was curious—about him, about why he was texting me, about what kind of person Thomas was when he wasn't hunched over his desk like a tortoise in a sweater vest.

The reply came faster than I expected.

Good. Care to meet for a drink sometime?

It felt like a trap, but a kind one, wrapped in soft words and good intentions. I wondered if Thomas had always been into me, if he'd spent those years sitting in his corner of the office, watching me and waiting for his moment. Or maybe my sudden disappearance had triggered something in him. Humans are like that. Always craving someone when they're no longer accessible to us.

The thought of seeing Thomas at a bar made me laugh hard so I agreed to meet him for a drink a few nights later. He was waiting for me outside, looking nervous, his hands stuffed in the pockets of his slacks like he didn't know what else to do with them. He smiled when he saw me, a hesitant, lopsided thing that made my chest ache in a way I didn't want to examine too closely.

"I'm glad you came," he said, holding the door open for me. His voice cracked, just a little, and I thought about how much courage it must have taken for him to text me. I liked how it made me feel. I carried that feeling with me the entire night.

Thomas was endearing. That's the word I kept coming back to. When I thought about it, I had always found him endearing. He reminded me of Sunday mornings, of lemonade stands, of a doe running in a field of flowers. He was small and innocent. Like he's never had a real bad thing happen to him ever.

He pulled out my chair and asked me questions about my life as if he really wanted to know the answers. I liked the way he laughed at my jokes, even the bad ones, his shoulders shaking with a quiet kind of joy that felt private, like it was meant just for me.

We only dated for a few months, but I still liked him the best out of everyone. He sat with me in my storm, quiet and steady, as if he believed it would pass if we waited long enough. But I was afraid he'd eventually see through me, past whatever charm or wit I was holding up like a shield, and find out that, underneath it all, I was empty. I didn't want him to see that. So I left before he could.

In the end, I didn't know what to do with someone like

Thomas. Someone who wasn't trying to take from me, who wasn't angling for control or dominance or whatever it is most men want when they talk to a woman. He was just Thomas, soft and awkward and sweet in a way that felt dangerous because it made me want to trust him. The reality of it was that he was too perfect, and I was afraid. Thomas had this earnestness, this unrelenting goodness that made me feel as if I was being held up to some kind of light, one in which I didn't want to be seen. I was too morose, too nihilistic for someone like Thomas. Even though he never said it, I knew deep down he wanted to motivate me, to pull me out of the pit of despair into which I was digging myself deeper.

How many jobs have you applied for today?

A few.

You'll get one, Gia. I know it.

But I didn't want that. I wanted to sleep. I wanted to ruminate. I wanted to sink. And I couldn't stand the idea of him watching me do it.

Sometimes I think about where my life would be in the future if I had not ghosted Thomas. Married, probably. We'd have a quiet ceremony, no more than thirty people since both of us don't like too much attention. He'd cry at the altar, and I'd laugh, wiping my tears with a tiny, delicate handkerchief. Two very well-behaved children would follow, kids with his soft eyes and my Type A personality. The kind of family you see in Hallmark commercials, staged but serene, everything in its right place.

I used to think about him in the middle of the night. I'd imagine reaching out to him. A message, a call, something to tell him that I'm sorry, that he didn't deserve to be ghosted by me and that I was treacherous for doing such a thing, and that I've thought about him more than I wanted to admit.

But I let it go. Again and again, I let it go.

I don't have a type. Before Thomas, there was Joshua, a handsome Black gentleman I met on Tinder. I hate apps. I want to meet people the old-fashioned way, the way the good Lord intended before we started outsourcing our chemistry to algorithms—in coffee shops, bookstores, catching someone's eye across a crowded room and feeling that rush, that pull. But that night, I felt restless, frisky, like I'd been locked in a room with no windows for too long.

Joshua was a banker and liked old cars and old music, constantly raving about Prince and Jimi Hendrix and Tom Petty.

He was kind but casual, the kind of man who didn't prod. He didn't ask a million questions, didn't make me perform my pain or dress it up like it was interesting. But in bed he softened, opened up, as though touching another person gave him permission to touch something inside himself. I liked that about him—how there was a version of himself he only let out during intimacy.

It lasted exactly three months. All my relationships are short. Bright and burning, and then nothing.

I wasn't keeping track, I never do, but I know we lasted exactly three months because it was during the summer, and I remember the feeling of him fucking me while it was bright and hot outside, how wrong it felt, having sex with the sun still out. I remember how much he sweated on me and how much I liked it. It felt illicit, hot. I remember it lasted exactly from June twentieth to September twentieth and I thought *oh how perfect that is* how it took me exactly three months to find out that he had a kid. He didn't tell me; he let me find out when I searched his name and found his Facebook.

There were at least a dozen pictures of him with food, holding up giant sandwiches the size of his head, hovering over enormous plates of barbecue and sitting at hibachi-style restaurants, always grinning wildly, always ready to dig in. He was one of those men who thought liking food was a personality trait. I scrolled past those photos with my eyes closed. They weren't attractive, and I didn't want to lose my lady boner for him. There were more photos of him at family outings, snapshots of him on a boat with his boys, all shirtless and gleaming. I watched a video of him doing a backflip off the boat and into the water four times. Suddenly my lady boner for him was stronger than ever.

And then . . . a picture of him with a young girl, no more than six or seven. Their heads lovingly smushed together, both bright and beaming. I wasn't mad about the kid itself—I didn't care. I wasn't trying to meet it, wasn't angling to be its stepmother. It was the hiding. That stupid, unnecessary lie. I thought back to and recalled a few times the subject of children came up, and he had never once mentioned he had one. It was like finding a scratch on something you thought was smooth, and you can't stop running your finger over it, feeling the jagged edge. I felt an overwhelming sense of melancholy when I stopped seeing Joshua. He was the only man who enjoyed watching *The Golden Girls* with me.

"These old broads are funny," he'd say as we settled in for a nightly marathon followed by raucous sex. And he was very good at it—better than most, to be honest.

Before Joshua, there was Matt. Matt was a bad boy with a neck tattoo who worked at the grocery store down the street. He sold weed and talked about golden showers like it was religion, like if he could just get me to pee on him, he'd ascend or something. He was reckless in that way that makes you feel alive and stupid at the same time, like jumping off a roof into a pool without knowing how deep it is.

We didn't last long—maybe three weeks—but for a moment Matt made me feel like I could be reckless, too. Like I could take things without consequence. He let me steal from his grocery store. He'd scan everything, but the packaged sushi would always slide under his hand and into my bag. That was the only thing I missed about him. Just the free grocery-store sushi.

Sometimes I think that's what all my relationships boil down to—the small, stupid things I miss when it's over. Free sushi. A good lay. Someone who doesn't make me feel embarrassed for liking a show about four old ladies cracking jokes. The rest of it is just noise.

I turn off the water and step out, the steam curling around me as I stare at my reflection in the mirror. My skin is red from the heat, my hair slicked back, my face stripped bare. I feel raw, unformed, like a thing still waiting to be made whole. And for a moment, I let myself wonder if Nathan will see that, too.

SIX

I've decided to straighten my hair, and regret has already settled in my chest. The flat iron hums in my hand like a living thing, accusatory in its heat. Each strand of thick, curly hair protests the transformation, the pull of the iron against my scalp feeling tender, raw, as though my hair itself is fighting back. I force it into submission, strand by strand, the tulle-like stiffness of straightened hair falling too heavy against my neck, reminding me with every tug that I've made a mistake.

This was my first misstep, and it's eating the time I'd carefully set aside to prepare. The seconds fall like tiny failures as I watch the clock tick toward inevitability. Each pass of the iron feels slower than the last, and already I know I'll be late. Not by much, but enough to matter. Enough for him to notice. Enough for him to judge. I can picture his face: the subtle downturn of his mouth, the tightening of his jaw. The silent calculation that I'm careless, disorganized, not worth the effort. My reflection glares back at me from the mirror, wide-eyed and frantic, my trembling hands betraying the tension coiling in my stomach.

Maybe I should've asked Nathan to meet closer to where I live; picked a place I know, a place I wouldn't have to rush to. But I didn't. I wanted to seem agreeable, unbothered. Easy.

Now I'm paying for it with an hour-long drive to some café I've never heard of. It's 11:15. I pause, running the numbers in my head. An hour and forty-five minutes to get there. Subtract the parking. Subtract traffic. Subtract the inevitable eight minutes I've already lost trying to straighten one strand of my hair.

The countdown looms. *Late. I will be late.*

The last strand of hair falls flat against my shoulder, and I click the iron off with a finality that leaves the air buzzing in its absence. My pulse thrums in my ears as I head to my room, each second slipping away like sand. My outfit is simple: black jeans, a white fitted t-shirt. Neutral. Effortless. Not too much, not too little. I glance at the dress hanging in my closet, the one that makes me feel good, confident. A dress meant for dinner, not coffee. A dress for later, if this goes anywhere at all.

I tuck a piece of my newly flattened hair behind my ear, fingers moving on autopilot, and look at myself in the mirror for two seconds—long enough to check my appearance but not long enough to find something I don't like. The clock reads 11:30. For a moment, relief flickers through me. I might still make it. But I know better than to trust moments like this.

I grab my bag and bolt. The doorframe catches my shoulder as I move too fast, my feet slapping against the pavement with the urgency of someone who's already late in her mind. The sunlight outside is too bright, the kind of sharpness that feels like punishment. And then—a metallic blur. A Buick. The blare of a horn shreds the air, sharp and hot, as I stumble out of its path. I don't stop to apologize, don't stop to look back. The car rolls past, its driver's frustration hanging thick in the air. I keep moving.

Somehow, I arrive downtown at 12:45. My feet carry me forward, automatic, toward the address Nathan gave me.

O'Malley's is nothing like I imagined. Not the light, airy café I had pictured, but a pub, dark and polished, with the faint smell of fried food and spilled beer lingering in the air. I hesitate at the door, feeling the weight of the place pressing against my chest. It's not right. This is not what I prepared for.

I slip inside anyway, scanning the room for a table in the back, somewhere quiet, somewhere I can disappear. The laughter spilling from the bar feels too loud, too much. All the back tables are taken so I opt for a table in the middle, pulling my phone from my bag. I scroll back through Nathan's messages, the word *coffee* staring back at me like an accusation. He definitely said coffee. The word is there, clear and unambiguous.

I glance down at my outfit. Jeans, t-shirt, black loafers. All wrong for this space. If I'd known, I might've worn the dress. The one in my closet that clings in all the right places. Maybe a red lip, something to assert my presence, to say, *I am here, and I am something.*

But it's too late for that now. The air feels heavy, the light too dim, and I sit there, waiting, pretending I don't feel the sweat gathering at the back of my neck.

Here.

I type the message, hit send, and set the phone down on the table as if it might bite me. My hands fold themselves neatly in my lap, a gesture meant to look calm, but my knees are bouncing under the table, my body already betraying me. Two seconds later, the restraint dissolves. I snatch the phone back up, thumb stabbing at the refresh icon like it owes me something.

The notification comes through faster than I expect, and his response is immediate:

What? Already? You're incredibly early. Lol.

The shame pools hot in my chest, sharp as a knife edge. My thumbs move again, this time careful, cautious:

I was anxious I'd be late haha. Sorry.

I refresh again, holding my breath until his next message appears, like a magician pulling a coin from behind my ear:

No worries. I was just hopping in the shower. I can be there in twenty minutes.

Relief washes over me, cold and fleeting, but I let it settle into my muscles for a moment. My shoulders loosen, my breath evens out.

I set the phone down, face up this time, and force myself not to pick it up again.

Exactly twenty-one minutes later, the door opens, and he walks in. He's taller than I imagined, his salt-and-pepper hair catching the dim light, his face lined but sharp, the kind of handsome that comes with age and effort. His grey t-shirt and jeans are unassuming, understated, and somehow that makes me feel less self-conscious about my own outfit.

The black watch on his wrist stands out, sleek and practical, as if it's a part of him. I like men who wear their time like a badge, who carry it around on their bodies as if they might lose it if they're not careful.

I stand too quickly, the wooden chair scraping loudly against the floor, and his smile spreads wide across his face, easy but intentional. He hugs me strangely—three quick firm pats on the back—as if I'm his buddy, as if he's congratulating me for winning a football game.

"Hi," I say, the word coming out smaller than I want it to, and as he pulls back and smiles at me I think, *Maybe this will be okay. Maybe.*

He slides into the seat across from me, his arms spreading out along the back of the booth as if he owns the place, as if the table between us is his territory, and I'm just here visiting. His mouth is slightly open. His eyes settle on me, and I feel exposed under his gaze, as if he's collecting data, measuring me against something I can't see.

"You are even more beautiful in person," he says, his voice low, tinged with surprise. "My God."

The words hit me like a sudden gust of wind, unbalancing me before I've even had a chance to find my footing. My brain goes into its usual loop: *Do I look that different from the pictures? Did I overdo it or underdo it? Is my hair okay? Should I have worn something else?*

But I force the thoughts down, swallowing them like bitter medicine. Instead, I smile—a smile calibrated to look effortless. He doesn't need to know how much effort it takes to seem effortless.

I cross my legs, my right ankle resting just above my left knee, the way I always do when I want to project calm, collected competence. His eyes are still on me, not judgmental, but assessing, as if he's trying to see past the mask I've so carefully constructed.

The space between us feels heavier than it should, the kind of weight that comes from too much thinking, too much planning. It's not fear. It's the constant awareness of all the ways this could go wrong. My fingers tighten around the edge of the table, and I tell myself to relax.

But I can't. Even relaxing feels like something I need to get right, something to break down into actionable steps. Inhale. Exhale. Shoulders back. Smile steady. Speak carefully. Don't say too much, don't say too little.

"You really think so?" I ask, my voice steady, but I know that there's a slight edge to it. I don't know how long it's been since he last spoke, but I say it anyway. I sound rehearsed, even to myself. He nods, leaning forward a bit, his eyes darkening with sincerity.

"Yeah," he says. "More beautiful than I expected."

I feel a strange surge of discomfort, a rush of warmth, and I think, *Why does this make me nervous?* It's not the compliment. No, it's never about that. It's the fact that he's *saying it*, and suddenly

I'm overwhelmed by the pressure of making it all fit, feeling that he might suddenly look at me and change his mind.

I shake my head slightly, just enough to release the tension in my neck. "I didn't expect to meet at a place like this," I admit, my voice softening. "I thought we were meeting for coffee."

He laughs, and it's warm, easy, the exact kind of laugh that belongs to a middle-aged wealthy white man who's never been burdened by anything. "Yeah, well . . . I thought a pub would be more comfortable. Coffee's fine, but it's kind of stiff, right?"

I smile, but it's more of a twitch, an acknowledgment that a sudden change in venue is fine and hasn't thrown me completely off. I glance at my phone, but not in the desperate, obsessive way I usually do. I'm only checking the time, trying to control it, trying to keep it in line with my mental schedule.

What should I say next?

I breathe out slowly and return my focus to him, to Nathan, to this moment. I wonder, fleetingly, if he knows how much work this takes. Being me.

I take a sip of water, the glass cool against my lips. "So," I start, my voice lower than I expect. "What are you looking for?"

I need to hear him say it. I need the words to make this real, to confirm that I'm not wasting my time. That I've made the right decision.

Nathan leans back in his chair, his arms crossing over his chest as if he's considering the weight of the question. The shift in his demeanor is subtle but tangible, the air between us tightening like a rubber band stretched too far. I've seen this before, the way people fold in on themselves when they're caught off guard, when they're forced into answers they're not ready to give.

But I hold steady. I've spent too much time trying to make sense of this arrangement to back down now. This is what I signed up for. I take a slow breath, the taste of the pub's faintly bitter air settling on my tongue. This is business, I remind myself. Nothing more.

"I mean, you're here for a reason, right?" My voice is steady, even, the words measured as if they've been rehearsed. "I just . . . I want to know what to expect. How much will I get paid for . . . this?"

The word *this* hangs between us, awkward and unavoidable. It feels too blunt, but it's out now, and I can't take it back. I watch him closely, studying the slight movements of his face. His lips tighten, the corners pulling in just enough to shift the balance of his expression. His fingers grip the edge of his glass, the subtle tension mirrored in his gaze.

"I—" he starts, but his voice falters. His brows knit together as though he's trying to form a response that won't land wrong. "I wasn't expecting you to just . . . ask like that."

I blink, the confusion blooming in my chest. *Why wouldn't I ask?* I think. Isn't that what we're doing here? Isn't that the whole point?

But I don't let the confusion reach my face. I press it down, forcing my voice to stay calm, measured. "I'm just trying to understand the dynamics," I say, the word *dynamics* feeling too clinical, too detached. "That's what this is about, right? You want someone to . . . be with, and in return I get money. It's simple."

The words fall flat, like a bad joke, one that leaves a silence heavy enough to fill the room. He shifts in his seat, his discomfort clear, and for a moment I feel it too—a flicker of guilt. Not because I think I've said anything wrong, but because I can see it now, the subtle misalignment between what I've imagined and what he's thinking.

"I don't think you're quite getting it," he says slowly, his voice quieter now. "This isn't just about money. At least not for me."

The irritation flares in my chest, quick and hot. *Of course it's about money.* That's the whole reason I'm here. That's the whole reason we're even having this conversation. Isn't it?

"But you're offering to take care of someone like me," I reply, my voice careful but firmer now. "This is a sugar-dating arrangement. I'm here because I need support. I've been out of a job for five months, and my savings are gone."

The admission sits between us, bare and uncomfortable. He doesn't respond right away, and the pause feels like a knife in my chest, sharp and unyielding. I shift in my seat, crossing my arms over my chest, trying to shield myself from the weight of the silence.

"Are you not interested in the . . . financial part of this?" I ask, though the question feels more like a plea now, my voice softer, more unsure.

His eyes stay locked on mine, steady and searching. "I'm not saying I'm not interested in helping you," he says finally, "but I don't want this to be transactional. I want a connection. A real one."

I blink, the meaning of his words sinking in like a weight dropped into water, rippling out in ways I can't control. "Isn't that what this is? Transactional?" I say, quieter now, the edge of confusion creeping into my voice. "You help me. I help you. We're both getting something out of it."

He sighs, the sound low and heavy, and looks down at his drink. For a moment, I think he might not answer, but then he looks back up, his eyes softer now, almost apologetic. "I didn't sign up for a business deal, if that's what you're asking. I want someone who's here because they want to be here. Not just because they need the money."

The words feel like a hand closing around my throat, squeezing tight enough to make breathing hard. What did I miss? What's happening here? I thought I understood the terms, the dynamics. I thought I knew what this was supposed to be.

"I'm just . . . not sure what you mean," I say, my voice faltering, the faux confidence I walked in with unraveling thread by thread. "I signed up for this because I need money, Nathan. That's all."

His expression softens, but he doesn't move, doesn't reach out. "Okay," he says quietly.

The pause that follows is suffocating, the silence wrapping around us like a fog I can't see through. I look at him, my mind racing, spinning with thoughts I can't untangle. I want to say something, anything to bridge the gap that's opened between us, but the words won't come.

So instead, I sit there, the weight of his gaze pressing down on me, wondering if I've already ruined this before it even started.

When I get home, the first thing I do is strip. Each piece of clothing is peeled away, a silent shedding of the day. The pants, the fitted white t-shirt, even the socks—all folded into perfect squares and stacked neatly in my drawer, their edges aligned like soldiers standing at attention. The order calms me, gives shape to a day that feels jagged and unfinished.

My phone is a weight I feel even without touching it, humming just beneath my skin. I want to grab it, to refresh the app, to see if Nathan's name has materialized on the screen. But I stop myself. Not yet. I cling to my routine, anchoring myself in its precision.

I wash my face, the lather cool and foamy in my hands. My fingers move in exact circles—three on the left cheek, three on the right, two for the chin. The rinse is cold, biting, sharp enough to pull me back into my body. I brush my teeth next, counting each stroke in my head. Ten on the left. Ten on the right. Ten for the middle. My mind drifts, replaying fragments of the day, Nathan's voice curling in the corners of my thoughts.

He was strange. Not in a way that made me uncomfortable, but in a way that made him impossible to pin down. I replay the conversation, dissecting each word, searching for the misstep. Why had he gone stiff when I mentioned the financial arrangement? Why had something so transactional, so agreed upon, suddenly felt fragile when spoken aloud?

It should be simple: he wanted companionship; I needed money. A clean exchange. But the balance felt slippery, like trying to hold water in my hands. Every time I thought I understood the terms, they shifted, leaving me uncertain, unsteady.

I finish my routine and sit on the edge of the bed, the sheets taut beneath me. My phone waits on the nightstand, its dark screen reflecting back at me. I reach for it slowly, the way you might approach something that could bite.

The first thing I see is another text from my father.

`I'm sorry, Gia. I've stopped drinking. Sober six months now. I want to be in your life again. Please let me try.`

The words land heavy, familiar in their emptiness. I've read this script before, each line an echo of something I've heard too many times. My thumb hovers over the message, but I don't respond. I swipe it away like an itch, ignoring the sting it leaves behind.

I open the app. The messages are waiting—new faces, new profiles, new men casting their nets with curated charm and carefully posed photos. None of them are Nathan.

I scroll until I find him, his name steady in the list. My fingers hesitate before tapping his profile, enlarging his picture. It's the one of him at his desk, the one where he looks the most real. He's leaning forward slightly, his gaze focused on something just out of frame. There's a stillness in his face, a quietness that feels like a balm against the noise in my head.

I stare at the photo longer than I should, tracing the lines of his jaw, the faint crease at the corner of his mouth, the soft streaks of gray in his hair. My chest tightens, my breath shallow. He feels close and impossibly far away all at once.

Please message me back. The thought presses into my mind. I press the phone to my lips, the screen cool and unyielding, as though the gesture might conjure him.

And then the tears come. Quiet, soft, the way they always do. They aren't violent, aren't messy. They slide down my cheeks in measured lines, a slow release that feels more ritual than reaction. I've cried like this so many times it's become muscle memory.

I kiss his profile picture once, gently, the way you might kiss a relic or a talisman. The phone feels cold and hollow in my hands, but the act feels necessary, a final step before I let the day go.

I sink into bed, curling into myself, pulling the comforter tight around my body. The room is quiet, the air heavy with my unanswered questions. But I cling to the small, fragile hope that tomorrow his message will come.

SEVEN

The phone rings, through the quiet. My body jolts, reflexive, as if the noise itself has teeth. Phone calls are rare, uninvited things that don't belong in the carefully built grid of my morning. My breath catches, my heart beating an uneven rhythm against my ribs as I stare at the screen. Unknown number. A puzzle I don't want to solve.

Who could it be? Kennedy, her voice bright and demanding? My father, another plea smuggled in apology? Spam? A wrong number? Or something worse, something urgent, clawing at the edges of my day? My thumb hovers, the moment stretching taut, heavy with indecision. I let it ring, the tension building with each chime until, finally, I answer.

The voice on the other end is clear, formal, and unexpected. A job offer. A courtroom-reporter position. The words land softly, almost tentative, before expanding, their weight settling in my chest. My thoughts scatter like startled birds, wings flapping frantic questions: *Can I type fast enough? Can I fit in? Will they see the cracks in me before I even start?* I push the doubts down, focus on the facts. "Yes, I'm interested." The words are out before hesitation can sink its teeth in, my grip tightening around the phone like it might fly away.

The details come quickly—a preliminary interview, though the woman on the other end assures me that I've already landed the position just based on my merits alone. I studied to be a courtroom reporter in college, back when I thought my hands could keep up with the world, back when I believed in the permanence of facts. I liked the precision of it—the way words became a record, how the right keystrokes could turn chaos into something neat and orderly. But I fell into accounting instead, something quieter, something that didn't demand so much of my body. Numbers were easier than people, and they didn't need me to listen so closely.

My breath evens out, the outline of possibility taking shape. A *job*. The thought lingers, solid and improbable. A flicker of hope.

When the call ends, I sit for a moment, the phone warm in my hand, the silence loud. That fragile swell of hope trying to push through the cracks. But the feeling doesn't last. The buzz of a notification snaps me back, its vibration rippling through the table like an electric jolt.

Nathan's name flashes on the screen.

My chest tightens, anticipation blooming sharp and fast, and I unlock the phone with a clumsiness that betrays me.

`Hey Gia. I'm sorry about yesterday, I am interested in seeing you again.`

The words are plain, unremarkable, but they hum with weight. *I am* instead of *I'm*—intentional, as though he's rehearsed this, chosen the phrasing carefully. He thought about me. He decided to try again.

I let the message sit for a moment, its implications spinning out, infinite and dizzying. My response has to be right—engaged, but not overeager; warm, but not vulnerable. I type. Delete. Type again. The words finally come together, compact and safe:

`Ok, sounds good. I'd like to see you again too.`

I read it three times, scanning for errors, for subtext I didn't intend. When I'm satisfied, I press send, my breath catching as the message leaves me. The phone rests on the coffee table now, perfectly aligned with the edge, its stillness mocking the storm in my chest.

The day feels suddenly expansive, possibilities stretching out in parallel lines, neat and straight, waiting for me to dig in.

I pull out my notebook, the blank pages humming with potential. I settle into my couch and the pen moves with purpose, carving order into the chaos in my head.

For the job interview: *What do courtroom reporters wear? Emphasize technical skills. Prepare for questions about accuracy.* I underline *first impressions* twice and scribble *practice typing test* in the margins.

For Nathan: *What to wear. How to act. What to say.* Everything will matter.

The cadence of my words. The ease of my smile. I list

scenarios, circling the ones that feel right, marking the ones I'll rehearse in front of the mirror.

The edges of the day feel sharp again, the mess contained. I breathe in deeply, let it out slowly, anchoring myself in the fragile structure I've built. A job offer. A message from Nathan. Two small certainties in a sea of unknowns. Two paths forward. For now, it's enough.

By the time I close the notebook, the day feels regimented, manageable; mine.

EIGHT

The following morning, I'm jolted awake by a series of knocks so forceful they feel personal, like the sound's been weaponized, calibrated to strike nerves I didn't even know I had. It ricochets through my body, cracking open some tender part of my chest where panic lives. My heart spikes, and my thoughts scatter like marbles on a hardwood floor, chaotic, impossible to pin down.

I sit up too fast, the room tilting for a moment before settling into place. My body feels stiff and useless, like the dissonance of the sound has sunk into my joints. I drag myself to the door, my fingers wrapping around the handle. The motion is slow, every second dragging with the weight of hesitation. I open it just a crack, peering through the narrow gap like I'm afraid of what might be on the other side.

There's no one there. Just a piece of paper slapped against the door, tilted at an angle like it's mocking me. The corners are curling slightly, the tape barely holding it in place. I pull it off with too much care, smoothing the edges instinctively, like that'll somehow soften what I know is coming. The words hit me in bold, unrelenting red: **NOTICE: FIVE DAYS TO PAY RENT OR QUIT.**

It lands in my chest like a brick, and it sticks there, heavy and immovable. I exhale sharply, the sound more habit than release, and mutter, "Damn it." The words evaporate as soon as they leave my mouth, as weightless as I feel right now.

I walk to the couch, drop onto it like the cushions might swallow me whole, and unlock my phone. My thumb hovers over the screen for a moment, indecisive, before I open the app and find Nathan's thread. It's the only tether I have to him—a string of messages that feel like both a lifeline and a trap. What I want is his number, something real and solid that doesn't exist in the cloud, but all I have is this, a digital breadcrumb trail leading back to nothing.

My fingers hover, then move quickly:

`Hey, are you able to meet up tonight? I need your help bad. Xo.`

I add my number to the bottom of the message, my thumb poised over the send button as if I'm holding my breath. When I finally press it, the action feels irreversible, a decision sealed in the space between one second and the next. I toss the phone onto the couch as if it's a grenade, as if putting distance between me and that message will soften whatever's coming.

The silence that follows is oppressive, the kind that swallows the room whole. I wait, the seconds dragging by in relentless cruelty. I pace, my steps a metronome marking the passage of time, the rhythm steady but my thoughts anything but. The phone rings suddenly, cutting through the quiet with a sharpness that makes me flinch.

I grab it from the cushions, my pulse hammering as I glance at the screen:

UNKNOWN NUMBER

I answer, my voice shaky despite myself. "Hello?"

"It's Nathan," he says, his voice so clean and crisp it feels as if he's standing next to me, close enough to touch.

"Oh. H-hi," I stammer, pacing again, my movements suddenly jerky and uneven. "I wasn't expecting you to call so quickly."

"Well," he says, and there's a laugh in his voice, low and familiar, as if it's something he's giving me for free, "you did say you needed my help tonight. What's going on?"

I glance around the room, my eyes landing on a smudge on the wall that looks like a tiny ghost of a mistake I can't fix. "I'd rather talk about it in person," I say, my voice steadying, grounding itself in the lie. "Are you free tonight?"

The pause stretches out, taut and unbearable, as if he's letting the silence do the talking for him. I count the seconds, each one pressing against me like a weight. Just when I'm about to fill the space with something—anything—he answers, and I explode.

"Yeah. I'm free tonight."

NINE

The dress is laid out like an offering across my bed, a black body-hugging thing that grazes the knees with a sweetheart neckline. I smooth my hands over the fabric, checking for wrinkles I know aren't there. It's the dress I've been saving, the one reserved for something important, something pivotal, and tonight it fulfills its purpose.

I slip it on carefully, the ritual precise: left arm, right arm, zipper drawn slowly, the click of teeth locking into place. I examine myself in the mirror, turning slightly to the left, slightly to the right, ensuring the dress falls just as it should. I take in the curve of my waist, the line of my shoulders, and whisper aloud, "Perfect," though I know I will check again in fifteen minutes.

I skip the flat iron this time, leaving my hair in its natural state—wild, spiraling, unpredictable. It feels wrong at first, the weight of the curls foreign against my face, but I tell myself it adds authenticity. I am not supposed to look too polished; I am supposed to look like a woman on the verge. The next task is practicing my face. I sit before the mirror, testing expressions like an actress preparing for her role. Sad, but not desperate. Vulnerable, but not weak. My mouth curves downward slightly, my eyes weighted just enough with sorrow. I practice furrowing my brow, tilting my head.

"Nathan," I say aloud, testing my tone. "I know we just met, but I need help. I'm being evicted. I don't know where else to turn." The words sound too dramatic, so I adjust. "Nathan, I don't know how to say this, but I'm in a tight spot financially. It's humiliating to even ask, but I thought maybe . . ." My voice trails off, and I nod. That's the one.

The preparation consumes me. My eyes flick to the clock every few minutes. Four hours until we meet. My hands itch for something to do, so I reapply my lipstick, blot, and reapply again. I rearrange the contents of my purse, ensuring everything has its place: wallet, phone, a compact for touch-ups, gum, a folded tissue for the tears I might summon if needed.

By the time I'm ready, the dress has been inspected ten times, the mirror rehearsals repeated until my expressions are muscle memory. I sit on the edge of my bed, rigid, knees together, hands folded neatly in my lap. I've allowed myself no room for error.

The hours crawl by, measured in small, compulsive tasks. I set an alarm for thirty minutes before I need to leave, then set a second alarm for ten minutes earlier, just in case. I refresh Nathan's messages, though I know there's nothing new. I rehearse my lines one more time, not because I've forgotten them but because I need to fill the silence.

By the time I finally step out the door, my mind is a well-oiled machine, every thought aligned in perfect sequence. My heels click on the pavement as I make my way to the car, the sound sharp, grounding. I've done everything I can to prepare, and yet a small, gnawing doubt lingers, whispering that it still might not be enough. The restaurant stands in stark relief against the darkening sky, its signage orderly, illuminated in soft white. *Gino's.*

I park three spaces away, ensuring enough room to open my door fully without grazing the neighboring vehicle. My engine hums for an extra five seconds before I turn it off, giving me time to prepare mentally.

I glance at the clock on the dashboard. Six p.m. One hour early. I allow the minute to tick over to 6:01 before I exhale and settle back into the seat. My purse rests squarely on the passenger seat, the clasp aligned with the seam of the upholstery. I run through my checklist: lines memorized, appearance checked, arrival accounted for. Still, the anxiety simmers, so I rehearse again.

"Nathan, I need to talk to you about something." Too abrupt. I try again, softer this time: "Nathan, I'm in a difficult situation, and I don't know who else to turn to." That feels closer, but I repeat it three more times to ensure it sticks.

My phone sits untouched for exactly four minutes before I pick it up, opening the sugar-daddy app as a way to occupy the idle time. Notifications spill across the screen: messages from men to whom I haven't responded, each one marked with a timestamp. I click into the first, scanning his profile for inconsistencies. He claims to own three properties in Dubai, but his photos look suspiciously like stock images. I delete the message without responding.

The next profile is more convincing. A CFO with a taste for fine art. I craft a response, playful but detached, careful not to betray any real interest.

Sounds interesting. What kind of art do you collect?

I hit send and the regret is immediate, sharp, like the sting of a paper cut you don't see coming. The question feels too much, too eager—a small betrayal of the indifference I was trying to cultivate. What does it matter what kind of art he collects? I don't care. Not really. But now I've turned the conversation into something that feels open-ended, something that requires attention.

The phone is heavy in my hand, a tether to something I can't name but to which I can't quite let go. I imagine his answer before it arrives, the familiar script. He'll list the artists, the pieces, each name a carefully chosen testament to his taste. Maybe he'll mention Rothko, because everyone knows Rothko, or some obscure name I won't bother to Google, a flex wrapped in pretense.

And then, the inevitable softening: *I really love supporting local artists, you know? There's something special about discovering someone before they make it big.* The sentence will be just the right mix of virtue and vulnerability, a self-portrait painted with words that say, *Look at me. Aren't I good? Aren't I generous?*

I imagine him curating this response, arranging it like an exhibition of himself, and something tightens in my chest. Not anger, not quite, but something adjacent—a bitterness, a knowing. Men like him don't just collect art; they collect admiration. They want to be seen not for who they are but for what they gather, as if a large collection of Funko Pops! or a room full of old sports memorabilia actually means something. Though collecting art isn't as egregious my thoughts still remain the same: *Very cool dude, but that doesn't mean you're a good person.*

The clock on my dashboard reads 6:15 p.m.. I've only killed fourteen minutes. I cycle through the app again, responding to three more messages, all variations on the same theme: polite, aloof, calculated. My interactions are clinical, a way to fill the time, though I know they're ultimately meaningless. After tonight, I tell myself, I won't need this app anymore. Nathan is different. Nathan is endgame.

At 6:35 p.m., I glance up at the restaurant. Couples filter in and out with steady rhythm, the door swinging on well-oiled hinges. I imagine Nathan's arrival: the sound of his shoes on the tile, the tilt of his head as he searches for me. My chest tightens.

I check my makeup in the visor mirror, not because I suspect it's flawed, but because I need to ensure it's perfect. Lipstick, smooth. Foundation, even. I adjust the straps of my dress for the third time, though they haven't moved. I'm stalling, I know, but the routine calms me.

At 6:50 p.m., I take a final look at the clock, allowing a single deep breath before I step out of the car. My heels click against the pavement in even intervals, a rhythm that feels grounding. I push open the restaurant door and immediately all my senses are pleased. It's nothing like the trashy Italian bistro Kennedy and I go to, with its sticky vinyl seats, it's loud pop-rock music always blaring over the speakers coupled with the back of the house kitchen staff screaming and cursing at each other.

Gino's is dazzling, blurry, old Hollywood beautiful. It was a place where big deals were made, where political figures dined, all of them drunk on whiskey and laughing loudly, it was a place where proposals were a show, they even made room for it—right in the middle of the restaurant where everyone can look on and clap and *ooh* and *aww* for the newly engaged couple. It was a place where groups of upperclass women who lied about how old they were turning gathered for birthdays, their pillowy lips blowing out bright, sparkly candles as they balanced giant garish tiaras on top of their heads. And it was precisely the type of place, where older wealthy men took their sugar babies for dinner.

I take a moment to adjust to the dim light, the ambient hum of conversation and then I approach the hostess stand with faux confidence, his name already forming on my tongue. "Reservation for two, under Nathan."

She smiles, checks her list, and gestures for me to follow. My heart pounds in steady beats as she leads me to the table. The symmetry of the dining room, the soft clink of cutlery, the orderliness of it should soothe me, but it doesn't. My chest feels tight, my thoughts spiraling into contingencies for which I haven't accounted.

I lower myself into the chair, smoothing my dress as I sit. I glance at my phone, refreshing Nathan's last message even though I've already memorized it. My hands rest neatly on the table, fingers interlaced. I tell myself I'm ready, but the voice in my head whispers otherwise.

The restaurant hums with a steady rhythm: forks tapping porcelain, muffled laughter, the rise and fall of voices. I scan the room, cataloging every detail as if I'll need to reconstruct it later. An elderly couple at the next table shares a dessert, their spoons clinking together lovingly. Across the room, a sweaty man who reminds me of the Pillsbury Doughboy leans too far over his plate, his tie dangling dangerously close to a pool of marinara. His date, who looks fabulous in an emerald-green dress, doesn't look impressed by him and I wonder for a second if we are kindred spirits.

My phone buzzes, jolting me. I look down and see Nathan's message:

`Hey, I'm here. Are you inside already?`

The words are casual, unassuming, but they send a ripple through my chest. I type back quickly:

`Yes I'm at a table near the back`

No punctuation—it feels too stiff, too formal. I hit send, my thumb hovering for a split second longer than necessary, and then I set the phone down carefully, aligning it with the edge of the table.

I reach for my water glass, the condensation cooling my fingers. I take a sip, then another, spacing out the motions as if

I can drink away the seconds. Two minutes pass, though it feels stretched thin, elastic and brittle. Then I see him.

Nathan steps into the room, his eyes scanning the space with quiet purpose. He wears a crisp white shirt under a charcoal blazer, tailored just enough to suggest care without effort. His hair is freshly cut—short and neat, with the slightest hint of product that catches the light. The sides look sharper, newer, and I imagine him in the barber's chair, leaning forward just slightly as someone sculpted his edges. It's the kind of detail that most people wouldn't notice, but I do.

He spots me, and I feel it immediately—the tension in my shoulders, the way my stomach tightens as though bracing for impact. I place the glass back on the table, centering it exactly where it was before, as if this small act will heal me.

When he reaches the table, he smiles, his teeth slightly uneven in a way that feels disarming. "You look great, Gia," he says, his voice warm but quiet, the compliment landing between us like something private.

"Thank you," I say, my tone steady, rehearsed. "You, too."

He sits down, adjusting his blazer as he does, and I notice the way his watch glints under the light. My eyes flicker to his hands—strong, capable, but not overly manicured. Everything about him feels curated, yet effortlessly so.

"I hope I didn't keep you waiting," he says, leaning back slightly in his chair.

"No, not at all," I say. The hour I spent in my car suddenly feels distant, irrelevant.

The waiter appears, dropping off two menus, and Nathan orders a glass of bourbon whiskey. I decline a drink, sticking to water. I never drink. Alcohol feels too risky—too unpredictable. It also reminds me of my father.

"So," he says, leaning forward now, his arms resting on the table. "How's your day been?"

The question is simple, but it catches me off guard. For a moment, I forget the lines I've rehearsed.

"Good," I say, my voice steady. "Productive."

He nods, waiting for me to elaborate, but I don't. Instead, I let the silence settle between us, watching him as he studies me. I wonder what he sees—if he notices the tension in my shoulders, the way my fingers rest too precisely on the edge of the table.

"Are you always this reserved? Always this . . . I don't know how to explain it." He waves his hands in the air as if he's casting a spell. "Stiff?" he finally lands on, a smile tugging at the corner of his mouth.

I feel my cheeks flush, and I let out a soft laugh. "Sometimes."

That's not true. I'm always like this, but it's an answer that satisfies him. He chuckles, and the sound makes me jump. For a moment, I forget why I'm here, why I'm doing this.

"So," he sighs, leaning back slightly, his arms crossing over his chest in a way that seems relaxed but which reads as controlled. His eyes search mine, and I know what's coming before he even says it. "You said you needed help. I'm assuming this is about money?"

My stomach flips, and I feel heat creep up my neck, but I

nod, forcing myself to maintain eye contact. The moment feels suspended, stretched taut, like the seconds before a rubber band snaps.

"Yes," I say, the word crisp and singular, leaving no room for ambiguity. My voice is steady, but my fingers twitch under the table, itching to trace the grain of the wood or the edge of my napkin.

He tilts his head, studying me, and I feel like a specimen pinned under glass. His mouth twitches—not quite a smile, not quite a frown. "Okay," he says, drawing the word out. "How much are we talking?"

I swallow, my throat dry despite the water I've been nursing. I've rehearsed this moment countless times, running through every possible reaction he might have, every tone he might use. "I'm behind on rent," I say, voice steady. "A couple of days late. It's twelve hundred dollars."

Nathan's brow furrows, his lips pressing together just slightly. His fingers tap the table once, a single, controlled motion. It's not nothing. I watch him closely, cataloging every movement, every micro expression, like data in an experiment I don't fully understand.

"And what happens after that?" he asks.

It's not the response I expected. "What do you mean?"

"What happens next month? Or the month after that?" he says, his voice the tone of someone accustomed to having the upper hand. "Do you plan to come to me every time you're short?"

The words hit like a flat stone in my chest, sinking with no ripple. I hadn't thought that far ahead—or I had, but I'd told myself not to, to let future me worry about it.

"I'll figure something out," I say too quickly, the words tumbling over themselves. They sound hollow, even to me. "This is just . . . a rough patch."

I consider telling him about the job interview, about the sliver of hope I've carved out for myself, but I keep it to myself. It feels too small to offer him, too flimsy to count as proof of anything.

He exhales through his nose and it sounds like a deflating balloon. He leans forward, his elbows on the table, closing the space between us, making me feel smaller by comparison. "Look," he says, "like I said the other day, I don't mind helping. But this"—he gestures between us, a vague motion that somehow includes the table, the space, the silence—"has to be clear. If this is about money, just say that. If it's something else, I need to know that, too."

"It's about money," I say, sharper this time. The words feel stark, naked on the table between us.

He nods, a slow, purposeful motion, as if he's weighing their truth. I feel a flicker of relief.

"Alright," he says, finally. "We'll figure something out. But I have something to show you before I decide to move forward with you."

The sentence is a puzzle, heavy with implications I can't yet name. I want to ask why he's even on a sugar-dating site if he doesn't want things to be about money. The question hangs in my throat, thick and bitter, but I swallow it down, smoothing the napkin on my lap.

I try to change the subject: "So, what do you do?" The question is light, casual on the surface, but I mean it with weight. I need specifics, a foothold in this uneven terrain. His profile says finance, but that could mean anything: investment banking, accounting, even one of those cryptocurrency schemes. I need details. Specifics. My fingers twitch under the table, wanting to write down his answer, to catalog it, analyze it later.

He hesitates, the smallest flicker of something unreadable crossing his face. "I work with portfolios," he says, each word neat but deliberately vague. "Helping clients manage their investments."

It's nothing, a placeholder answer that leaves no room for real understanding. It irritates me in a way I didn't expect, makes me want to press harder, but before I can, the waitress interrupts with a smile that feels pasted on.

"Have you two decided?" she asks, pen poised.

"Two spaghetti Bolognese," Nathan says, his voice quick, authoritative. "And a bottle of red."

I blink, caught off guard. He ordered for me. My brain stumbles over this, the presumption of it. I don't even like Bolognese. I've already imagined the acidic sauce staining my lips, the mess of it lingering too long. It feels too uncouth for sugar dating. I wanted oysters or crab cakes, something sexy. Spaghetti Bolognese is for couples on the brink of divorce.

"Thank you," I say to the waitress reflexively. She widens her eyes at me. *Get a load of this guy.* I smile and cartoonishly widen my eyes back at her before she leaves the table. I love how we can telepathically converse like that. It is one of the only things women have that men can't take away.

"You like Bolognese, right?" Nathan asks, a faint curve of amusement at the edge of his mouth.

"Sure," I lie. The word feels sour in my mouth.

I sip my water again, this time more slowly. I'm holding it too tightly, I realize, my fingers tense around the rim. I set it down carefully before I break the glass.

"Have you always been in finance?" I ask, redirecting the conversation into safer waters, though my pulse quickens at the thought of him dodging again. I want something real from him, something I can pick apart later.

I wanted an arrangement for money, but even in that, I still want to know with *who*. I still want to look across the table and see a person instead of an outline, to hear something real in the spaces between the practiced lines. Men can sleep with anyone without knowing their name, their favorite color, what keeps them awake at night. They can touch a body without wondering about the life that inhabits it.

But women—women require more. Not much more, not always, but enough to tether the act to something tangible. It's not just the mechanics of connection; it's the context, the shape of the person behind the hands. Who are you when you're not here, sitting across from me? What's your damage, your desire, your history? What do you see when you close your eyes at night? I'm not asking for love or even for vulnerability. Just something sharp enough to make the moment stick. Something to make me feel as if I'm not vanishing into nothingness the second this ends.

Because that's what it feels like, being here with him. He is a smoothed-over surface, glossy and opaque, withholding just enough to keep me at bay. And I hate how much I care. How much I want to peel him apart, layer by layer, until I can see the raw, messy thing underneath. It's not romance—it's curiosity. It's wanting to know who I will be giving myself to.

He nods, but his answer is noncommittal, the details slipping away like sand through my fingers. I don't like the slipperiness of it, the way he refuses to let me pin him down.

The pasta arrives, steaming and rich, and I force myself to smile, to mirror his calm. But my mind spins, replaying his words, dissecting his gestures, the uneven power of this arrangement laid bare between us.

The restaurant hums with a quiet, mechanical efficiency, the kind that smooths over the chaos of human presence. Forks scrape against porcelain. The low hum of ambient jazz muffles laughter. Voices rise and fall like waves, colliding, dissipating, and disappearing into the fabric of the space. I keep my gaze fixed on my plate, my fork absently tracing the edges of the pasta I've barely eaten. Nathan doesn't comment on it. Doesn't ask if I enjoyed the meal or why I've basically left it untouched, only taking a few small bites. He just signals for the check, and when it comes, he throws down a stack of money like it's nothing.

"Ready?" he asks, shrugging his blazer back into place as he stands. I nod, my throat too tight to form words.

Outside, the air bites at my cheeks, crisp and sharp in a way that feels violent. "Follow me in your car?" he says, gesturing toward the sleek black sedan waiting for him at the curb, the valet holding the door open like a scene from a movie.

I nod again, my head bobbing mechanically. My legs carry me toward my car, each step feeling heavier than the last. Inside,

I grip the steering wheel until my knuckles pale. What does he want to show me? Is this some kind of test? A game? My chest tightens at the thought, and for a moment, I consider turning around, driving home, erasing the night from memory. But then the image of the eviction notice flashes in my mind and something in me pulls tight. I put the car into gear and follow him.

The city falls away quickly, the bright lights and crowded streets replaced by wide, tree-lined avenues and the quiet, measured order of suburban wealth, and then eventually the middle of nowhere. Each turn feels like a step deeper into something I don't understand, a path I can't retrace. I count them anyway—right, left, left again—committing the route to memory, a lifeline I might need later.

Twenty minutes pass, and then we're pulling into the driveway of a secluded house that doesn't look real. It's too big, too polished, its windows glowing softly against the darkening sky. I park behind him, my breath catching as I step out of the car.

"This way," he says, his tone light, casual, as if he's not subjecting me to whatever this is. I follow him up the path, my heels clicking against the stone, the sound unnervingly loud in the silence.

Inside, the house is immaculate, every detail curated to within an inch of its life. Clean lines, muted tones, furniture that looks as if it's never been touched. It smells faintly of cedar and something sharper, like a strong cleaning solution. It doesn't feel like a home. It feels like a set.

He leads me to a room at the back of the house, flicking on the light. The space is small, intimate. A study or an office, though the desk is too pristine, the bookshelves too perfectly arranged. There are two lounge chairs, black leather, their surfaces gleaming under the soft overhead light. He gestures for me to sit in the one by the window. I hesitate, my gaze drawn to the far corner of the room. That's when I see the cage.

It is big, larger than any I've seen before, with thick metal bars painted a dull black. My eyes fix on it immediately, and my mind starts cataloging the details: the latches on the door, the way it sits perfectly parallel to the wall, the faint sheen on the surface that suggests it's been recently cleaned.

"Do you have a dog?" I ask. I don't particularly like dogs—their unpredictability, the mess they bring. If we were to end up in a long-term arrangement, this is something to which I would need to adjust. I make a mental note: *Research dog breeds, behavioral traits, nearby dog parks. Find ways to tolerate them.*

He smiles faintly, shaking his head. "No, no. I don't have a dog."

His answer should be comforting, but it isn't. The absence of a dog doesn't explain the cage, its size, its strange placement in the corner of an otherwise meticulously curated room. I force myself not to stare at it for too long, but my eyes keep drifting back, tracing the clean lines of its frame, the way it commands the space without being intrusive.

"Oh," I say simply. I don't ask any follow-up questions,

though the urge to know—to understand—is nearly overwhelming. I make another mental note: *Don't press. Let it go.*

But I can't let it go, not entirely. The cage looms in the corner of my vision, a quiet enigma. I tell myself there must be a practical explanation. Storage, perhaps, or something left behind by a previous tenant. My mind begins constructing scenarios, each one more plausible than the last.

He watches me closely, his gaze steady but unreadable, as though he's waiting for me to ask something more. But I don't. Instead, I force a small smile and fold my hands neatly in front of me, fingers laced tightly together, as though holding them still will keep my thoughts from spiraling.

He sits across from me, his eyes fixed on mine, glinting faintly in the dim light of the room. The silence between us stretches, each second marked like the tick of a clock. I feel the weight of his gaze, steady and unblinking, and my hands curl tightly in my lap, fingers pressing into my palms in rhythmic beats to ground myself.

Finally, he rises, his movements calm, calculated. He crosses the room with purpose, the sound of his shoes soft against the hardwood floor. My eyes follow him as he reaches for something hung up behind the door, something I cannot see at first. My breath catches as he turns, and for a moment, the edges of the object blur in the low light before coming into sharp focus.

A collar. Black leather, gleaming with silver studs.

He approaches me slowly, holding it in both hands as though

it's something precious, sacred. My pulse quickens, each beat overwhelming, as I try to process what I'm seeing.

"Stand up," he says gently, his voice low and calm, the kind of tone one might use to soothe a child or an animal.

I hesitate, my mind racing through possibilities, none of them clear. But my body responds before my brain can catch up, and I rise to my feet. The chair scrapes softly against the floor, and I flinch at the sound.

He steps closer, and I can feel the heat of his presence. He moves behind me, his hand brushing against my hair as he gently pulls it to one side. The action is intimate, and my breath catches in my throat. I hear the faint click of the clasp as he secures the collar around my neck. It's snug but not tight, resting against my skin like an unfamiliar weight.

He steps back in front of me. His eyes are low now, his gaze heavy. I recognize the look immediately, though I have little experience with men like him. It's primal, hungry, and unmistakable. Every woman knows that look.

"You look amazing with that on," he says in a voice that's barely above a whisper, deep and smooth like a blade slicing through the air.

My hand rises automatically, fingers brushing against the leather. It's cool to the touch. "What—what is this?" I ask, my voice unsteady, almost inaudible.

He stares at me, the faint glimmer of a smile tugging at the corners of his mouth. But his expression shifts, darkening, his features hardening into something sharper, more sinister. My stomach tightens, and my fingers curl around the edge of the collar, the smooth leather suddenly feeling oppressive.

"This," he says, pausing as if savoring the moment, "is your audition." The words hang in the air, heavy and sharp. I blink, my thoughts spiraling, searching for meaning. "Get on your hands and knees," he says, his tone still calm, almost coaxing. "And bark like a dog."

I stare at him, the words not registering at first, my brain stalling as it tries to catch up. My breathing quickens, my chest tightening with confusion and disbelief.

This is what he wants. This is what he's into. The realization lands heavily, the puzzle pieces clicking into place.

I don't move. I can't. I stand there, frozen, my thoughts spiraling into a loop of questions I can't answer, possibilities I can't predict. The weight of his request settles over me like a thick fog and my mind spirals, calculating every angle, every consequence. *Do it, don't do it, what happens if I refuse, what happens if I don't?* The questions loop endlessly, each one louder than the last.

His gaze doesn't waver. It is calm and steady, as though he already knows what I'll choose. I inhale deeply, the leather of the collar pressing lightly against my throat. Slowly, I lower myself to the ground. My knees press against the hardwood floor, my hands following, palms flat against the cool surface. I feel absurd. My hair falls into my face as I glance down, my fingers trembling slightly. My heart pounds in my chest, each beat a relentless rhythm that matches the tempo of my spiraling thoughts.

"Good," he says softly, his voice low and approving.

I take another breath, deep and steady, and then I do it. A soft, tentative bark escapes my lips, barely audible at first. It feels strange, surreal, and my cheeks flush with heat as the sound hangs in the air.

"Louder," he says, and there's something almost gentle in his tone, as though he's coaxing me forward.

I try again, the bark louder this time, the sound bouncing off the walls of the small room. I feel silly, exposed, but I force myself to stay in place.

When I finally rise to my feet, brushing my hands against my dress to steady myself, I look up and see him smiling. It's not the faint, polite smile I've seen before. It is wide, genuine, and warm, the kind of smile that transforms his face, making him seem less calculated, less controlled.

"You did great, Gia," he says, his tone lighter now, almost playful.

I swallow hard, the heat still lingering on my cheeks, but his approval feels like a small victory, an odd sense of relief blooming in my chest. He liked it. That much is clear.

I touch the collar lightly, my fingers tracing the studs as I force myself to meet his gaze. "That's what you wanted, right?" I ask, reveling in the validation. My voice is steadier now, though the words feel surreal even as I speak them.

"Yes," he says simply, his smile never wavering. "Exactly what I wanted."

For a moment, the tension in the room shifts, the air feeling less heavy. I stand there, back straight, my hands clasped together in front of me, the spiraling questions in my mind momentarily quiet. "As you can see, I have a very interesting sort of fetish," he says slowly.

"I *do* see," I say, my voice sounding far away, detached.

He nods, his gaze never leaving mine. "I'm looking for someone to be my dog," he continues, pausing as if to let the words settle. "For eight hours every day."

The sentence lands heavily, each word clear and sharp, and my mind begins spiraling immediately, dissecting his tone, his posture, the exact phrasing he used.

Eight hours. Every day. Dog. The words loop in my head, a strange, rhythmic pulse I can't shake. "Eight hours?" I repeat, as though clarifying the logistics that will make the concept more digestible. "That's . . . a full workday."

He chuckles softly, a sound that feels too light for the weight of the conversation. "Exactly. I believe in treating it like a job—because it is. A role with expectations, structure, and, of course, compensation."

The word *compensation* pulls me back into focus. I nod slowly, processing, calculating. My hands fidget against the fabric of my dress, the leather collar still pressing lightly against my skin. "And what, exactly, does being your dog entail?"

His smile widens slightly, and he takes a step closer, his presence filling the small space between us. "It's simple. You'll wear the collar, spend the day as my pet. No talking, no standing on two legs, no human behavior unless I explicitly allow it."

I swallow hard, the collar tightening around my throat. My mind floods with questions, each one branching into another. *How would this work? What are the boundaries?*

But one question was the most important.

"And the pay?" I ask, my voice low, controlled, though my pulse is quickening.

"Generous," he says, his tone almost playful. "Enough to cover your rent—and then some. I am willing to pay off all your debt."

I take a step back, needing space, needing air. My fingers brush against the edge of the desk behind me, grounding me.

"I thought you said you didn't want anything transactional?"

He smiles again. "That was a test." He steps closer to me. "And besides, it's not *really* transactional. I get more satisfaction from a beloved Girl Pet than anything."

His words settle heavy in my chest until I feel as if I can't breathe and the room is spinning. "I'll . . . need to think about it," I hear myself say as I look around the room. Anywhere but directly at him.

"Of course," he replies smoothly, as though he expected nothing less. "But I'll need your answer soon. This kind of opportunity doesn't come around often."

His words hang in the air, a mix of promise and pressure. I nod again, my thoughts spiraling, unable to focus on anything but the weight of the collar around my neck and the faint glint in his eyes as he watches me.

"Well," he says, his voice light and steady, as if this

conversation hasn't been anything but extraordinary. "Since you need time to think about it, I'll bid you adieu, my lady. Shall I walk you out?"

The casualness of his tone catches me off guard. My mind latches on to it, dissecting every word, every inflection, as though it might reveal some hidden meaning. I have so many questions—too many to organize neatly in my head. But I don't ask any of them. Instead, I nod, my body responding automatically even as my mind whirls. He steps behind me and unbuckles the collar around my neck and then he leads me back through the house, his pace measured, his posture unhurried. The sound of his shoes tapping against the floor is sharp, rhythmic, each step an echo that feels oddly final. I count them instinctively—ten to the hallway, thirteen to the door.

When we get outside, I reach for my car handle, eager to leave, to escape the overwhelming weight of everything that has just happened. But before I can open the door, I feel his hand on my shoulder.

His grip is firm, not forceful, but enough to make my heart hitch forward, a beat out of sync. He turns me around, and for a moment, I can't meet his eyes. I focus instead on the sharp line of his blazer, the faint glint of his watch, before I feel him press something into my hand. It's heavy, firm. I look down, my mind already categorizing the texture and size before I fully process what it is. A roll of cash, thick and tightly bound.

"Twelve hundred," he says, his tone even, almost clinical. "Enough to pay your rent this month."

I stare at him, my thoughts scrambling to connect the dots, to make sense of the gesture. The sheer physicality of the cash feels jarring, real in a way that the rest of this evening hasn't.

"There's more where that came from," he continues, his voice steady, calculated. "You'll be getting double that. Every week."

The words reverberate in my head, repeating in perfect loops. *Double. Every week.* I feel the edges of the bills pressing into my palm, grounding me.

I manage a nod, though it feels mechanical, disconnected from the storm inside my head. "Thank you," I say, the words soft and automatic, devoid of meaning but necessary to fill the silence.

He steps back, his hand falling away from my shoulder, and I turn quickly, sliding into the driver's seat of my car. The door closes with a satisfying click, and I immediately lock it, pressing the button twice to ensure it is secure.

I start the engine and pull out of the driveway.

The drive home is silent, the roads dark and empty. My mind loops through the same thoughts, dissecting every moment, every word, every action. $1,200. Enough to pay rent. $2,400 every week after that. And he's willing to pay off all my debt, whatever that means. The numbers click into place like puzzle pieces, the logic undeniable. That kind of money—it changes everything.

But then the other details intrude: the collar, the cage, the absurdity of barking, crawling, submitting to his strange requests. My chest tightens, and I grip the steering wheel harder, counting the ridges beneath my fingers as a way to steady myself.

Can I do this? Eight hours a day, every day, acting like a dog?

The thought circles endlessly, intersecting with images of overdue bills, eviction notices, and Nathan's steady, confident gaze.

I pull into my driveway, aligning my car perfectly with the curb. I sit for a moment, staring at the roll of cash before finally picking it up. My fingers run over the smooth edges of the bills, the weight of them both reassuring and overwhelming.

TEN

The crisp envelope, stuffed with rent money—actual, physical cash—felt heavier than it should have in my hand as I drove to my landlord's house. The bills were perfectly aligned, crisp and fresh, sealed inside with a neatness that felt like absolution. I'd imagined this moment for days, the small victory of catching up on rent, of watching his face when I handed it over.

And he didn't disappoint. The look on his face when he opened the door was priceless—shock, maybe a little confusion, like he couldn't believe I had paid it. I smiled, wide and confident, handing him the envelope.

"I'll never be late again," I said, the words smooth, like a mantra I was trying to believe myself.

He grunted something in response, something that might've been "good" or "okay," but it didn't matter. I'd done it. I turned and walked back to my car with a spring in my step, the cool air brushing against my cheeks, sharp and electric. The relief was almost overwhelming, a physical thing that loosened the tightness in my chest. But there was something else, too—a faint unease that lingered in the back of my mind.

The drive home was quiet, the city slipping by in blurred fragments of light and shadow. My mind wandered, circling back to Nathan, to the cage, to the black collar that still felt like a phantom weight against my neck. The memory was sharp and intrusive, but it didn't fill me with dread. If anything, it felt oddly comforting. Predictable. A challenge with clear rules, a role I could step into if I just practiced enough.

Once home, I sit at my desk and open up my laptop. My fingers fly over the keyboard as I type *dog behavior tutorial* into the search bar. The results flood the screen: videos on training dogs, analyzing their movements, understanding their instincts. I begin clicking through them, one by one, absorbing the information like a sponge.

I learn quickly that different breeds behave very differently. Border collies are energetic, almost frantic in their movements. Labradors are playful, friendly, and eager to please. Dobermans are sleek and purposeful. After some deliberation, I narrow my focus to one breed: golden retrievers. They're gentle, easygoing, loyal—qualities I think I can emulate.

I clear a space in the center of my living room, pushing the coffee table against the wall so I have room to move. I set my phone on the floor, propped up on a book, and start recording myself.

First, I get on all fours, my hands flat against the carpet, my knees pressing into it. The position feels unnatural at first, my body stiff and awkward. I watch the video tutorial again, mimicking the way the golden retriever lowers its head and wags its tail. I don't have a tail, of course, but I sway my hips gently from side to side, trying to replicate the motion.

"Good dog," I whisper to myself, my voice soft and coaxing. Next, I practice walking on all fours. The tutorial emphasizes smooth, fluid movements, so I focus on coordinating my hands and knees, ensuring each step is balanced. I crawl across the room, turn, and crawl back again, repeating the sequence until it feels less awkward. Then comes the barking. I watch the dog in the video tilt its head and let out a sharp, playful bark. I pause the video and mimic the sound, my voice hesitant at first.

"Woof," I say softly. It doesn't sound right. Too human.

I try again, this time louder, more forceful. "Woof!"

It's closer, but still off. I rewind the video and listen again, studying the pitch and cadence of the dog's bark. I practice over and over, adjusting the tone and volume until I'm satisfied.

Finally, I add the tail wag to the bark, performing both simultaneously. I crawl to the center of the room, sit back on my heels, and let out a soft "woof" while swaying my hips. I feel silly, but there's something calming about the repetition, the focus required to perfect each motion.

I review the video I've recorded, taking notes on my posture and movements. *Back too stiff. Hands too far apart. Bark needs more energy.* I adjust accordingly, repeating the sequence until I see improvement.

When I finally stop, my knees ache, and my palms are red from pressing against the floor, but I feel accomplished. I sit back on the rug, my legs crossed, and replay the video one more time. I have been doing this all day.

"I can do this," I whisper, a small smile forming on my lips. "I just need to practice more."

The thought feels reassuring, almost comforting. With enough repetition, enough preparation, I can perfect the role. I can be the best dog Nathan has ever seen.

I haven't officially accepted the offer yet, though my mind is already consumed by the details. Every time Nathan asks—four times now since our date—I give the same answer: *Maybe. I have more questions.*

And I do. The questions churn in my head, relentless and specific, each one growing sharper the longer I think about it. The first one came late at night, the thought too urgent to ignore: `Can I use the bathroom?`

His response was quick, firm: `Yes, you can use the bathroom. I am not cleaning up your shit.`

The bluntness of it startled me, the words cutting through the vague, almost playful tone of his earlier texts. I stared at the screen, my fingers trembling as I typed my next question.

`What if I cough or sneeze? Does that count as breaking character?`

He replied almost immediately: `Yes. Unless it's unavoidable, I expect you to stay in character. Any slip will be punished.`

The word *punished* lingered in my mind long after I read it. My heart raced as I typed back: What kind of punishment?

His reply came slowly this time, the three dots lingering far too long. That depends on how serious the infraction is. You'll learn.

I stare at the words, feeling a knot tighten in my stomach. I didn't press further, but my mind raced with scenarios, each one spiraling into the next.

The next question surfaces like a wave, impossible to hold back: Will I be able to leave when I want?

This time, there is no immediate reply. The silence stretches, unbearable. My thumb hovers over the screen, refreshing my texts.

Finally, after what feels like hours, his answer appears:

Yes.

What about water? Will I be able to drink from a glass, or do I need to use a bowl?

Bowl, he responds, without hesitation. You'll eat and drink from the floor, like a dog. You can only stand if I allow it.

The finality of his tone is unshakable. Each rule he lays out feels like a wall closing in, limiting my movement, my options, my autonomy. And yet the boundaries are also oddly reassuring. They give structure to the chaos of my thoughts, parameters I can follow. I ask another: What about leaving the room? Do I need permission?

Always, he replies. You don't move without my say-so.

I pause, staring at the screen, the collar I'd worn at his house flashing in my mind. My breathing quickens as I type another question, the most important one yet: `What if I mess up? What if I'm not good at this?`

His response is fast, cutting off my train of thought: `You won't mess up. You'll learn. Quickly.`

I stare at the text for a long time, my fingers brushing against the edges of my phone. The firmness of his answers both terrify and intrigue me. Each message cements the role he wants me to play, stripping away any room for doubt or misinterpretation.

Deep down, I know I'll say yes. I always knew. But the finality of it still looms, the decision sitting heavy on my chest as I close the message thread and stare at the ceiling, imagining what it will feel like to fully step into the role.

ELEVEN

Kennedy's backyard is pristine, curated like an Instagram feed with the saturation turned up—symmetry in every corner, perfection draped over the mundane. The lawn is shaved into uniformity, its green so bright it feels artificial. The patio furniture is arranged like a showroom, all sharp lines and coordinated cushions, and even the bounce house, riotous in its colors and its cacophony of children, feels intentional, a controlled chaos to complement the order. It is Liam's third birthday, and his parents are making a show of it.

I sit stiffly on the edge of a wicker chair, my iced tea sweating onto the glass side table. The condensation pools into tiny circles that refuse to stay contained, slipping into one another until they form a jagged mess of moisture. I swipe at them with my finger, but the smear it leaves behind is worse, a half-erased mistake that only draws more attention to itself.

Kennedy is effortless beside me, her laughter cutting through the sound of children's shrieks as they hurl their tiny bodies against the walls of the bounce house. Her mojito sits balanced in her hand, the glass already frosted, the mint crisp and vibrant.

"I still can't believe you have a kid," I say, my eyes drifting to Liam, his sweaty face scrunched in pure, unselfconscious joy as he launches himself into the air. His hair is plastered to his forehead, a shoe dangling precariously with one strap undone, flapping against his heel like it's protesting every jump. The urge to fix it rises in me, unbidden, as if order could be imposed on his wild, untethered joy.

Kennedy laughs lightly. "I know, right? Sometimes I can't believe it either. But hey, life moves fast."

Life moves fast. The words hang in the air, gilded with meaning that's not meant to land on me but does anyway. Kennedy's life has sprinted ahead, gathering itself into milestones and accomplishments: marriage with a successful real-estate guy, a child, a house with a lawn so green it borders on satire. My life, meanwhile, has unraveled slowly, as though it wanted me to feel every thread loosen before it fell apart completely.

She turns to me, her eyes too bright with curiosity, cutting through the safety of my iced tea. "So," she says, her voice pitched too high, too casual. "How's the sugar dating going?"

My stomach tightens reflexively, and I take a sip of tea, the cold liquid coating the discomfort in my throat. I stall, letting the silence stretch just enough to seem contemplative, not evasive. "Not much luck on that front," I say finally, shrugging as if it doesn't matter. "But I've got a job interview tomorrow."

The words taste strange in my mouth, like an offering that isn't entirely mine to give.

Her face lights up, her mojito wobbling dangerously in her excitement. "Oh my God, Gia, that's amazing! I knew you'd pull through. What's the job?"

I hesitate, setting my glass down with care. "Courtroom reporter," I say, the words smooth and polished, already rehearsed. The tightness in my chest grows, but my face doesn't betray it.

Kennedy beams, her hand grazing my arm. "See? I told you. You're too smart, too talented to . . . you know," she says. "I mean, not that there's anything wrong with it, oh my God," she adds quickly, placing a well-manicured hand on my arm.

I smile tightly, nodding along as though her pride in me isn't slicing me in half. The truth hums just beneath the surface. This morning, I sent two words that changed everything: I'm in.

Nathan responded almost immediately. Marvelous. Let's start tonight.

I've been replaying it all day, letting it knot itself into the fabric of my thoughts. I wonder if Kennedy would understand—if she could fathom it—me pretending to be a dog for eight hours for a man I met online.

Her hand is warm on my arm, grounding and unbearable all at once. "This is such a huge step forward for you," she says, her voice still honeyed with pride. "You're going to kill it, babe."

"Thank you. I hope so," I say, my voice thinner than hers, brittle at the edges. I look past her to Liam, who is still jumping, his shoe strap flapping defiantly with every leap. I count his bounces, anchoring myself to their uneven rhythm, as though their chaos might somehow steady me. I'm still perched on the wicker chair, my spine too straight, like a guest at an interview I didn't apply for. My iced tea is sweating on the glass table beside me, the condensation pooling into shapes I keep trying to fix, but they resist, spreading out into jagged lines. Every moment feels like it's designed for scrutiny.

Across the yard, Kennedy moves as if she owns the sun. Her dress is linen, loose enough to suggest she's untouched by the heat, and she laughs lightly at the dad jokes being lobbed by her husband who is standing next to some other dad wearing boat shoes. She tosses her hair, a single stubbornly out-of-place piece flying free from what is otherwise a curtain of gold. She's effortless in the way that makes me hyper-aware of my body, my sweat, the way my Forever 21 dress sticks to my thighs.

"Liam, fix your shoe!" she calls, her voice cutting through the din. Liam looks over, his hair plastered to his forehead, one shoe halfway off, and grins defiantly before launching himself against the rubber wall. He knows she won't leave her audience.

I press my hands against my thighs, the sweat slick against my palms, and glance at the other parents clustered under the pergola. They hold cocktails and conversations like weapons, their laughter forced into neat bursts that signal camaraderie but stop short of authenticity. They talk about things like school districts and organic snacks and the best way to get crayon off a wall, and the sound washes over me like static. I don't belong here. Not in this house, not in this backyard, not in this domestic-bliss life.

Kennedy turns her attention back to me, her mojito barely touched, the mint still green and perfect. She sits back on the edge of her chair, her presence spilling over into my space.

"Isn't this amazing?" she says, gesturing to the scene like a general surveying her army. "I can't believe we pulled this off. Liam's going to remember this forever."

I nod, my throat tight, the words stuck somewhere between polite agreement and the urge to laugh. Liam will forget this party by next week. What he'll remember, what will live in his bones, is the hum of Kennedy's relentless perfection, the way it shapes and shadows everything around her. The perfect mother. He doesn't know how lucky he is.

"Did you see the cake?" she asks, her eyes bright with pride. "It's a three-tier fondant masterpiece. Took me weeks to find the right baker."

I glance toward the dessert table, where the cake stands like a trophy. It's shaped like a train, its details so intricate it looks like something from a magazine. Liam doesn't care about the cake. He's still bouncing, his shoe finally flung off, his laughter floating through the air.

"It's beautiful," I say.

Kennedy beams. "I wanted something memorable, you know? Something that says, *'You're special.'*" Her voice dips into a conspiratorial whisper. "You'll understand one day."

I smile, tight-lipped, and take another sip of my tea. The

sugar grates against my teeth at the thought. Do I even really want a child? A family? The notion of it is so far removed from my current life that the thought almost feels illegal, like I shouldn't be allowed to think about these things.

The party churns on around us, the soundtrack of children screaming and some adults pretending to care, others caring way too much. I watch a woman who I vaguely recognize snatch her young daughter away from the bounce house with a bit too much force. *Sweetie. Sweetie. Sweetie, come here. You're getting too rowdy. Please put down your dress — you are not a boy.*

Someone cranks up the Bluetooth speaker, and a pop song spills into the yard, its manufactured cheer adding more excitement to the scene. A kid starts crying, the sound piercing, and Kennedy's head snaps toward the noise like a predator sensing weakness.

"Excuse me," she says, standing again with the kind of grace that turns even basic movement into performance. She strides toward the chaos, her voice rising in a soothing coo that carries over the din. The other moms watch her, their faces carefully blank, but I see the calculation behind their eyes. They're clocking her—her dress, her tone, the way she bends without breaking.

I sit alone, my hands gripping the arms of the chair, the iced tea forgotten beside me. My gaze drifts back to Liam, his body a blur of motion, his hair a mess of sweat and joy. His freedom is something wild and untamed, something this backyard can't quite contain. It's the only thing here that feels real.

★ ★ ★

When I get home, the words *I'm in* feel heavier, as if they've been waiting for me to notice their weight. I imagine Kennedy tucking Liam into bed, smoothing his hair, her life folding neatly into place like an average thirty-something-year-old woman. And then I imagine myself on all fours, barking, the collar around my neck a tangible reminder of the choices I've made.

I wonder how long I can keep these worlds from touching, how long I can keep their orbits from colliding. For now, they spin separately, unevenly, tethered only by the fragile gravity of my denial.

TWELVE

I get ready for the night, my movements as automatic as the hum of the refrigerator. I toss a few things into a bag—my purse, Chapstick, a hair tie—each one useless. Dogs don't carry purses, and their lips don't get chapped. I know this, but packing calms me, even as the absurdity of it scratches at the back of my neck. It's not about utility. It's about the ritual, the illusion of control, like cleaning a room before a fire burns it down.

I hadn't thought I'd start tonight. I'd imagined a more traditional schedule—something solid and predictable. Eight to four. But Nathan was clear: it's overnight, and it starts now. The word *now* sticks to my ribs, prickly and wrong, even as I pretend I don't feel it. I grab my phone and type fast, thumbs skipping over each other. `What should I bring?`

His reply is instant. `Nothing. Yourself.`

I read it twice, then again. The words settle somewhere low, weightless but dense, as if they've hooked onto the space between my lungs. No bag, no things, no armor. Just me.

I clean the kitchen to drown it out. I scrub until the counters gleam, not because they need it but because I do. I organize the dishes in the drying rack—big plates first, then the little ones, the mugs in a line like soldiers. I know I'll be back by morning, but the work steadies me, makes me feel like this is just another night, just another thing that will end. I wipe down the last plate, and for a moment I feel lighter, as if I've hit a reset button somewhere deep in my head.

At the table, I open my laptop and stare at an email draft I've been avoiding. It is addressed to the woman who called me about the courtroom stenographer interview. I type without thinking, fingers moving as if possessed: Hello, after much consideration, I have chosen not to attend the interview tomorrow. Thank you for the opportunity.

I hit send too fast, like pulling the trigger before you've aimed. The regret blooms immediately, settling heavy in my stomach. The courtroom job wouldn't pay much at first, but it would've built to something stable, something honest. But Nathan's offer—weekly cash, no questions—dangles in my head like a carrot tied to a stick. I can't stop imagining the bills in my hand, their crisp weight. It feels real in a way the future never does.

I cling to that vision as if it's already mine, let it carry me to the bathroom. The water is scalding, almost punishing, but it feels good to have control over something. I shave slowly, the razor gliding over my legs and bikini line. My thoughts drift to Nathan, to the cage, to the terms. Sex seems inevitable. I tell myself it's just part of the arrangement, part of the job. I have ruined myself for far less. It's nothing I can't handle.

SHY GIRL

When I step out of the shower, the steam clings to my skin. I pull my hair into a tight bun, practical and clean. No makeup—it doesn't feel right to look polished. Dogs don't wear eyeliner. I dress in a black t-shirt and yoga pants, clothes that don't mean anything, that won't get in the way. When I glance in the mirror, my reflection looks stripped down, utilitarian. I feel like I've stepped outside myself, like I'm preparing a mannequin for something it won't remember.

I take a deep breath, hold it for a count of four, let it go. My heart drums against my ribs, but my hands stay steady as I grab my keys. I open the door to the cool night air and lock it behind me, double-checking the knob twice, pressing against it with my palm.

The walk to my car is slow, each step measured. I slide into the driver's seat and grip the wheel, my knuckles whitening under the pressure. I sit there for a moment, listening to the silence, trying to feel normal. But nothing feels normal. Not the air, not my skin, not this moment, where the streetlights buzz faintly and the night seems to lean in, watching.

This is it. There's no turning back now.

YEAR ONE

THIRTEEN

I step out of the car, the cool air folding over me like a second skin. The lock clicks softly, the sound almost reassuring. I press the button again, needing the confirmation beep, the small punctuation that says everything is secure, everything is in its place. My purse hangs lightly at my side, and I think about leaving it behind, but the thought won't stick. *What if I need something?* The question loops, nonsensical but insistent, its weight heavier than the bag itself. The walk to the front door stretches. Each step feels choreographed, my body carrying me forward while my mind stalls in place. The faint glow from inside frames the door like an invitation, and I pause, my hand hovering just shy of the wood. The knock feels heavy in my chest before it even lands.

Nathan opens the door almost instantly, as if he's been waiting just beyond it, his silhouette etched in the frame as if it's part of the architecture. He's casual in a way that feels considered—dark jeans, a gray sweater with its sleeves pushed up to his elbows.

"You're on time," he says, his voice low, edged with faint

amusement, as though my punctuality surprises him. He steps aside, and the space opens behind him. "Come."

I nod, the words caught somewhere between my chest and my mouth. I step inside, and the scent hits me first: polished wood, faint cologne, and something colder, sterile, like an echo of something recently scrubbed away. The house is immaculate, each object curated, the kind of cleanliness that feels untouchable. The air is still, oppressive in its order.

"Follow me," Nathan says, his voice a steady current that pulls me along. I obey without hesitation, my feet moving automatically, my purse swaying lightly at my side. His gaze flickers to it, a quick tilt of his head that sharpens the weight of it against my arm. He doesn't say anything, but I feel the disapproval settle in the quiet between us.

He leads me down the hallway, the shadows pooling in the corners, softening the edges of the pristine walls. The room at the end is just as I remember. The cage sits waiting, its metal bars gleaming faintly in the soft light, unapologetic in its presence. My chest tightens, my breath shallow as the reality of this night presses down on me.

Nathan turns to me, his face unreadable, his expression carefully calibrated. "Give me the purse," he says, the command laced with a calm finality that leaves no room for argument.

I hesitate, my fingers gripping the strap like it's the only thing tethering me to my real life. Slowly, I hand it over. He takes it. "You'll get this back in eight hours," he says, and then lifts it up and down as if he is weighing it. "Is your phone in here?"

I nod, the motion small.

"Good," he replies. Then, his gaze sharpens, cutting through the air between us. "Now undress down to your underwear."

The words land like a weight. My hands move before my mind catches up, trembling as they pull off my jacket, and then pull at the hem of my shirt, and then my pants. I fold them into a neat pile, an attempt to impose control on a situation where I have none. When I'm left in just my bra and underwear, I cross my arms, my body folding in on itself as if it's trying to disappear.

Nathan watches me with a detached focus, his movements like liquid as he pulls the collar from his pocket. Black leather, silver studs, a piece of art in its own right. He steps closer, and I hold still, my breath catching as he wraps it around my neck. The buckle snaps shut in a way that feels intimate, his fingers lingering just long enough to make the air between us feel too full.

"Kneel," he says, the word cutting through the moment like a blade.

I drop, my knees meeting the floor with a dull thud, my palms resting flat against my thighs. He circles me, his steps soft, the floor creaking faintly beneath his weight.

"No standing, no speaking, no human behavior," he begins, his tone steady, authoritative. "You are to remain in character unless I say otherwise. Understood?"

I nod.

"Speak," he commands, his voice sharper now.

"Woof," I reply.

"Good," he says, a flicker of a smile pulling at the corner of his lips. "You'll get better."

He gestures toward the cage, the door swinging open with a faint groan. "Inside," he says simply, stepping back to watch.

I crawl forward, my movements slow, as I step into the small space. Nathan closes the door behind me, the latch clicking into place with a sound that feels final, unyielding. "Good girl," he says. "This is your bed for the night," he says, his voice even, as though he's pointing out something mundane, like a coat rack or a spare chair. "Get comfortable."

I lower myself onto my stomach, the mat beneath me thin and unkind, the cage bars pressing cold and rigid against my skin whenever I move. My first position doesn't work—the collar catches awkwardly at my throat, and the angle feels wrong. I turn onto my side instead, curling inward, my knees pulling tight to my chest. The collar shifts slightly, settling in a way that feels no less strange, but that at least doesn't constrict. I close my eyes, but my mind won't quiet. It moves instead, rapid and analytical, replaying every detail of his instructions, every nuance in his tone, every flicker of expression that might've hinted at what's next.

He lingers for a moment, watching me, his shadow cutting across the soft light. When he leaves, the sound of his footsteps fades slowly, each one an echo of presence retreating into absence. The house hums faintly around me, a low, constant vibration that settles like static in the corners of the room. I breathe evenly, counting the inhales, holding the exhales, trying to tether myself to the rhythm.

Eight hours, I think. *I can do this.*

The cage is too small, the mat barely a buffer between me and the hardness of the floor. Every time I shift, a new ache blooms—my knees pressing against steel, my back stiff from the forced curvature of the space. Even so, I stay as still as I can, my breath shallow, my body compliant. I tell myself it's part of the work, part of the deal, but my thoughts loop, circling back to the thinness of this arrangement and the weight of it all at once.

Time stretches and contracts in uneven increments, elastic and unmeasured. Every so often, I hear the faint creak of footsteps in the distance, a signal that Nathan is near. My chest tightens with each approach, and when he finally returns a few hours later the anticipation solidifies into something sharp and unrelenting. The cage door swings open with a sound that feels louder than it should, and he clips a leash to my collar, the cold metal brushing against my neck.

"Come," he says, his voice calm.

I follow on all fours, the leash pulling taut but never jerking. My hands and knees move in time with the rhythm of his steps, each one anchored to the soft pad of his soles against the hardwood. He leads me to his bedroom, the space a study in masculine—deep grays and blacks, clean lines, an absence of warmth.

"Up," he says, gesturing toward the bed. I hesitate for a

fraction of a second, then climb onto the mattress, my movements careful, my body hyper-aware of his gaze. He watches me with a focus that doesn't waver, his expression unreadable as he begins to undress. His movements are deliberate, unhurried, as though this is more ritual than routine. When he joins me, his touch is firm but gentle, his voice steady as he murmurs, "Good girl," the words soft but charged.

The sex surprises me. I had expected something rough, something unkind, but instead it's careful, intimate in a way that feels almost romantic. He doesn't rush. His hands are sure, his movements measured, and the repeated cadence of "Good girl" punctuates every moment, a refrain that threads itself through the air, making it heavier, denser. I don't hate it. That fact alone catches me off guard, a realization that settles somewhere I can't quite reach.

When it's over, he doesn't leave me to clean myself up. He disappears into the bathroom and returns with a warm, damp cloth, his hands precise as he wipes me down. His touch is impersonal, detached, as though this is just another part of the arrangement. Still, there's something jarring about it, the intimacy of being tended to even in the absence of care.

"Good girl," he says again when he's finished, his voice softer now, almost a whisper. The leash clicks back into place, and he leads me down the hallway again, the cage waiting like an inevitable destination.

"Sit," he says once we're back in the study, his tone sharp but even. I drop to my knees, my body moving before my mind catches up. My hands rest on my thighs, my posture stiff, waiting.

"Beg," he says next, gesturing with his hand. It takes me a moment to understand, but then I raise my hands in front of me, mimicking the motion of dogs I've seen on the videos I studied. He watches closely, his gaze intent. "Higher," he says, and I adjust, lifting my hands closer to my chest.

"Good girl," he says again, the words landing differently each time, shifting from praise to command to something else entirely. He moves through more instructions—"roll over," "crawl to me," "stay"—each one executed without question. His approval follows every act, consistent, predictable, and I find an odd kind of solace in the structure of it, in the absence of ambiguity.

When it's over, he gestures toward the cage again, and I climb in without hesitation. The latch clicks shut, the sound final, and I curl up inside, my body folding into the tight space. The bars press against me in uneven intervals, and the thin mat beneath me does little to ease the ache, but I stay still, my breath shallow, counting each exhale as though it might tether me to something solid.

The house hums again, low and steady, and the light above me cuts through my closed eyelids. I think about asking him to turn it off, but the thought loops in my head, circling until it exhausts itself. I stay silent, unmoving.

FOURTEEN

The hours stretch thin, each one a wisp of thread pulled too taut. The house creaks around me—footsteps in the hall, water falling somewhere distant, the faint groan of a chair leaning under him. He doesn't come back until the air feels stale with waiting. When he does, his voice is a flat blade. "Wake up."

I surface slowly, the weight of sleep heavy on my skin. Light leaks in through the window, pale and forgiving, and I know the night is over. Relief is a gentle thing, pooling in my chest. Eight hours. I made it.

The cage door groans open, and the leash is back—cold metal clipping into place with a finality that presses against my ribs. I wait for him to say something like, "You're done for the day," but the words don't come. Instead, his voice is steady, like a hand pressing my shoulder. "Let's get you to the bathroom."

My body protests as I crawl out, vertebrae grinding in their sockets, each movement a reluctant surrender. Palms and knees hit the floor in rhythm, the leash pulling softly as he leads. I follow, focusing on the scrape of skin against wood, the small noises that tether me to the present.

The bathroom is too bright. The tiles gleam like they've been waiting for me, and my stomach churns. *Germs.* The word sits heavy in my mouth, a sour taste I can't swallow. I've crawled here, dragged myself across this floor, and now it sticks to me, clinging like a second skin.

I move as quickly as my body will allow. The water runs scalding as I scrub my hands, once, twice, digging the soap under my nails until the sting feels earned. Behind me, the door is cracked just enough for him to watch, though we both pretend not to notice. His presence hangs in the space like steam.

When I'm done, he's there, leash in hand, waiting like he always does. My stomach twists at the sight of it, but I drop back to my hands and knees, the motion instinctual now. The floor meets me like an old habit, cold and unyielding, and I crawl back to the room, each step a quiet surrender.

The cage looms again, its edges sharp in my periphery. Relief flutters at the thought of leaving, of shedding this skin. My bed waits for me somewhere else—soft sheets, warm water, a version of myself that doesn't exist on all fours. But he doesn't say I can go. Not yet.

Instead, he watches, his silence a knot pulling tighter. The words that follow are quiet. "I've changed my mind."

The air stills. My hands press against the floor, grounding myself against the weight of his voice. I look up, the question caught behind my teeth, the rules keeping it there. He doesn't wait for it.

"You're not free to go," he says, the leash swaying lightly in his hand. His tone is steady, as if this is nothing, as if my world isn't tipping on its axis. "I think I'll keep you."

The words hollow me out. *Keep me?* The thought splinters, fragments of panic lodging themselves deep. The door feels farther now, the walls higher. The air thickens as he kneels, his shadow spilling over me.

"You're doing so well," he murmurs, his hand brushing a strand of hair from my face. The touch is too light, too human, and it burns. "It would be a shame to stop here."

I nod because it's what I know to do, the motion automatic, reflexive. Inside, my mind twists, searching for a way out, a crack in the walls of this moment. Eight hours. That was the deal.

"Do you understand?" His voice cuts through the haze.

My head jerks in another nod, frantic and small, though every part of me recoils. "Speak," he commands, and his eyes pin me there, waiting.

"Woof," I whisper, the sound barely a breath. It feels foreign, hollow, but I say it again, louder this time. "Woof."

The word hangs in the air between us, and I feel it settle into my chest like a stone.

"Good girl," he says, the words gliding off his tongue like a thread pulled smooth, his smile a faint curve that settles somewhere between comfort and command. Approval, gentle but sharp-edged, like a blade wrapped in silk.

He rises, straightening, looking down on me. "This is your home now," he says, his voice low and final, as if the decision had been made long before I arrived, before we even met.

The words echo, each syllable a stone dropped into the still pool of my mind. I press my hands harder into the floor, the cool surface biting back, but the grounding doesn't come. My stomach knots itself tighter, my thoughts spilling over in a tangle of questions.

What does he mean by "keep"? What happens if I say no?

But the words never make it to my lips. They fold into themselves, collapsing under the weight of his gaze.

The cage door is open, yawning wide. It waits for me like a familiar ache. I glance at it, at him, at the space between us that feels narrower than ever. He doesn't speak. His silence blooms, thick and unbroken, until it swallows the room whole.

With a quiet click, the leash falls away, and I crawl back inside. The bars press against me, cold and certain, as he closes the door with a soft, almost thoughtful finality. The sound lingers, stretching thin and bright like the light overhead, which now feels too watchful, a pressure I can't escape.

I fold into myself, curling tight as though I could shrink small enough to slip through the cracks. My knees press into my chest, my breath a careful rhythm, my focus narrowing to the smallest things—the texture of the floor, the metal at my back, the slow pulse of time as it drags.

The rules, the leash, the cage—they're the only truths I can touch now, the only things I can trust to stay the same. But his words are still there, circling like vultures, their wings heavy with meaning.

You're not free to go.

I think I'll keep you.

They loop endlessly, settling deeper each time, carving out a hollow I don't know how to fill.

FIFTEEN

I wake to the light, harsh and bright, carving itself into the room. My body is stiff, aching in places I didn't know could ache. For a moment, I am unmoored, the soft fog of sleep a balm against recognition. But then the collar shifts, a slight pressure at my throat, and reality snaps back into place. The cage, the leash, Nathan's voice like a blade slipping between my ribs: *I think I'll keep you.*

The hours are long gone, the ones on which we agreed. I glance toward the wall where the clock used to hang, but it's gone. He's removed it. Of course he has. The absence of it feels dark, like a hand pressed over my eyes. Still, I've been tracking time in other ways: the rhythm of his steps, the stretch of light shifting through the window, the groan of the house as it wakes. It is well into the afternoon now. I'm sure of it.

I tell myself it's nothing, that it's just him testing me. Pushing my limits. A first-day trial to see if I'm worth the effort. This is what I repeat, over and over, like a mantra. This is fine. This is normal. He's testing me.

But my body protests, each movement stiff and reluctant, my muscles shrieking against the cold press of metal bars. I shift, curling tighter, grounding myself in the steady rhythm of my breath: in for four, hold for four, out for four. My head swims with fragments of his words, each one heavier than the last.

I think I'll keep you.

He couldn't mean forever. Forever is absurd. This is an agreed-upon arrangement. A thing with boundaries and terms. Eight hours, payment at the end of the week. That was the deal.

But the words don't leave me. They loop in my mind, cutting into my certainty, pushing doubt into the soft places I'd hoped to protect.

I want to call out, to ask if my time is up, but my voice isn't mine to use. The rules are clear, and I know better than to break them. Instead, I press my palms to the floor, cold and hard beneath me, and try not to think about how the bars feel like an extension of my skin.

The footsteps come at last, faint at first, then louder. Relief blooms sharp and uneasy. I uncurl, just enough to peer through the bars, my heart caught in the tension between dread and hope.

The door creaks open, and there he is, his expression calm, unreadable. He stands there for a moment, watching me as if he's considering something I can't see.

"Good afternoon," he says, his voice smooth and even.

I nod. My throat tightens against the words I want to spill, the questions clawing their way to the surface.

"Did you sleep well?" he asks, his tone so casual it feels like a joke.

I nod again, though my dreams were anything but restful. They were tangled things, filled with commands that stuck to me like a second skin.

He crouches, his eyes meeting mine. "Let's see how much you've learned," he says.

The commands come, one by one, and I obey without hesitation. My body moves before my mind can register, each motion smooth from repetition. *Sit. Beg. Stay.* The words slice through the air, and I mold myself to fit them. When he nods in approval, I feel the weight of his gaze linger, heavy as the collar at my throat.

I am hungry now, my stomach a raw ache, the sound breaking free in a low growl that startles us both. Nathan's eyes flick toward me, amused. I lower my gaze instinctively, a flush creeping up my neck. I want to go home. To oatmeal, blueberries in a perfect circle, something real and mine.

Instead, I bark. The sound is sharp, ripping through the silence, and I feel it leave me like a piece of myself.

Nathan tilts his head, his smile faint and cutting. "What is it, girl?" he asks, his voice playful, mocking, and I feel the edges of myself fray.

I raise a hand, point toward my mouth—a small rebellion, a plea.

His smile disappears, replaced by something cold and dangerous. "Dogs don't point," he says, his tone flat, edged with warning.

My hand falls instantly, my body folding into itself, eyes wide and pleading. *This isn't funny anymore.*

He studies me, his gaze heavy, the air thick enough to choke on. Then, like a crack in glass, his expression softens into a smile. It's casual, almost warm, but it doesn't ease the tension coiled in my chest.

"I get it," he says lightly, as if we're sharing some unspoken understanding. "You're hungry."

He crouches to my level, his knees cracking faintly, and pets me, his hand dragging over my head and down my back. The touch is dehumanizing in its softness. My body stays rigid beneath his hand, every nerve electric, but I don't flinch.

"Don't worry, girl," he says, his smile curving wider, something gleaming beneath the surface. "I've got just the thing for you."

He stands, the leash clipping onto my collar with a familiar click, and the sound lodges in my stomach like a stone. "Come," he says, and I follow. My hands and knees drag across the floor, the hard surface scraping at my skin, my muscles burning from hours of this. Hunger twists sharp in my belly, a hollow ache that makes the world blur at the edges. I focus on the rhythm of crawling: left, right, left, right.

The kitchen is bright and clinical, the air sterile and sharp. He stops in the center of the room and points to a spot on the floor. "Stay," he commands, his voice low and firm, the word pinning me in place.

I sink back onto my heels, watching him move. He hums

softly, almost cheerfully, as he busies himself at the counter. His movements are light, unhurried, as if he's enjoying some private joke. I track him, my eyes following the way his hands pull out a metal dog bowl, the scrape of it against the counter making me wince.

The sounds are vague but visceral—clinking metal, the wet smack of something sliding out of a can. It's enough to make my stomach churn, the hunger warping into nausea.

He sets the bowl down in front of me, a faint smile tugging at the corner of his mouth. "Here you go, girl," he says, stepping back like he's waiting for applause.

I hesitate, leaning forward just enough for the smell to hit me. It's sour, rancid, a sharp slap of canned dog food. My stomach lurches, and instinct takes over. I jerk back, nearly knocking the bowl over.

"Oh God!" The words rip out of me, raw and unguarded, before I can stop them.

The air shifts instantly. Nathan's smile vanishes, replaced by something colder, sharper. He steps closer, his eyes narrowing.

"What did you just say?" His voice is quiet, but the edge in it cuts clean through me.

My breath catches, my heart pounding as I freeze under his gaze. The silence stretches, thick and suffocating, and I drop my eyes to the floor. My fists clench against the tile, nails digging into my palms.

His voice slices through the tension. "Now you'll have to be punished." The words settle in the air like lead, heavy and inescapable. He snatches the bowl from the floor. "No food until tomorrow," he says.

That's it. The thought rises, unbidden but steady. *I'm done.*

Pain shoots through my legs as I push myself upright, my knees trembling, my back stiff and unforgiving. But I stand tall.

He turns, his face a mask of fury, his movements slow as he closes the space between us. "What do you think you're doing?" he asks, his voice low, crackling with warning.

I hold his gaze, my breath coming in shallow bursts, my chest tight with the force of it. "I'm done," I say, the words trembling but firm. "I want to go home."

For a moment, he doesn't respond. His eyes stay locked on mine, searching, calculating. The silence presses in, wrapping itself around me like a noose. Then he sighs, the sound heavy with exasperation.

"Okay," he says finally, the word soft, almost resigned.

The relief is immediate, rushing through me like a flood. My knees threaten to buckle under the weight of it. He steps back, his movements measured, his face unreadable.

"You're free to go," he says, his voice calm, even.

I nod, my body trembling, my hands curling at my sides as if bracing for something that doesn't come. His words hang in the air, and I cling to them as I back away out of the kitchen. Each step backward is cautious, measured, my eyes glued to his. His silence clings to me, thick and unbearable, his gaze dissecting me.

"I understand if you don't want me anymore," I say, my voice fragile, trembling under its own weight. "This . . . this is too much. I can't do it."

The words unravel as I back away, each one pulled taut by fear. His face doesn't change. The intensity in his eyes doesn't waver, and the stillness of him is louder than anything I can say.

"I'm sorry this didn't work out," I add quickly, the apology tumbling from my lips like loose thread.

Still nothing. His silence is a living thing, filling the space between us as I turn, stiff and mechanical, toward the hallway. My feet quicken, and I count my next moves in my head: *Clothes. Purse. Out.*

His presence trails me, a shadow stitched to my heels. I don't look back. I can't. The air feels heavy, pressing against me as I reach the study and fumble for my clothes. My hands shake as I pull them on, the fabric sticking to my skin, every movement jagged with panic.

My eyes scan the room frantically, heart hammering as I search for my purse. "Hey, where's my—" I start, the words bursting out before I can think.

Pain.

It's sudden and blinding, a fist slamming into my stomach, and my body folds in on itself like paper crumpling under a heavy hand. Air flees my lungs, leaving me gasping, clutching at my abdomen as the room swims in and out of focus.

I blink through the haze and see him, standing over me, fury carved into the lines of his face. In his hand, something small and black. It takes a moment for my brain to connect the dots, but then the prongs glint under the light, and fear floods every corner of my body.

The taser crackles before I feel it, the electricity tearing through me, locking my muscles in a violent spasm. I scream, raw and guttural, the sound tearing through the room. My body shakes uncontrollably, the aftershock leaving me limp and gasping on the floor.

"Speak again! I dare you!" he snarls, his voice a jagged edge cutting through my disoriented thoughts.

I try to form words, anything to pacify him, but my throat tightens. No sound comes, just the desperate heaving of my breath. His hand twists into my hair, yanking me upright, and I stumble, knees scraping the floor as he drags me toward the cage. The sting from the taser lingers, radiating through my body in sharp, pulsating bursts.

Before I can resist, he shoves me inside. My body crumples awkwardly against the cold metal bars, the cage a fist closing around me. The door slams shut, the lock clicking with brutal finality.

Tears stream down my face as I curl into myself, the sobs coming in ragged, broken waves. My hands tremble as they press against the cage's unforgiving floor. The collar around my neck feels tighter, heavier, as if it's pulling me under.

Nathan stands above me, the taser still in his hand, his chest rising and falling with sharp, measured breaths. His eyes bore into mine, unreadable but searing. "You don't get to decide when this ends," he says, his voice cold and precise, every word a shard of glass. "I do."

I shrink away, my body folding tighter, but his gaze doesn't relent. The room seems to close in, the air thick and stifling, the bars pressing into my skin like a brand.

He leans down, his face inches from mine, his voice soft but terrifying in its calm. "You're going to learn the rules," he says, the words curling around me like smoke. "And you're going to learn fast."

I nod instinctively, the motion automatic, a reflex born of fear. My mind races, spinning with questions that lead nowhere. How did this happen? What do I do now?

Nathan straightens, his grip on the taser firm, and steps back. The sound of his footsteps fades as he leaves the room, the door clicking shut behind him.

I sit in the cage, my tears falling freely, my body trembling from the pain, the fear, the weight of it all. I tell myself this isn't real, that it can't be real, but the cold bite of the metal bars and the lingering ache in my abdomen tell me otherwise.

SIXTEEN

The next morning, I jolt awake to the sound of banging—loud and rhythmic. It slices through the haze of hunger and exhaustion, vibrating through the floor and into my spine. My body screams in protest as I shift, every joint stiff from a night curled up in the cage. For a moment, I think the noise is a dream, something dredged up from the same twisted corner of my brain that invents reasons to stay here. But then it comes again, louder this time. Hammering.

I hear footsteps, heavy and purposeful, moving closer. My heart stumbles into a faster rhythm, and I brace myself, pressing my body into the bars as if they might open if I push hard enough. The door creaks, and I curl into myself instinctively, expecting the worst.

But I couldn't have expected this.

Nathan steps into the room, his smile stretched thin. His eyes glint with something bright and unnerving, as if he's savoring a joke only he knows. His presence fills the space, sucking the air out of it, and for a moment I can't see anything else. Then she crawls in behind him.

It all happens in slow motion. The first thing I notice is the leash, taut in his hand, the loop wrapped casually around his wrist like an afterthought. The second is her—the way she moves, low and fluid, her body arched in a way that's both unnatural and practiced. Her limbs bend as if she was made for this, as if she's been doing it forever.

She's gaunt, her frame painfully thin, her ribs casting shadows across her pale skin. Bruises bloom along her arms and legs, some fresh, others fading into yellows and greens, like they've been layered over time. Her blonde hair is tied into neat pigtails that feel cruel, too childish for the hollow-eyed woman beneath them. She's wearing a light blue babydoll dress that clings to her like a second skin, the fabric absurdly frilly, as if she's been dressed up as someone else's idea of innocence.

My eyes catch on the collar around her neck, the pale blue leather perfectly matched to her dress. A small metal tag dangles from it, catching the light. *Cupcake.* The name is engraved in delicate cursive, sweet and diminutive, so at odds with the bruises and her sharp, feral movements.

But it's not just her appearance. It's the way she crawls, the way her body shifts with an eerie, animalistic grace that sends a shiver down my spine. She doesn't hesitate, doesn't falter. There's no awkwardness, no shame—only the smooth efficiency of someone who has been remade into this, who has forgotten what it is to move any other way.

Her eyes snap around the room, wide and unblinking, as if she's searching for something that's constantly just out of reach. They're blue, almost too bright, and they shine with a feverish intensity that sits uneasily between fear and madness. Her mouth hangs open slightly, her tongue darting out to lick at the corners, saliva pooling and dripping onto the floor as she pants audibly, loudly.

I can't look away. My mind stumbles over itself, trying to make sense of what I'm seeing, but it refuses to settle. I don't know how long she's been here, but her body tells the story clearly enough: a long time. Long enough to forget how to stand. Long enough to become this.

Nathan tugs gently on the leash, and she snaps her head toward him, her movements jerky and immediate. She wriggles slightly, a tremor passing through her body, as though she's bracing for a command. My stomach lurches as I realize she's been trained to anticipate him this way. To need him this way.

"This is Cupcake," Nathan says, his smile stretching wider. His voice is calm, almost proud, as if he's introducing a beloved pet. "This is who you're replacing."

The words hit me like a punch to the chest. *Replacing?* My eyes flick back to Cupcake, who is trembling faintly, her ribs rising and falling with shallow, rapid breaths. Her head lowers again, her eyes darting to him before dropping to the floor.

"Cupcake is sick," Nathan continues, his tone softening, a strange affection creeping into his voice. "She can't stay here any longer." He crouches beside her, petting her head gently, his hand moving down her back in slow, lazy strokes. She leans into his touch, her body shivering, and I feel sick.

I can't stop staring at her, every detail burning itself into my brain: the hollows of her cheeks, the tremble in her limbs, the way she pants like an overworked animal. She's about my age, I realize, and the thought makes my chest tighten. *What happens to someone after years of this?*

Fear settles in next to pity, wrapping itself around my ribs like a tightening vice. *How long does he plan to keep me? How long before I become her?*

Nathan gestures to the cage. "I'm transitioning her space to yours," he says lightly. "This is just temporary." He waves his hand dismissively at the cage, as if it's beneath discussion. "You'll have a room soon. A real one. Prettier than this."

He steps closer, his hand reaching through the bars to pet my head. The touch is deceptively gentle, but it doesn't feel like affection. It feels like ownership.

"You'll love it," he murmurs, his eyes locking on to mine. The intensity in them makes my skin crawl. Then he straightens, his tone shifting into something more casual. "I need to take care of Cupcake," he says, tugging lightly on her leash. "I'll be back in two days."

His words barely register. He's leaving? For two days? What does he mean by *take care of her*?

Panic floods my chest, and I grab the bars of the cage, shaking them violently. "Wait!" I scream, the sound tearing out of me before I can stop it.

Nathan halts, the air around him tightening like a coil. He turns slowly, his smile gone, leaving only a face carved from ice.

His hand tightens on the leash, and Cupcake collapses inward like a dying star. She knows I messed up.

"What are you going to do to her?" The words burst out of me, raw and trembling, desperation bleeding through every syllable. My voice cracks under its own weight. "Please. Don't hurt her."

Nathan's eyes find mine, narrowing like a predator homing in on prey. He steps deeper into the room, and crouches until his face is level with mine. The space between us collapses into something suffocating. He says nothing at first, the silence stretching, its edges curling closer. When he finally speaks, his voice is low, coiled tight with something cold and precise.

"You broke a rule."

The words strike like a slap, stealing the breath from my lungs. I recoil, my hands falling away from the bars as my body folds inward, instinctively trying to make itself smaller. Tears well in my eyes, blurring his face into something unrecognizable.

"Please," I whisper, the sound fragile, disintegrating on my tongue.

He straightens, towering over me now, his face devoid of warmth. His grip on Cupcake's leash doesn't waver, and she trembles at his side, her breaths shallow and quick.

"I'll deal with this later," he says, each word cutting like a scalpel. "For now, stay quiet. Don't make me regret leaving you alone."

The finality in his tone closes the space between us, and my stomach knots as he turns, leading Cupcake away. Her movements are quick, frantic, her body clinging to the ground as though afraid to rise too high. She doesn't look back. She doesn't hesitate. She follows him into the void.

The door clicks shut, the sound reverberating through the room, and the silence that follows is heavy, oppressive. It settles over me like smoke, thick and choking.

I collapse onto the floor of the cage, my body wracked with tremors, the bars cold against my skin. The sobs come hard and fast, tearing through me, echoing in the empty room until the sound feels like it belongs to someone else.

Nathan's words linger, circling like vultures: *You broke a rule.*

The silence stretches, unbroken, swallowing me whole.

SEVENTEEN

The punishment was absence. A week of silence that thickened and swelled, folding itself into the corners of the house like mold. It pressed against my skin, filled my lungs, and became a kind of second body I had to wear. The quiet wasn't still—it groaned and hissed, the house shifting in the cold, the hum of the fridge swelling to a roar. At first, I measured time, trying to twist it into something I could hold. But by the third day, it unraveled, the hours dissolving into a fog where everything stretched and snapped. Time became a creature with no boundaries, coiling into itself.

When I hear the front door open, it is a knife cutting through the haze. Relief comes first, hot and sick, swelling in my chest until it spills out as tears. I hate myself for it, for the pathetic tremor of gratitude that blooms like rot. Gratitude for the man who had left me here, who had let the silence sink its claws into me. But my body didn't care about principle. It cared about survival. It wanted food, water, warmth—something, anything, other than the monstrous nothingness of waiting.

He had left me a bowl of water, and it kept me alive. I rationed it in small sips, imagining it lasting forever, but by the fourth day, it was gone, the metal bowl dry except for the bitter tang of its residue. My throat burned, raw and hollow, my tongue thick and useless. I swallowed air as if it might soothe the ache.

By the second day, I pissed myself. The shame was distant, a faint sting compared to the gnawing hunger. The cage reeked, the sour stench clinging to my skin. It didn't matter anymore. My body was a machine failing piece by piece, hoarding every ounce of energy. I hadn't defecated once. There was nothing left to lose.

By the fourth day, I broke. The dog food sat there, congealed into a rancid, gelatinous heap. At first, the sight of it made me gag, but my hunger soon sharpened me into a different kind of beast. When I finally lowered my head to the bowl, it wasn't a decision—it was instinct. The taste was metallic and foul, like swallowing rot, but I forced it down, one bite at a time. Each swallow carved me into something less human, but it gave me another hour, another breath.

By the fifth day, I wasn't a person anymore.

Nathan's footsteps echo closer, and my heart stutters, caught between relief and dread. I press myself to the bars, weak and trembling, my breath shallow, uneven. The door creaks open, and there he is, his presence swallowing the room whole. He looks the same, untouched by the time that has dismantled me.

Tears streak my face before I can stop them. My chest heaves with the awful realization: *He's back. He's back.*

Nathan doesn't acknowledge my tears. He opens the cage and pulls me out with a grip that is firm but not cruel. The leash clicks onto my collar, the sound too loud, too final. He doesn't look at me, doesn't speak, and I don't dare break the silence. The questions sit like stones in my throat, heavy and jagged: *Where is Cupcake? What did you do to her?*

But I already know. He killed her. Of course he did.

As if reading my thoughts, Nathan glances down. His voice is flat, detached. "Took her to a hospital," he says, the words landing with a hollow thud. "She's fine."

I don't believe him. The weightless way he says it, the way his eyes don't quite meet mine—it doesn't match the violence I know that lives inside him. But I stay silent. There's no space for questions, and even if there was, my voice is not something I can use.

I stop crawling for a moment, lost in the spiral of thoughts, and the leash snaps taut. He tugs sharply, a reminder that my body is no longer mine. My knees scrape against the floor as I follow, the rhythm automatic, the submission reflexive.

He leads me to the bathroom, where the air is thick and warm, the tiles slick with condensation. Steam rises from the tub as he turns on the faucet, testing the water with his hand. He adds soap to the water and it smells of lavender, a detail so small but it reminds me of my old life back home and it makes me want to scream.

I wait, knees pressed to the cold floor, the silence wrapping itself around us like a noose.

He stands over it, turning the faucet, his hand dipping into the water like a sculptor testing clay.

"Get in," he says, his voice flat, the edges clipped clean.

The water looks too still, too perfect, like it's waiting to pull me under. I step in. The heat bites first, sharp and invasive, a punishment in itself. I flinch, gasping, but lower myself further, the water softening into something kind. It wraps around me, melting the grime from my skin, clouds of dirt swirling in delicate patterns. For a fleeting moment, I feel human, weightless in the warmth.

Nathan watches without speaking, his presence filling the room. Then he moves. He doesn't undress fully—just strips to his boxers—and the sight of him climbing into the tub makes my stomach turn, though I don't fully understand why. My hands grip the rim of the tub as he kneels, picking up a sponge.

He begins scrubbing me, his motions steady, detached. It's not rough, but there's no tenderness, no connection—just the mechanical efficiency of a man washing his car, inspecting every inch for flaws. His focus is singular, starting with my arms, working down my back. When he reaches my hair, his fingers comb through the tangles with a care that feels almost out of place. The warm water cascades over my scalp, and for a moment, I let myself drift. I imagine this is normal, a scene pulled from someone else's life, something gentle. He's my boyfriend, and this is love, a quiet intimacy shared in the steam.

But the silence is loud, and his presence is a weight I can't escape.

His hands move lower, between my legs. The rhythm doesn't change—still detached, still efficient—but his eyes meet mine for the first time. They are cold, sharp as glass, and the contact slices through me.

"I'm not happy you spoke," he says, his voice low and flat, like a stone thrown into still water.

The words hit harder than his hands ever could, and my chest tightens. My gaze locks on his, frozen, my lips pressed shut as though any sound might shatter me completely. He waits, his eyes daring me to respond, but I know better than to speak.

His tone sharpens, each syllable a whip. "Didn't you learn from last time?"

I nod, my entire body rigid under his touch. The water, once soothing, now feels like a weight pressing me down, the heat stifling, choking. I drop my gaze to the ripples on the surface, watching them distort the reflection of his hands, trying to anchor myself in their rhythm, trying not to shatter.

The sponge slips from his grip, the sound of it hitting the water breaking the silence. He doesn't move to pick it up. Instead, the quiet stretches between us, thick and unbearable, the tension clinging to my skin.

I stay still, submerged, waiting. The water laps at my body, the warmth now a mockery of comfort. At least, for now, I'm clean. At least, for now, I'm still here.

The weeks fold into one another, indistinct, their weight pressing down on me in a continuous, seamless stretch of time. I no longer track the days. Light seeps through the windows, pools on the floor, fades to darkness, and returns again, but its rhythm is meaningless. Time is no longer mine. It belongs to Nathan—his commands, his footsteps, the soft click of the leash, the intervals between his movements. Even when he's not in the room, his presence fills it, heavy and pervasive, as though the air itself carries him.

The dog food comes thick and pungent, spooned into the same dull metal bowl, turning my stomach before it touches my lips. I tell myself I won't eat it again. Each refusal feels like a small victory until the hunger sharpens, hollowing me out, its edges gnawing at my resolve.

Once, he tossed me a dog biscuit, his lips curving into a faint, amused smile as it clattered to the floor. Another time, a piece of steak fell from his plate—accident or intention, I couldn't tell. He gestured with lazy authority, his voice soft and mocking.

"Go ahead, girl," he said. "You've earned it."

SHY GIRL

I hesitated, caught in the web of his tone, scanning for traps in the way his eyes followed me. When he nodded, I crawled forward, lowered my head, and picked up the steak with my teeth. I ate it quickly, the salt and fat almost unbearable, a bitter reminder of every meal I've ever turned down, when I had the luxury of saying no.

The cage is always cold, the thin mat beneath me offering no protection from the chill of the bars. I curl into myself, knees to my chest, arms wrapped tightly around my body, but the cold seeps in, steady and relentless. My back aches from the hours spent hunched, my knees burn, and my wrists throb. Every part of me is a reminder of how much space I've lost, how my body has been reshaped by confinement.

Sleep comes in shards, shallow and restless. The overhead light drills into my skull, unrelenting, and the muffled sounds of Nathan's movement in the house pierce the thin veil of rest. Each creak of the floorboards sends a jolt through me, snapping me awake. Even when I drift off, my dreams fracture under the weight of this reality—cages, collars, Nathan's face looming in the periphery, always watching.

I haven't spoken since the morning I met Cupcake, since my voice betrayed me. I wanted to ask: *Why are you doing this to me? What do you want? Why can't you let me go?* I still think that sometimes if I could just talk to him, reason with him, I might find some crack in his resolve, some humanity buried deep inside.

But I know better. His punishments are too cold, too exact. The rules are etched into the walls of my mind: speak, and you will suffer.

So I focus on survival, on the small rituals that make me feel human. I drink from the water bowl he leaves, the taste metallic but necessary. I follow his commands—*sit, stay, beg*—and lower my head when he strokes my hair, the motions automatic. I crawl when he calls, bark when he demands. The sound of my voice turned animal feels foreign in my mouth, yet it passes my lips with practiced ease.

Sex is frequent. Even when I'm dizzy, exhausted, barely able to keep myself upright, he takes what he wants. My body struggles under his weight, my joints groaning in protest, my muscles screaming for relief. Sometimes I pass out mid-act, my consciousness retreating to a safer place. When I whimper, it's no longer feigned; the sounds of distress slip out, raw and uncontrollable. Either he notices, or he doesn't care. My guess is the latter; he does not care.

I try to create order from the chaos, dividing my days into fragments: *this is morning light, this is evening light, this is his dinner hour, this is his resting hour.* But even that slips away. Time bends and warps, its edges frayed. The days stretch, and the nights swallow them whole.

I survive, though. I endure the cold, the hunger, the exhaustion. I tell myself this can't last forever, that something will break before I do. But when the thought creeps in—that this might not end, that I might stay here, in this cage, in this life, until I disappear completely—the spiral begins.

I bite down on the panic, hard, and anchor myself to the small, mechanical acts that keep me sane: breathe in for four, hold for four, breathe out for four. Repeat.

EIGHTEEN

Nathan strides into the room, grinning, his teeth sharp and predatory. The smile isn't joyful—it's a weapon, a gleaming blade honed with control, satisfaction glinting in his eyes like the punchline to a joke only he finds funny.

"It's done," he says, his tone light, conversational, like he's telling me the weather or what's for dinner. The casualness of it cuts deeper than anger ever could.

He pulls me out of the cage. The leash snaps onto my collar, the click louder than it should be, reverberating in the taut silence between us. My knees tremble as I follow him, each movement hesitant, my body braced against the weight of his words.

We stop in front of a door I've never seen open. It has loomed there since I arrived, a part of the house I trained myself to ignore. Nathan places a hand on the handle, turning to me with that same unnerving grin, and then swings the door wide.

The room is pink—*violently* pink. It punches me in the chest, a pastel assault so sudden my eyes squint against it. Bubblegum walls framed with frilly white trim; a plush pink rug spreads across the floor like candy floss. The sweetness of it clogs the air, so cloying it makes my stomach twist.

The furniture looks ripped from a nightmare of childhood nostalgia. A small white bookshelf overflows with children's books and there's a battalion of stuffed animals in a small wooden chest, their button eyes unblinking, fixed on me. But the bed—small, twin-sized, absurd—is the centerpiece. Its pink quilt is edged with lace, a confection of faux innocence, but it's the headboard that anchors me: two pairs of silver handcuffs dangle from its edges, glinting in the soft light.

The windows are boarded up, the planks painted pink to blend in with the walls. The effort to disguise the room's suffocation only amplifies it. The entire space feels toxic, a grotesque trap, sweetness layered over steel.

"This is your permanent room," Nathan says, stepping back, his voice rich with satisfaction. He gestures like a game-show host presenting a prize. "Go on, girl, climb up on the bed."

He unhooks the leash and waits, his grin unwavering. My body obeys before my mind catches up, crawling onto the bed in hesitant, jerking motions. The mattress is too firm, the lace scratching my skin with every shift, a reminder that I can't escape it.

"You'll sleep here every night," he continues, matter-of-fact, like he's explaining a schedule. "When I'm gone for long periods, you'll be handcuffed to the bed. Until I can trust you."

Trust. The word twists, hollow and sharp, its weightless

promise pressing into me. His tone is casual, but the permanence in it is a cold hand around my throat.

"You have a bed. A room. Isn't that great?" His voice turns falsely enthusiastic, his grin stretching wider. He waits for me to agree, the absurdity of his excitement curling my stomach into knots.

"Woof," I say flatly.

Nathan claps his hands, pleased. "I have another surprise for you," he says, disappearing through the door.

For the first time, I'm alone and not on a leash. My eyes dart to the boarded windows, the toy chest, the room itself, scanning for something—*anything*—that might help me escape. But the door swings open again before I can move, and Nathan returns, holding something in his hands.

A collar.

It's pink, thick, with a silver heart dangling from the center. The charm glints in the light, the word *Shy Girl* engraved in delicate cursive.

Nathan holds it up like a trophy, his grin now sharper, crueler. "You are no longer Gia," he says, his voice steady. "From now on, your name is Shy Girl. Got it?"

I nod, the motion quick, mechanical. "Woof," I say, my voice trembling but firm enough to satisfy him.

He steps closer, unclips the old black collar from my neck, and replaces it with the new one. The leather is soft, but it feels heavier, the heart charm pressing coldly against my skin. His fingers move methodically, fastening the buckle like a ritual, his eyes scanning me with detached satisfaction.

"Perfect," he murmurs. Then, without warning, he pushes me back onto the bed. My body moves automatically, offering no resistance.

When it's over, he straightens, adjusts his clothes, and steps back, his expression serene. "You're free to roam around your room," he says, almost cheerful.

My eyes dart again to the boarded windows, hope flickering faintly, but Nathan follows my gaze. He points to the corner, where a small black security camera blinks steadily, its red light cutting through the pink haze.

"But don't try anything sneaky," he warns, his voice darkening. "I'm watching you. If I see you standing, you'll be punished. If you try to escape, you'll be punished."

The words land heavy, sealing the air.

"Woof," I whisper, my throat dry, the sound barely audible.

Nathan grins one last time, satisfied, and leaves the room. The door locks behind him with an echoing click, and the sound reverberates like a final note.

I sit on the bed, the lace scratching at my skin, the charm at my neck pressing into my collarbone. The camera blinks steadily, a constant reminder that there is no freedom here, no privacy. The weight of the room, the collar, the name—all of it settles over me, suffocating in its violent pinkness. I curl into myself, the reality of my new life sinking deeper with every breath.

NINETEEN

I don't know how long I've been in the Pink Room when Nathan walks in, grinning. Time here is elastic, pulling me apart, snapping back with no warning, leaving me dizzy. I've read every book on the shelf at least ten times, the words eroding into hollow shapes I trace with my eyes just to fill the space. The bed is better than the cage—enough room to stretch without folding into origami—but it doesn't change the fact that I'm dissolving, piece by piece, into nothing.

The sound of the door unlocking clicks through the fog. My head jerks toward it, then lowers instinctively as he steps inside. My shoulders hunch, my hands knot into themselves, as if I could shrink small enough to disappear into the fibers of the rug.

Something flutters to the floor in front of me. It lands softly, harmlessly, but the air in the room shifts, changes. I glance down, my breath catching.

It's a missing person's poster.

It's me.

The bold letters of my name hit me first. Then my picture,

taken at work, the version of myself that looks like a stranger now. My eyes stare back at me, tired but whole, framed by details: my height, my weight, the mole near my left ear, the scar from the bike accident when I was twelve. My chest tightens as the realization crashes over me, cold and jagged.

Nathan sighs, theatrical and heavy, yanking my attention back to him. "I thought I'd covered all my bases with you," he says, his tone casual, as if he's annoyed about a stain on his shirt.

I don't speak. I can't. My throat feels tight, my breath uneven.

"I know you don't talk to your family, so they weren't an issue," he continues, pacing slowly, like this is a story he's been waiting to tell. "I wrote your landlord a letter. Said you were leaving the country. Even included four grand in cash—generous, right? Told him to toss or sell your stuff." He pauses, tilting his head as if waiting for applause, his eyes glinting with control.

I stare back, my chest rising and falling with shallow, frantic breaths. My hands clench into fists.

"But I missed something," he says, softer now, almost amused. "Your college friend. Kennedy."

Her name lands like a blow, reverberating through the room. The pink walls close in, the sweetness turning sour. My chest aches with something sharp, unfamiliar—a flicker of hope tangled with despair. Kennedy. *He knows about Kennedy.*

Nathan studies my face, a faint smirk curling his lips. "Apparently, she's been looking for you since you went missing six months ago."

Six months.

The number unravels me, a thread pulled too tight. *Six months of pink walls. Six months of nothing.* The weight of it fills every corner of the room, pressing down on me. Tears spill, hot and unstoppable, streaking my face. Nathan watches, his amusement crackling in the space between us.

"Luckily," he says, his tone light, conversational, "you didn't tell her anything about me. I know because I checked your texts. You know, for someone who's supposed to be your best friend, you didn't tell her much." He chuckles, low and cruel. "If I'd known you two were so close, I would've written her a letter. Told her you were off starting some fabulous new life abroad. Actually . . ." He pauses, tapping his chin. "I still might do that."

Guilt slams into me. *I should've told her something. Anything.* If I had, maybe she'd know. Maybe she wouldn't still be looking.

Nathan crouches in front of me, his face inches from mine, triumphant and mocking. His voice drops, dark and cutting. "Not that it matters. The police aren't taking your disappearance seriously. They think you ran off. Even your dad gave up. Sent a text saying he'd leave you alone—figured it's what you wanted."

The sobs come harder now, shaking my body as the poster blurs in front of me. It's an accusation, a mirror, a monument to the version of me that's vanished. Nathan rises, brushing off his hands like he's finished tidying up.

"It's amazing," he says, his tone breezy, almost impressed. "You disappear, and the world just moves on. You made it so easy for me."

His words are knives, and I can't stop bleeding. My chest heaves as the sobs tear through me, my tears pooling on the rug. Nathan's smile fades slightly as he watches, his amusement dimming, replaced by something bored, disinterested. Without another word, he turns and leaves, the door clicking shut behind him.

The deadbolt slides into place, final and cold.

I stare at the poster, its details smudged by my tears. My face stares back, warped and distant. *Kennedy is looking for me. Six months. She's been looking for six months.*

And she won't find me.

YEAR TWO

TWENTY

The next year drags by slow and jagged, each day bleeding into the next with no clean edges, no seams to tell one from another. Time here doesn't move forward—it is a heavy, pink-tinted void where nothing begins or ends. The books on the shelf have long stopped being stories. Their words dissolve as I read them, the letters turning into shapes, the shapes into noise. But I read them anyway, over and over, hoping the repetition will tether me to something real. Anything.

But the only real thing is my voice, thin and trembling in the dark, whispering apologies to a father who will never hear them.

I didn't think about my dad much before this room. He was always on the periphery of my life, a figure of quiet disappointment. He lived in the sighs he let out when I told him I wasn't coming home for Thanksgiving, knowing he'd get drunk and unravel the night. But now, in the pink glow of this room, he is everything.

At night, when the silence wraps itself around me like a second skin, I lie on the bed with its scratchy quilt and press my face into the pillow. I whisper to him, my voice breaking on the same promises, over and over: *If I get out of here, the first thing I'll do is call you.*

I hold his face in my mind like a photograph I'm scared to lose. The crow's feet that deepened when he smiled. The way he'd squint at the horizon, refusing to admit he needed glasses. His hands, rough and steady, fixing things I didn't know were broken.

The last time I saw him, he hugged me awkwardly, his arms too loose, like he wasn't sure I wanted to be held. I replay that hug constantly, looping it like a lifeline, imagining what it would feel like to step into it again.

Some nights, Kennedy finds her way into my thoughts. I imagine her at her kitchen table, scrolling through my dead social media accounts, trying to stitch together clues that don't exist. Her determination feels like both a gift and a curse. I wonder if she's angry with me, if she hates me for leaving without a word. I hate myself for all the things I didn't say, every message I didn't send. If I could go back to that afternoon in her backyard, I would tell her everything. Maybe she would have stopped me.

The rest of my life slips away slowly, like a photograph left too long in the sun. My apartment, with its drafty windows and creaky floors, feels distant, its colours blurring. I can't remember the exact shade of my couch, the smell of my favorite candle, or the way the light spilled through the blinds in the late afternoon. The details fade, one by one, until my life feels like a dream I once had but can't hold on to.

Master Nathan's moods swing like a pendulum. His grin, wide and bright, is as unpredictable as his anger. On his good days, he lets me crawl into the kitchen for a bowl of lukewarm oatmeal. On his bad days, he locks the door behind him and makes me sit in silence as he lectures me on obedience, his voice slicing the air, sharp and unforgiving.

But it's not the punishments that hurt the most. It's the absence of everything else. The way the world beyond this room collapses in on itself, shrinking until it feels as if it was never real. It feels like trying to remember a melody I haven't heard in years—familiar but just out of reach.

I start talking to the stuffed animals on the bookshelf. The rabbit becomes my favorite, its stitched eyes lopsided, its fur dirty and matted. At night, I clutch it to my chest, its small, soft body soaking up my tears.

If I ever get out of here, the first thing I'll do is call my dad. I whisper it like a prayer, like an incantation.

My voice cracks, trembling under the weight of words I don't know how to say. I bury my face into the rabbit's fur, whispering so softly it feels like the room itself is swallowing my voice. "I'll tell him I miss him."

Some nights, in the quiet, I think I hear his voice. It comes faint, like a thread stretched too thin, but steady. *Gia*, he says, low and certain, as if he's standing just outside the door. *It's time to come home.*

TWENTY-ONE

The first time I try to escape, it's raining. The sound is relentless, rhythmic, pressing against the boarded windows like a memory of the world outside, like the world is knocking softly, waiting for me. The rain reminds me that there is something else—something beyond the pink walls and stuffed animals with unblinking eyes.

Master Nathan's snores rumble from the next room, uneven and thick, like a machine choking on itself. He's been drinking himself into oblivion for weeks now, his movements slack, his grip on control slipping. Last week, he forgot to bathe me. He forgot to even *look* at me. In the mornings, he shuffled me to the bathroom, leash dangling loose in his hand, his mind somewhere far away. Then he locked me back in the Pink Room without a word. The neglect wasn't kindness; it was weakness. A crack in the foundation.

Tonight, his snoring is louder, wetter, the smell of whiskey still heavy in the air, sharp and sour. When he led me back to my room, his hands fumbled with the lock. I held my breath, listening for the deadbolt's finality—but it didn't come. He didn't lock the deadbolt. I sit on the rug, my hands pressed flat to my thighs, staring at the door. The leash is off. The camera blinks in the corner, its red light steady, patient, as if it knows I'm always watching it back. I've studied its angle, memorized its blind spots—or convinced myself I have.

The snoring continues, deep and rhythmic.

I crawl to the door, my knees sinking into the softness of the rug, my movements slow. My body feels too large, too loud, every creak of my joints amplified in the stillness. When I reach the door, I stand. My legs tremble, my knees crack, the sound sharp in the quiet.

I wait. The snoring doesn't falter.

The handle is locked. Of course it's locked.

I reach for the bobby pin I've kept hidden, tucked into the hem of my dress for weeks. My fingers shake as I work it into the lock, the metal cold and unfamiliar. My breath comes in shallow gasps, my mind whirring with failure after failure.

This has to work. This has to work.

The lock clicks open, the sound deafening in the silence. I freeze, waiting for the house to wake. But the snoring continues, and the rain drums on, steady and insistent. I exhale, shaky and uneven, and push the door open just enough to slip through.

The hallway is dark, a nightlight near Nathan's room casting pale shadows that stretch and bend like they're alive.

As I pass his door, I hold my breath, counting my movements in my head. One. Two. Three. The door is cracked open, a sliver of light spilling out, but I don't look inside. I don't need to. I can feel him there, heavy and oppressive, radiating through the walls.

The front door is ahead. The rain is louder now, closer, the sound pressing against the wood as if it's trying to get in. My fingers graze the frame as I reach for the lock. My entire body trembles, every nerve screaming for me to move faster, quieter, to *go*.

Then the snoring stops.

The silence crashes down, thick and immediate. My breath catches in my throat, and I freeze, my mind a static hum. I wait for footsteps, for the creak of his door, for the end.

Nothing. Then, faintly, the bed creaks, and the snoring resumes—jagged at first, then falling back into its uneven rhythm.

I let out a silent breath, my hands shaking so hard they slip from the handle. My knees ache, my muscles burn, but I force myself to stay still. My mind spins through the possibilities—the failures. The door will make noise. A rush of air, the hinges groaning, a sound loud enough to pull him from sleep.

But then I see it.

The back door.

It's ajar, just slightly, a gap so small it's almost undetectable. My breath catches as I crawl toward it, my body moving without thought. I push it wider, the air rushing in cool and sharp against my skin, carrying the scent of rain and earth.

I step outside.

The grass is slick under my bare feet, the mud pulling at me as if to slow me down, but I move. The rain clings to me, soaks through my nightdress, my hair plastered to my face. The air is too big, too alive, and it steals my breath, my freedom too heavy to hold.

I run.

I don't know where I'm going. The forest stretches out, endless and dark, but it doesn't matter. As long as I'm not in that house, it doesn't matter. The sound of the rain swallows everything, until it doesn't.

A yell cuts through the night, sharp and guttural, followed by a gunshot that splits the air like a wound.

I freeze. The sound echoes in my head, reverberating through my body. My legs give out, and I collapse into the mud. The rain pours down in relentless sheets, mixing with the tears streaming down my face, carving rivers into the earth. I tilt my head back, staring at the sky. The rain blurs the world—trees, ground, the faint silhouette of Nathan in the distance, shotgun in hand.

For a moment, I let myself feel it. The air on my skin. The open sky. The freedom I know I'll never have again. These are my last minutes of being alive, and I hold on to them, tight, even as they slip through my fingers.

YEAR THREE

TWENTY-TWO

One day, Nathan brings me a full-length mirror, its size commanding the space in the tiny room. The frame is intricate, gold filigree twisting like veins, the kind of thing you'd see in a museum or a house too large for one family. He doesn't explain. He doesn't even look at me. He props it against the wall with a grunt, adjusts it until it's perfectly straight, and leaves without a word.

At first, I try not to notice it. I keep my head down, eyes fixed on the floor, the way I've been taught. But the mirror is impossible to ignore. Its presence hums, pulling at the edges of my attention, turning the room into a trap of reflections and empty space. It feels alive, as if it's watching me even when Nathan isn't.

Days pass. The mirror becomes a weight, an unspoken thing pressing on my chest every time I move. Finally, I give in. I crawl toward it slowly, the way you might approach an animal you're not sure will bite. My knees burn against the floor, but I barely notice. All I can think about is the mirror and what it might show me.

When I reach it, I lift my head. And there I am.

The reflection knocks the air out of my lungs. This is the first time I am seeing myself—really seeing myself—in three years. I don't recognize myself. My hair hangs in tangled clumps, greasy and matted. My body is hunched, my shoulders caving in like they're trying to disappear. Bruises spread up my arms and across my back. They look almost purposeful, like a grotesque mimicry of something natural. The pink collar gleams against my skin, snug and unrelenting, a perfect symbol of everything I've let myself become.

I reach out, my fingers trembling, and press them to the glass. The reflection blurs under the smear of my hand, but it doesn't go away. I pull my hand back and let it fall to the floor, my gaze dropping with it. My knees, raw and calloused, stare back at me like an accusation.

Nathan enters. I don't hear him at first, but I feel him—the weight of his presence shifting the air in the room. My body stiffens. He stops behind me, his reflection towering over mine, and the room feels suddenly smaller.

"What do you see, girl?" he asks, his voice calm, measured, but sharp enough to cut.

I stare at the floor, unsure if I'm supposed to answer. The silence stretches, and when it becomes unbearable, I let out a soft bark just to appease him.

He crouches beside me, his hand brushing against my shoulder. His eyes meet mine in the mirror, and I hate the way it feels like he's searching for something, like I'm a puzzle he's trying to solve.

"I see potential," he says. His tone is low, almost tender, but it sticks in my throat like something sour.

The words sit heavy in my chest, their weight spreading, suffocating. His hand lingers on my shoulder, the pressure just shy of comforting, before he stands and leaves. The door clicks shut behind him, but the sound doesn't break the spell the mirror has cast.

I stay there for a long time, my eyes locked on the stranger in the glass.

I sit in front of the mirror for hours, the floor gnawing at my knees, the reflection in the glass warping as the light shifts in the room. The golden frame gleams faintly, mocking, its ornate details curling like fingers around the truth it holds. My mind drifts, unmoored and slippery, to the app. To the flicker of messages. Names and faces blurred together now, like smudged ink.

I think about the other men. The ones who called me beautiful, who promised to treat me like a queen, who filled my inbox with carefully crafted lines about respect and affection. The ones who wanted nothing more than a warm body across the table, a companionable laugh over wine that tasted like money. The ones who wanted more but dressed it in velvet, wrapped it in promises of fun, of ease, of no strings.

I scroll through those memories like a faded photo album. The man with the yachts, his profile picture a sunlit grin, who wanted someone "spontaneous." The one who signed every message with a rose emoji, "darling" spilling from his fingers like a reflex. The man who quoted poetry like he owned it, who wrote in sprawling paragraphs about art and soulmates and destiny.

None of them had felt real. Too smooth, too curated, as if they'd rehearsed their lives for an audience. Too eager to show me the spotlight without asking if I wanted to be seen.

Then there was Nathan.

Nathan didn't bother with poetry. He didn't wrap his intentions in silk. His messages were short, blunt, carved clean with the precision of a scalpel. He didn't promise adoration or indulgence.

And now here I am. Kneeling on this cold floor in the gilded cage he's built for me, staring at a reflection that barely feels like mine. My hair is limp, my posture hunched. The bruises on my skin—some yellowing, some dark and purple—cast shadows across my arms, legs, and back. The collar gleams in the glass, a perfect circle trapping me where I am.

I wonder if I chose wrong—or if I'd ever had a choice at all. What were the odds, out of everyone on that app, that I'd choose Nathan, and Nathan would choose me?

This was fate, and I am cursed. Terrible luck of epic proportions. Cosmic karma for something I did in my past life. It is the only explanation.

He was the first message I got on the app. The first ping in the empty, cavernous inbox. His words were direct, no flowers, no fluff, just a plain introduction that didn't even bother with a compliment.

It was almost as if he could feel the desperation radiating from me through the screen, as if I had unknowingly sent out a telepathic plea to every man on the app: *pick me, choose me, save me.* His message cut through the static like a blade. No *hi beautiful,* no roses, no pretense.

I could have had the man who wanted me for my smile, for the way my face glows in candlelight. The man who would've draped diamonds around my neck, who would've flown me to Paris just to watch me sip wine beneath the Eiffel Tower. And even though I wasn't looking for any of those things, it sounded nice. Meeting someone who would've kept me intact, untouched, unchanged. But I didn't.

I chose the man who wanted not who I was, but who I could become.

A pet.

A prisoner.

I'm dreaming of a feast—pizza and chicken salad sandwiches and burgers and little mini donuts and big steaming bowls of ramen—when I hear Master Nathan scream, a raw, guttural sound that rips through the house and claws its way into me. It startles me awake, my body jerking, my heart pounding as if it's trying to escape. His grief is so loud it feels alive, heavy and thrashing, filling the air with its weight. My stomach knots, instinct taking over. I feel the guilt before I understand it, a sharp, reflexive thing burrowing deep, as if somehow this is my fault—as if I've failed him in a way I can't even name. The walls seem to close in tighter, the pink trim mocking in its sweetness, and I sit frozen in the dark, every muscle tense, waiting for his grief to turn its head and find me.

A couple of hours later, I get my answer. Nathan staggers into the room, grief etched deep into his face, his hair sticking up on all ends, his breath thick with whiskey. He moves as if his body has forgotten how to hold itself upright, dragging himself to the edge of the bed and collapsing there, head hanging low. I lie frozen, every muscle locked, afraid to even breathe. My heart hammers in my chest as the silence stretches, heavy and endless.

Finally, he speaks. He turns his head, and his eyes—red and raw—find mine. "My mother was murdered yesterday," he says, his voice flat, stripped of anything but the weight of the words. He looks back down, his fingers twitching against his knees. "She got robbed at gunpoint in a grocery store parking lot. They got away with her purse and still fucking shot her."

The words hit the air like stones, heavy and sharp, and I can feel their weight pressing into the space between us. I stare at him, my breath catching in my throat. There's a knot in my chest, tight and unfamiliar, and I can't tell if it's pity or fear or some awful combination of the two.

He sniffs, a wet, broken sound, and for a moment, it's as if I'm staring at someone else—a child who lost his mother, not the man who's turned me into this, who's stolen the shape of my life and forced me to crawl. His face crumples, his body shaking as he breaks down into tears, loud and wrenching, his grief spilling out in waves.

And then he grabs me. His arms wrap around me with a force that steals my breath, and he holds me against him, his face buried in my shoulder. His sobs are loud and raw, soaking through me like rain.

For a second, I think maybe this is it. Maybe this will crack him open, make him see himself for what he is, for what he's done. Maybe this will change him, make him realize that holding me here, stealing my life, was monstrous. Maybe he'll let me go.

I hold my breath, my heart pounding as his tears soak into my skin. *Please, let this be it*, I think. *Let him see.*

But his grip only tightens, his sobs turning into muffled, guttural sounds. And I stay still, trapped in the silence of his grief, in the terrible, fragile hope that this might be the moment that saves me.

The next morning, Nathan is stone, hard and emotionless, as if the man who cried into my shoulder never existed. His grief is gone, or maybe it's buried so deep it's turned into something else—something sharp and jagged. He doesn't look at me when he unlocks the door. His movements are brisk, mechanical, his face a mask of blank indifference.

I sit there, waiting for a crack, for the softness that had briefly flickered through him the night before. For a moment, I think maybe I imagined it, that the version of him who shook and sobbed into my skin was some trick of the dim light. But then I reach out, hesitant, my fingers trembling as they hover near his arm.

He turns and slaps me across the face so hard that I topple over.

"You're a fucking *dog*," he says, his voice low and venomous, each word landing like a stone thrown into a well. The room feels smaller, the air sucked out, and my cheek burns hot under his hand.

I stare down at the bed, my heart pounding in my ears. The tears threaten to come, but I choke them down, swallowing the lump in my throat. He stands there for a moment, breathing heavily, his hand still raised as if he might strike me again. His eyes are hollow, his expression cold, as if he's already erased what happened yesterday.

Losing his mother hasn't softened him. It hasn't changed him. Whatever part of me dared to hope for that feels small and stupid now, shriveling under the weight of his anger.

He doesn't say anything else. He just grabs the leash, clips it to my collar so he can take me to the bathroom. My knees hit the floor, the rug scratching at my skin, and I crawl after him, my body moving on autopilot, my mind frozen in the slap, the burn of his hand, the words hanging in the air like smoke.

He's harder now, harder than he's ever been, and I know, deep down, that whatever softness I thought I saw in him was a ghost. Whatever version of him that held on to me last night is gone, buried under the weight of himself.

YEAR FOUR

TWENTY-THREE

"Shy Girl, come here," Master Nathan calls, his voice slicing through the thick quiet of the house. It echoes easily from the kitchen to the living room, where I'm sprawled on my pallet, tracing shadows on the ceiling until their edges blur and fade. His tone is casual, but it hooks into me, pulling me upright without hesitation.

I crawl toward him, knees brushing the rug, each movement automatic now. He's at the counter, stirring something in a pot, the scent curling through the air—warm, savory, the kind of smell that awakens a low, desperate hunger. My stomach tightens reflexively, clenching around the promise of food I know he won't share.

"I'm having some company over tonight," he says, his voice light, as if he's telling me we're expecting rain. "I'm going to need to handcuff and gag you, so hurry up and eat your dinner."

The bowl lands with a dull thud in front of me, its contents glistening in the dim light—a single piece of chicken breast, shriveled and overcooked. I stare at it for a moment too long before lowering my head.

Company. The word feels foreign here, a sharp contrast to the near silence that's ruled this house for almost four years. My mind stumbles over it, twisting it into shapes I don't want to name. Someone else. A replacement. Someone better, someone newer.

The spiral starts, clawing its way through me. What if tonight is my last night in the Pink Room? What if he's done with me, tired of the version of me that's become too fragile, too worn? My chest tightens, and the panic rises fast, pressing against my ribs, but I swallow it down. I force my face into blank obedience. Don't let him see it. Don't let him know.

"Woof," I murmur, barely audible, and lower myself to the bowl.

The chicken is tough, dry against my teeth, but it's warm, and it's not the unsettling mush of dog food. That's enough. I chew quickly, mechanically, swallowing it down without letting myself think. Protein keeps me standing. The scraps of human food he gives me are rare, erratic, but they've kept me from slipping too far, from crumbling completely. My ribs still press against my skin, a sharp reminder of what I've lost, but I'm satiated. For now.

I glance up as I eat, watching him. His movements are hurried like his guest might arrive any minute, wiping the counter in big, circular motions, his focus somewhere far from this room. The questions press at my lips, begging to be spoken—*Who's coming? What do they mean to you? What will happen to me?*—but they stay locked behind my teeth.

The last time I asked a question, it cost me three days of bruises and silence. That was three years ago. I asked what happened to Cupcake.

When I finish, he turns to me, nodding once, a gesture so slight it feels like an afterthought. "Follow," he says, his voice clipped, and I crawl after him, my knees scraping against the hardwood, the air between us taut with unspoken weight.

The Pink Room smells of cleaning spray, the kind he uses when he's too drunk or too tired to wash me. The sweetness clings to the air, sharp and artificial, failing to mask the deeper rot underneath. He gestures to the bed, and I climb up without hesitation, spreading my legs before I can stop myself, my body moving faster than my mind.

He chuckles softly, a sound that's almost kind, almost cruel. "Not that, Shy Girl," he says, his voice coaxing as he presses my legs closed, his touch light but firm. "Not right now."

The handcuffs are next, their metal glinting faintly. They bite cold against my wrists as he snaps them on, securing them to the headboard with a decisive click. The ball gag follows. "Open," he says, and I obey, my jaw trembling as the rubber slides in, its chemical taste bitter and invasive, spreading like rust across my tongue.

"Shh," he murmurs, brushing his hand against my cheek in a gesture that pretends tenderness but that reeks of control. He lingers there, his eyes heavy on mine, his expression unreadable, before flicking off the light. The room plunges into darkness, the door clicking shut behind him, the deadbolt sliding into place like a blade drawn clean.

I lie still, my breaths shallow, uneven through my nose. The gag forces me into small, measured inhales, each one tightening the ache in my chest. The cuffs dig into my wrists, biting into my skin with each slight movement. My body feels like a cage within a cage, trapped in itself, every sensation amplified—the sting, the pull, the exhaustion crawling up my spine.

Who is it? What does this mean for me?

The questions churn, circling like vultures. The silence presses against me, thick and suffocating, broken only by the faint murmur of his voice on the phone, muffled and indistinct. I strain to hear more, to find an answer in the fragments of sound, but nothing comes.

I focus on the slow rhythm of my breath. In. Out. In. Out. It's the only thing I have, the only thing I can control. The questions don't stop, though. They chip away at me, each one sharper than the last, each one carving away another piece. Time folds in on itself, stretching and collapsing, and the room shrinks, the silence heavy and unyielding.

I lie there, trapped in the waiting, in the dark, in the endless, suffocating ache of not knowing.

About an hour later, I hear it: the front door opening and the sound of a woman's laughter, light and melodic. My chest tightens, and my ears strain, every muscle in my body tensed, waiting. Her heels click sharply against the floor, a crisp rhythm that makes my stomach turn.

Their voices drift faintly through the walls, indistinct but alive. Hers is warm, bright with amusement, while his is steady, deeper. Laughter spills between them, hers more frequent, like he's coaxing something out of her.

The questions come fast, cutting through me like splinters. *Has he told her yet? Does she know what he likes? Has he shown her the cage?*

I see it in my head before I can stop it—Nathan leading her down the hall, his hand on the small of her back, the door to the study opening. Her face when she sees it, the way her expression would shift, the dawning horror. His grin, sharp and cruel, as he waits for her to understand.

I try to shut it out, to focus, to hear them more clearly, but their voices stay muffled, their laughter distant and veiled by the walls.

Time stretches thin, and I lie there, the cuffs biting into my wrists, the gag heavy in my mouth, my jaw aching with the weight of it. My body aches, stiff and sore from the stillness, but I don't move. I just listen, clinging to the rhythm of their voices, trying to brace myself for what's coming.

Finally, their footsteps echo down the hallway, uneven and stumbling, her heels tapping out a disjointed melody. My heart pounds harder, each beat a sharp thud against my ribs. *This is it.*

But they don't stop at the study. They stop in front of Nathan's bedroom. The laughter fades, softens, mutates into something else—low murmurs, breathy sighs. Then the bed creaks.

The sounds that follow are unmistakable. Rhythmic. Loud. Her moans pierce the quiet, sharp and relentless, like a knife scraping against bone. The bed creaks in time, a jarring metronome I can't escape.

I close my eyes tight, pressing them shut as if I could block it out, but the noises burrow in, filling every corner of the room. I flinch with every sound, every gasp, every guttural groan, my body recoiling even as I stay still.

It goes on forever, the minutes stretching into something unbearable. When it finally stops, the silence is sudden, ringing in my ears. Her heels click again, harder now, faster, and then the front door slams shut.

She's gone.

Nathan's footsteps follow, slower, heavier, his weight

dragging against the house. He fiddles with the locks, and the door to the Pink Room swings open. Light floods the space, harsh and intrusive, making me squint.

"Stuck-up bitch," he mutters, his words slurred, thick with whiskey. For a moment, I think he's talking to me, and my body tenses, bracing for his hand, but then I realize it's about her.

"I can't keep her," he says, frustration seeping through his words. "She's not the right girl."

I feel something shift inside me—confusion, maybe, or a flicker of relief, faint and bitter.

Nathan stumbles toward the bed and sits heavily beside me, his weight making the frame groan. He reaches out, his hand finding my head, his fingers threading clumsily through my hair. His touch is strange, sloppy, pretending tenderness but loaded with possession.

"She's not obedient like you, Shy Girl," he says, his voice softening, almost warm. "I can't find anyone like you."

The words settle over me, thick and suffocating, pressing into my skin like a brand. *You mean someone desperate enough. Someone who gave up trying to fight.*

Nathan sighs, a long, heavy exhale, his breath warm against my cheek as he leans back. His head hits the pillow, and his hand stays tangled in my hair. Within minutes, his breathing evens out, slow and rhythmic, his snores filling the silence.

I stare at the ceiling, my wrists aching from the cuffs, my jaw tight against the gag. His body sprawls across the bed, his man-sized frame claiming most of it, leaving me perched on the edge like an afterthought. My limbs are stiff, my back screaming in protest, but I don't move.

The hours stretch, the silence heavy except for the sound of his breathing, and my thoughts spiral in tight, endless loops. *Who was she? What does this mean for me?*

I count his breaths—one, two, three, four—until the rhythm steadies me, pulling me away from the noise in my head. I lie there, trapped in his shadow, waiting for the morning to come, waiting for anything to change. But I know it won't. Nothing ever does.

YEAR FIVE

TWENTY-FOUR

The pain started small, a dull throb at the back of my jaw, the kind of ache you can tuck away and ignore if you're used to worse. And I am used to worse. Pain here has its own hierarchy, and this was so low on the ladder it barely registered. But by the second week it intensified. Every movement of my mouth sent a jolt through my skull, white-hot and unrelenting, carving itself into the back of my head.

I didn't tell Master Nathan. Complaining only leads to worse things, his punishments always heavier than the pain itself. I thought I could outlast it, thought the tooth might just fall out on its own. But last night, when he threw me a bowl of oatmeal, the mushy weight of it pressed against the raw nerve, and I couldn't swallow. Couldn't even try.

He noticed. Of course, he noticed.

"Open your mouth," he barked, his voice already sharp with irritation.

I hesitated for half a second, and his hand shot out, grabbing my jaw, forcing it open. His nails dug into my cheeks as his eyes narrowed, scanning the swollen, angry wound at the back of my mouth.

"Christ," he muttered, shoving me back with a force that felt like a warning. "You've got a fucking tooth infection."

Before I could process his words, he was gone, his footsteps echoing unevenly down the hall. When he came back, he wasn't empty-handed. He carried a pair of pliers, rusted and grimy, the kind you'd find at the bottom of a toolbox, sticky with oil and neglect.

"Sit," he said.

I sat.

There was no pretense of care, no antiseptic, no rag to bite down on. Just him, the pliers, and the sharp smell of whiskey on his breath. His fingers twisted into my hair, jerking my head back until I was staring at the ceiling.

"Open," he ordered.

I obeyed, my mouth falling open, the air slicing into the raw ache of my gums. The pliers clinked against my teeth, loud and jarring, as he forced them inside.

"Which one is it?" he asked, his tone flat, bored, like he was picking out a nail to pull from a wall.

I tried to answer, but the metal pressed against my tongue, muffling the words into a useless grunt. He sighed, annoyed, and jabbed the pliers at my molars.

"This one?" he said, the scraping sound of metal against enamel making my whole body flinch.

I couldn't help it—the pain shot through me, a sharp, searing thing—and he grinned. "Got it."

The next few moments blurred into noise and agony. The pliers clicked shut around the tooth, the squeal of metal against bone reverberating through my skull. His grip tightened in my hair, pulling my head back further as he yanked.

The pain was immediate, blinding, a white-hot explosion that ripped through my jaw. It felt as if he was trying to unhinge my skull, nerves screaming as the tooth refused to give. My muffled scream caught in the metal, my body jerking against his hold, but he didn't stop.

When it finally tore free, the sound was wet and sickening, a nauseating mix of tearing flesh and cracking bone. Blood filled my mouth instantly, warm and metallic, spilling over my lips and dripping down my chin.

Nathan held the tooth up to the light, grinning like a hunter admiring his kill. The root dangled jagged and streaked with gore, a cruel monument to my suffering.

"Look at that," he said, shoving it in front of my face. "No wonder it hurt, huh?"

I couldn't answer. I was too busy choking on blood, my body trembling, the pain radiating through me in waves. He let go of my head, and I collapsed forward, spitting onto the floor. The thick, viscous mix of blood and saliva pooled beneath me, dark and sticky.

"Stop being dramatic," he said, tossing the tooth onto the

counter like it was trash. The dull clink of it landing sent a shiver through me. "You'll feel better tomorrow."

I didn't respond. I couldn't. My mouth was too full of blood, the empty space where my tooth had been throbbing in time with my pulse. I spat again, the puddle on the floor growing larger, the metallic tang thick in the air.

Nathan didn't care. He was already in the fridge, rummaging for a beer, the bottles clinking together as if this was just another night.

I stayed on the floor like that for twenty minutes, the room spinning, blood dripping steadily from my mouth. When I finally dared to touch the hollow space, my fingers came away slick and red. I stared at them, the sticky warmth staining my skin, and thought, *This is it. This is what's left of me.*

I closed my eyes, trying to anchor myself in the dark behind my lids, but the pain roared on, unrelenting. I counted my breaths—one, two, three, four—but the ache drowned out everything else. It would still be there tomorrow, long after the blood stopped flowing. Long after he moved on to the next thing to take.

YEAR SIX

TWENTY-FIVE

The tooth doesn't heal neatly. The hole in my gums is a constant throb, a dull ache that sharpens with every attempt to eat. I don't dare ask Nathan for anything to soothe it. He's been walking around with that smug look, like yanking it out with pliers makes him a hero. For two days, I spat blood into the corner of the Pink Room, the acrid tang heavy on my tongue, clinging to everything, making the air taste like rot.

I hear him before I see him—his uneven footsteps, the clink of a bottle hitting the wall, the shuffle of a man coming undone. The smell reaches me next, sharp and sour, spilling through the cracks before the door swings open. Light floods the room, making me squint, and there he is: hulking in the doorway, his silhouette swaying, his grin loose and crooked.

"Shy Girl," he slurs, leaning against the frame. His smile spreads wide, but it doesn't reach his eyes, which are glassy and dim, like the bottom of a drained bottle. "Been a while, huh?"

I freeze, my body locking instinctively. Even the ache in my jaw dulls beneath the flood of adrenaline. He doesn't mean the tooth. We haven't had sex in almost two weeks.

He stumbles into the room, the door clicking shut behind him. The sound feels final, a closing chapter, a locked fate.

"Get on the bed," he says, his voice low and rough, the words cutting through the fog of his drunken haze.

I crawl onto the bed, my limbs trembling, my movements automatic. I arrange myself the way he likes: legs spread, arms limp at my sides, head tilted slightly, eyes fixed on the ceiling. A pose I've rehearsed a thousand times, each one erasing a little more of me.

He doesn't bother with pretense this time. There's no soft touch, no muttered "Good girl," no illusion of gentleness. He's clumsy, rough, his weight pressing down on me like a slab of concrete. His hands grip too tight, his nails digging into the soft flesh of my thighs. When he pushes inside me, I bite down hard on my lip, the taste of blood blooming like an old, bitter friend.

It doesn't last long, but it feels endless. Each thrust is mechanical, a thoughtless rhythm, his breath hot and erratic against my neck. I fix my gaze on the ceiling, tracing the cracks in the plaster, clinging to anything that pulls me away from the pain, the humiliation.

When it's over, he collapses beside me, his breathing ragged, his sweat slick against my skin. I stay still, my body aching, my muscles locked as I wait for him to leave. But he doesn't. Not immediately. Instead, he chuckles, a low, humorless sound that vibrates in my chest.

"The audience has been complaining you're boring," he says, his tone so casual it feels surreal. "So I thought I'd give them a little afternoon treat."

The words hit like a punch, knocking the air from my lungs. For a moment, they don't make sense. They hang there, impossible, until he sits up, fumbling with his pants. His movements are slow, unsteady, but his words are clear.

"You've been good, Shy Girl," he murmurs, almost tender. "But we're going to have to make things more interesting."

He stands, wiping his hands on his jeans, swaying slightly. Then he's gone. The door shuts behind him with a quiet click, the deadbolt sliding into place, locking me in but leaving me exposed.

It hits me all at once, the weight of his words crashing over me, pulling me under. My chest tightens, my breath coming in short, sharp gasps. *The audience has been complaining.* My eyes dart to the camera, the steady red light blinking in the corner of the room.

It's been there the whole time. I'd trained myself not to see it, to file it away with the rest of the horrors. But it wasn't just watching. It wasn't just recording.

It was *broadcasting*.

The realization crawls over my skin, hot and cold, sticky with shame. Every moment. Every humiliation. Every violation. Someone was watching. People were watching.

I retch, my body heaving, but there's nothing in my stomach. The bile rises anyway, burning my throat as I curl into myself, knees to my chest, arms wrapped tight like I could hold myself together.

The tears come fast and hard, spilling over before I can stop them. They soak into the mattress, into the room, into everything. The sobs are loud and raw, a sound I haven't let myself make in years. They tear through me, leaving my chest hollow, my body trembling.

The camera blinks on, indifferent, unrelenting, its gaze heavy and eternal. It watches as I shatter, as I fold into myself, as I cry until there's nothing left but a husk.

The questions claw at me, sharp and endless. How many people? How long? Has it been the entire time? But there are no answers, only the suffocating silence of the room, the weight of the truth pressing down on me. I lie there, staring at the red light, its steady pulse burning into me. For the first time, I feel completely naked. Not stripped of clothes, but of myself, my dignity, my humanity.

And I know, deep down, that nothing will ever feel safe again.

TWENTY-SIX

I wake up to the prickle of something foreign against my back, a sharpness pressing through the sheets like an accusation. Half asleep, I trace the feeling to its source, my fingers brushing the unfamiliar texture of fur. I think back to the last time Nathan shaved me—it's been weeks. But as I push the covers back, the truth stares at me: patches of dark, coarse hair, not the soft peach fuzz of neglect but something thicker, wilder. It sprouts on my arms, my thighs, a small tuft curling just above my hip.

I run my fingers over it, marveling at the texture, the way it resists me like it belongs to something untamed. Panic feels distant, abstract. Instead, there's a strange calm, quiet *okay, this is happening*. I crawl to the mirror and tilt my body to inspect the patch growing on my shoulder blade, the coarse bristle standing defiantly against my pale skin.

I think, *This is new*, then pull my shirt back down and move on. Ignoring it feels like a relief, letting it blend into the chaos already carved into my life. Nathan notices the same day. Of course he does. It's during one of his inspections, the ones that feel more like inventory than affection, his hands skimming over my skin with the dispassionate ownership of a man checking his possessions. His fingers pause at the patch on my lower back, and I feel his body stiffen behind me, his breath catching in a way that makes my stomach twist.

He doesn't say anything at first. He retrieves an electric razor from the bathroom, clicking it on with a steady hum.

"Hold still," he says, his voice low, not unkind, but threaded with something I can't name.

I hold still. The buzzing fills the room, slicing through the silence as he shaves me clean. The fur falls away in soft clumps, landing like shadows on the floor of the Pink Room. He finishes quickly, pats my hip like I've done something obedient, and leaves. No questions, no comments.

But a week later, the fur comes back. Thicker. Darker. This time, it's on my forearms too. I see him notice it during dinner, his fork hovering mid-air, his jaw tightening as I scarf down my food, the dog bowl scraping against the tile.

That night, he shaves me again, his movements slower, more deliberate, his lips pressed into a thin, tight line. I catch the flicker of concern in his face, the way he mutters, "It keeps coming back," like a confession he doesn't mean for me to hear.

The weeks stretch on, and the fur refuses to be tamed. It spreads across my body like moss creeping over stone, stubborn and alive. At first, Nathan tries to keep up with it, the razor buzzing against my skin every few days, but eventually, he stops. Instead, he dresses me in long-sleeved dresses, the fabric falling just below the knee, hiding the patches on my thighs, my arms.

At first, I think it's practical—easier to hide than to shave. But then I notice the way he avoids looking at me, the way his gaze skips over my body like it's something foreign. When we fuck, he keeps the lights dim, his eyes fixed on some point in the distance. His hands, once possessive, now hover just above my skin, hesitant, trembling slightly before pulling away.

He's not fully hard most nights. Not really. The fur bothers him, pushes him into some corner of himself he doesn't want to face.

I can't help but laugh, quietly, bitterly, at the absurdity of it. Isn't this what he wanted? A pet. A dog. I'm becoming one in real time, and he's recoiling, unprepared for the reality of his fantasy. He'll still call me "good girl," still buckle the collar tight around my neck, but the fur is too much. It's real in a way that makes him flinch, a mirror in which he doesn't want to see himself.

At night, I run my fingers through the patches, feeling the way they soften, thicken, become more than just rogue clumps. The fur spreads, wrapping me in its quiet defiance, covering the parts of me I no longer want to recognize.

I don't mention it, and neither does he. But the silence grows louder between us, the air charged with the weight of this thing neither of us can control. I start to notice the way he avoids me now, the distance in his eyes when he looks my way, like he's searching for the girl he once took and finding only this.

And I wonder, late at night, when the house is quiet and the fur brushes softly against my skin: *Who did he want in the first place? A girl pretending to be a dog? Or a dog pretending to be a girl?*

And I wonder which one I am.

The fur started in stubborn patches, growing darker, thicker, spreading across my skin like an invasion. At first, it's just patches on my arms, my thighs, the back of my neck where his hands linger too long. But then it moves to my belly, my chest, crawling up my jawline in thin tendrils that prickle against my touch. The texture changes, soft and wiry in places, coarse and rough in others. At night, I lie awake and run my fingers over it, feeling it creep further, becoming something impossible to ignore.

My nails start to change next. I don't notice at first, not until one breaks and refuses to crack cleanly, splitting into layers that thicken and curve. The tips harden, darken, the smooth crescent of each nail warping into something blunt and sharp. I sit on the bed, staring at my hands, at the way the fur creeps toward my knuckles, the way my nails seem foreign, dangerous.

Nathan doesn't do anything, he just watches. His eyes are different now—not disgusted, not afraid, but something worse: fascinated. He doesn't touch me as much, but when he does, his hands are rougher, less measured. He doesn't talk to me like he used to, doesn't call me "good girl" in that coaxing tone that once made my stomach twist. Now it's sharper, clipped, like he's reminding himself of what I'm supposed to be.

"Sit," he says one night, his voice steady, the leash taut in his hand.

I sit.

"Stay."

I stay.

It feels different this time, the command settling into my body like instinct, like it's no longer a choice. My legs fold automatically, my body curling into the position before I can think. He smiles, and the sight of it makes my stomach churn.

The changes come faster after that. My teeth ache constantly, the dull throb of something shifting beneath the surface. One day, I wake up to find my canines longer, sharper, pressing against the inside of my lips. They catch on the gag when he straps it in, drawing blood, the taste disgusting and warm.

My voice changes too. I try to speak. It comes out wrong—hoarse, guttural, a low growl that doesn't belong to me. It sounds like a real bark. Nathan freezes when he hears it, his hand tightening on the leash, his eyes narrowing.

"Do it again," he says, his tone unreadable.

I do, and it comes out deeper, raw. He stares at me for a long moment, then mutters something under his breath, dragging me to the Pink Room.

"You'll be fine," he says, but his voice lacks conviction.

My legs ache constantly now, the muscles tightening, the joints stiffening into unnatural angles. My arms feel longer, my shoulders shifting forward, pulling me into a permanent crouch.

The first time Nathan sees me like this, he doesn't say anything. He just watches, his face unreadable, his hand twitching at his side as if he wants to reach for me but doesn't know how.

At night, I can't stop scratching. My nails—or claws,

now—rake across my skin, tearing at the fur, at the itch that spreads beneath it. My back arches involuntarily, my body contorting in ways that feel alien.

I wake up one morning to find my ears different. They're longer, the tips pointed, the cartilage hardened into something stiff and unfamiliar. I touch them hesitantly, my claws brushing against the edges, and I want to scream, but the sound that comes out is a low, guttural whine.

Nathan hears it from the hallway. He opens the door slowly, his gaze locking on to me, and for the first time, I see fear in his eyes.

"What the fuck," he whispers, stepping closer, his movements cautious.

I try to speak, to explain, to beg, but the words don't come. Only a deep, rasping growl, low and menacing, filling the space between us.

"Stay," he says, his voice trembling slightly.

I stay. Not because I want to, but because I have to.

The leash is gone now. He doesn't need it anymore. I follow him without thinking, my body moving on instinct, my limbs folding into the rhythm of something primal. He doesn't touch me unless he has to, and when he does, his hands are hesitant, his grip loose.

One night, I catch my reflection in the mirror. The face staring back isn't mine. It's something between human and animal, the fur thick and dark, my eyes gleaming with a sharpness that makes me recoil. My mouth hangs open slightly, my canines glinting in the dim light, and I realize I'm panting, short, shallow breaths fogging the glass.

I don't know what I am anymore. A girl pretending to be a dog, or a dog that once thought it was a girl. Nathan doesn't know either. He watches me now with a mixture of fascination and revulsion, his movements cautious, his commands fewer.

At night, I curl up on the floor, the fur on my arms brushing against the rug, my claws scratching at the wood. I feel the weight of the camera's gaze, the red light blinking steadily, and I wonder if they can see it too—the thing I've become.

I wonder if they're waiting for the moment when there's nothing human left at all.

YEAR SEVEN

TWENTY-SEVEN

I'm pregnant. The knowing sits in me, low and heavy, coiled tight like dread. There's no confirming it—no test, no clinic—but I feel it in the way my body has betrayed me, shifting in ways I can't control. The nausea rolls over me every morning, tidal and relentless. My skin stretches tighter, my belly rounding just enough for me to notice, but not yet enough for Nathan to see. Not yet.

He doesn't know, and I've turned my life into an exercise in hiding it. I've learned to vomit silently, crouched over the toilet, my breaths shallow so he doesn't hear. I scrub my mouth, wipe away the evidence, and swallow the taste like penance. I chew slower now, swallowing the dog food in measured bites, willing it to stay down. If he realizes—if that dark calculus in his mind clicks into place—I know what happens next.

He will kill me.

It repeats in my mind like a pulse, like a law. *He will kill me.* He won't do it in anger or heat but with the same detached efficiency he used the day he dragged Cupcake out of the house. I remember the taut leash around her neck, her trembling body, and his face, calm and unreadable, when he returned alone.

I haven't bled in five years. I thought it was the stress, the starvation, the slow erasure of my body's ability to claim itself. I believed I was barren, that this house had made me incapable of giving life. But this thing growing inside me is proof that my body has a will I don't understand. It defies the hunger, the deprivation, the cruelty, and yet it feels like another betrayal, another way for this place to consume me.

Lately, Nathan has been kind. His kindness is never a gift; it's a lull before the drop, a prelude to something worse. He lets me crawl into the backyard now. He's given me air, a sliver of freedom so thin it feels like a trick. His voice has softened, his commands quieter, as if he's testing the depth of my submission. He thinks I don't want to leave anymore. He thinks he's won.

But I don't forget. I can't. I hear his voice in my head, calm and detached, the day I met Cupcake: *She's sick, and she can't stay here anymore.*

I understood then. He only keeps what he can use. The moment something doesn't serve him—when it breaks or strays too far from his control—it's discarded. Efficiently. Quietly.

This pregnancy is a crack in the system, an anomaly he won't tolerate. It's not part of his plan. I've seen how he reacts to things he can't control. I can't let him find out.

At night, when his snores rumble through the walls, I press my hand to my stomach, to the small curve that feels like a question with no answer. I whisper apologies into the dark, my voice trembling. *I didn't ask for you. I didn't choose this.* The words hang in the still air, heavy and futile.

The fetus complicates everything. My body is no longer mine—it's a battleground. The fetus is an unwelcome guest, carving out space in a house that isn't big enough for three. There's no room here for me and Nathan and this thing growing inside me. It needs to go.

I lie awake, my thoughts circling, quick and insistent. How much time do I have? What will I do when he finds out? How do I stop this before he stops me?

The answers don't come, only the cold, unshakable truth that this house was never built for survival. Hope doesn't live here. Hope is what gets you dragged out back, the leash tightening around your throat as you're led to where no one will find you.

I press my hand harder against my stomach, the faint swell a secret I can't carry much longer. The nausea stirs again, and I swallow it down, staring into the dark, waiting for the moment when I run out of time.

The yard is slick with sun, the air syrup-thick, sweet and heady with the musk of summer heat. It clings to my skin, seeps into the folds of this moment, too lush, too alive for the small brutality that's about to happen. Nathan's voice drifts from the porch, low and barbed with frustration. He's on the phone again, pacing, bourbon glass rattling faintly against the side table every time he sets it down too hard. His foot bounces, his body wound tight as if the call is pulling him apart one syllable at a time. He isn't watching me.

I crawl along the edge of the yard, the grass bristling against my palms, overgrown blades curling rebelliously at the edges like the wild reclaiming its space. My head stays low, my movements fluid, unremarkable. The leash is slack, forgotten in the heat of his distraction. His focus is elsewhere, split between the bourbon in his glass and the static impatience of the person on the other end of the line.

That's when I see it.

The rat.

It is round and fat, trembling in the shade of a bush, its black eyes gleaming like dark marbles, reflecting the stretch of my body moving closer. Its chest heaves, frantic and rhythmic, its tail flicking against the dirt like a whisper of panic. My breath catches, my body lowering instinctively. My fingers hover just above the earth, splayed like a trap about to spring.

The rat watches me, its gaze locked with mine, something feral meeting something broken. The air between us thickens, the space charged with the electric hum of recognition. Two animals sizing each other up: its quick, shallow fear against the deep, quiet hunger that's been building in me for years.

It shifts forward, cautious, its tiny nose twitching, its body a fragile bundle of nerves and instinct. The moment stretches, taut and delicate, and then—when the creature turns to retreat—I lunge.

My hand squeezes around its body, its warmth shocking against my palm. The rat squeals, high-pitched and piercing, its claws scraping desperately against my skin. Its tail whips, a frantic blur, but I hold firm, pressing it to my chest like a secret I can't let go. Without thinking, without hesitation, I lower my head to its belly.

The first bite tears through the fur cleanly, the skin splitting with surprising ease, the warmth flooding my mouth before I even register the taste. Blood coats my tongue, drips down my chin, pools on the grass beneath me in dark, uneven streaks. The rat writhes, its body a desperate, thrashing pulse in my hands, but I don't stop. I can't stop.

Each bite is a jolt, a shock of something primal and consuming, raw and undeniable. My teeth sink deeper, through sinew and bone, the slick heat of its organs spilling onto my tongue. The blood smells like iron, like earth, like survival. The fur catches in my throat, coarse and bristling, but I swallow it down, the texture foreign, the taste strangely addictive.

It is horrifying. It is delicious.

The realization slides under my skin like a knife. After seven years of crawling, barking, begging, something in me has tipped, shifted into a shape I don't fully recognize. I've worn the collar, the leash, the obedience like a costume stitched into my body, but this isn't a game anymore. The fur spreading across me is proof. The way my jaw aches with want as I tear through the rat's flesh, the way my breath heaves low and guttural in my chest—it's all proof. This isn't pretending.

This is instinct. Raw, relentless, and real.

The rat lies still in my hands, its final twitch a faint ripple under my fingers, a fragile echo of the life I just extinguished. Its tail hangs limp, a pale, sickle-thin curve that catches the sunlight. Its blank eyes don't see me, don't accuse me. The grass beneath me is damp, sticky with the blood I spilled, with the saliva that clings to my chin, dripping in thick strands onto the ground.

The smell of it—metallic, pungent—saturates the air, so heavy I can taste it even when I'm not chewing. My stomach churns, twisting in slow circles, but I don't stop. I swallow. Again and again, the warmth coursing down my throat, spreading through my chest, pooling in my belly like something molten, something alive.

It grounds me. Anchors me.

I don't wipe my mouth. I don't look away from the rat, its limp form cradled in my hands like something sacred. This is survival, I tell myself. This is an adaptation.

I think of the fetus and the thought crystallizes sharp and bitter. Rats carry diseases. Filth. Poison. I chew harder, my tongue exploring the insides of its belly, seeking out the tender insides, the slippery pieces.

Please let this end it.

Let this end the thing growing inside me before Nathan ends me first.

And then I hear him. The sound of footsteps, crushing the gravel behind me. I freeze, my breath hitching, the rat's limp body still clutched in my hands. The taste of blood is thick on my tongue, pooling warm and sticky in the corners of my mouth as I turn, slowly, to face him.

Nathan stands there, bourbon glass tilted in his hand, his face frozen in something between confusion and horror. His eyes flicker over me—over the blood streaked across my cheeks, the rat's gutted body, the red stains on the grass. His jaw tightens, and for the first time, I see it.

Fear.

It glints in his eyes, sharp and unfiltered, cutting through the thin veneer of control he wears like armor.

I smile.

It stretches across my face in a way that feels like both defiance and surrender.

The rat slips from my hands, its body falling with a soft, wet thud, and I don't look away. The taste of blood lingers, and I feel it—something feral, something ancient, something powerful unfurling in the pit of my stomach.

Nathan doesn't move. He just stares, fists clenched, the bourbon glass trembling slightly in his grip.

Let him see it, I think. *Let him see what he's created. Let him see me.*

TWENTY-EIGHT

Master Nathan is not happy with me. The bathroom feels smaller with his anger in it, his displeasure radiating in tight, controlled waves. He grips my arm harder than he needs to, yanking me toward the tub as if he's pulling a piece of furniture. The faucet hisses, spitting out steam, the heat fogging the mirror and blurring my reflection into something abstract.

"Get in," he says, his voice sharp enough to cut, and I lower myself into the water without hesitation. It's scalding, biting at my skin, but I don't flinch. The warmth loosens the dried blood, letting it slough off in thin, diluted ribbons. The water turns pink almost immediately, swirling around me like some macabre watercolor.

He doesn't waste time. He grabs the sponge, the cheap, stiff kind that scratches more than it cleans, and starts scrubbing. "What is wrong with you?" he mutters, the words low and clipped, his frustration simmering just beneath the surface. "Bad girl. Bad."

I don't respond. He scrubs harder, the sponge rough against

my arm, and I watch the pink water deepen into red, slowly blooming outward. "Do you have any idea what kind of disease you can catch?" he growls, his nose wrinkling as he works at a particularly stubborn patch of dried blood.

The irony is almost funny. Diseases are exactly what I want. I hope for them, beg for them, something invisible and insidious to rid me of the thing inside me. But I keep that to myself. I just watch the water, the way the blood moves in soft, hypnotic spirals before disappearing into the murk.

His disgust is palpable. He doesn't look at me—just at the mess, the streaks of dried blood and dirt he's trying to erase, as if scrubbing me clean will fix whatever he thinks is broken. His lips press into a thin, pale line, and his grip on the sponge tightens. And then, out of nowhere, the thought comes, sharp and electric, cutting through the monotonous rhythm of water and sponge.

I want to rip him open.

The idea is immediate, visceral, so vivid it makes my teeth ache. I imagine leaning forward, sinking my teeth into his arm, tearing into his flesh the way I tore into the rat. The image blooms in my mind like a sickness: blood pooling in thick, rich streams, spilling over my lips, warm and metallic. His skin splitting cleanly beneath my teeth, the soft give of muscle, the crunch of tendon.

It's overwhelming. The thought loops, spiraling tighter and tighter until it's all I can think about. I imagine his chest cracked open like a carcass, ribs splayed like a cage, his heart faintly beating before I bite into it. It would be heavier than the rat, meatier, the taste richer, more satisfying. Would his blood taste the same or more bitter because he is evil? The warmth of the idea spreads through me, grounding me, a thrill I haven't felt in years.

He's still talking, but I don't hear him. My mind is elsewhere, chewing on the image, gnawing at the fantasy. I imagine how long his body would twitch before going still, how his entrails would feel on my hands, on my tongue.

I force myself to focus. I stare at the water, the sponge, the repetitive motion of his hand as he drags it across my skin. I count the strokes—one, two, three—like a lifeline, trying to anchor myself, trying to keep the thought from devouring me whole. But it's there, simmering just below the surface, refusing to let go.

Nathan moves to my back, his hand pressing firmly against my shoulder to keep me still. "Don't ever do something like that again," he says, his voice tight and cold, like he's struggling to hold his temper.

I nod, quick and small, my head dipping just enough to appease him. But my mind is still elsewhere, still gnawing on the idea of him torn apart, reduced to something raw and bloody and powerless, to just meat.

The bathwater is murky now, darker than it should be, the faint scent of blood still clinging to the air despite the soap. Nathan pauses, his hand still for a moment, and I glance up to see him inspecting a streak of blood on his wrist, his face twisting in faint disgust.

I look away quickly, biting the inside of my cheek to keep from smiling. When he stands and mutters something about getting a towel, I wait until the door creaks open. As soon as he's gone, I lower my head beneath the surface of the water.

The warmth envelops me, muffling the world, and I open my mouth. The bloody bathwater rushes in, thick and metallic, sliding down my throat in heavy gulps. It tastes like the rat, like dirt and iron and something faintly bitter, and I swallow it all, letting it fill me.

A few days later I'm in pain. It is relentless, radiating through my body like a warning, like punishment. It's no longer something I can ignore or compartmentalize. It's raw, loud, pressing into every nerve, and I'm folded up in the Pink Room, knees drawn tight to my chest, the frilled hem of my dress soaked with sweat. My stomach twists in cruel waves, each one worse than the last, and it feels as though something is alive inside me, something angry, something foreign. Something other than the fetus. I start to writhe on the bed as I claw at my face, my neck, my arms, leaving deep bloody scratch marks on my body.

When the screams tear out of me, it feels like surrender. It's not intentional; it's ripped from me, sharp and animal, cutting through the oppressive stillness of the room. The sound of my scream slices through it, clean and bright, and then the door bursts open.

Master Nathan stands there, backlit, his silhouette stark and menacing. His face is tight, etched with frustration, his eyes narrowing as he takes me in.

"What is it?" he snaps, crossing the room in two quick strides. "What's wrong now, girl?"

He kneels beside me, his hands rough as they grab my face, tilting my head up so he can look at me. His grip is bruising, and I can feel the callouses on his fingers scraping against my skin. His expression changes as he examines me, his irritation curling into something sharper, darker.

"My God," he mutters, his voice dropping low.

I whimper, the sound involuntary, pulled from somewhere deep and raw. Words are impossible—have been for years now—but even if I could speak, I wouldn't know what to say.

His eyes stay locked on mine, narrowing as though he's trying to solve a puzzle. And then his lips curl, his voice turning cold, dripping with venom. "You know what you did when you ate the rat? You stupid, stupid girl."

Before I can bark, his hand clamps around my arm, dragging me off the bed. The floor is cool against my knees, a brief reprieve from the heat roaring through my body. My limbs feel boneless, but his grip is unrelenting. He yanks me out of the room, dragging me down the hallway, his steps heavy and purposeful. The bathroom is blindingly bright, sterile, the fluorescent light buzzing faintly as he shoves me inside.

"Stay," he commands, his voice sharp as he pulls open a drawer. His movements are clipped, methodical, as he pulls out a small hand mirror. Its edges are dull, scratched from years of use. He crouches in front of me, holding it up with one hand, the other gripping my chin to force me to look. "See for yourself," he spits.

I hesitate, my hands trembling as I take the mirror from him. Slowly, I lift it, angling it toward my face. My reflection stares back at me, gaunt and pale, the shadows beneath my eyes stark against my skin. And then I see it.

Behind my eyes, thin, white, almost translucent strings shift and writhe, their movements sinuous and alien. They're alive, burrowing beneath the surface, and the sight of them sends a wave of nausea crashing over me. I scream, the mirror slipping from my fingers, clattering against the tile floor.

Nathan doesn't flinch. "You gave yourself parasitic worms," he says, his voice flat, dripping with disgust. "Fucking brilliant."

I want to claw at my eyes, to rip them out, to rid myself of the invaders crawling beneath my skin. My hands twitch with the urge, but I don't move. I'm frozen, trapped in the horror of my own body.

Nathan shakes his head, muttering under his breath. "Hold still," he barks, pulling a pair of tweezers from the counter. The metal glints under the harsh light. He doesn't ask permission. He doesn't warn me. He just moves, gripping my chin again, tilting my head back as he brings the tweezers to the corner of my eye.

The first press of metal against my skin is unbearable, sharp and invasive. I flinch, but his grip tightens, his fingers digging into my jaw. "Stop moving," he growls. "You want these things out or not?"

I nod, my breath coming in short, shallow gasps. The tweezers slip beneath the edge of my eyelid, and the sensation is worse than pain. It's a deep, intimate violation, a scraping against something that should never be touched. And then I feel the tug.

The scream rips out of me before I can stop it, raw and guttural, my body twisting in agony. My eye feels as if it's being plucked out, the pain searing and bright. Nathan doesn't stop. His face is set, his focus absolute, as he pulls. The first worm emerges slowly, inch by inch, pale and glistening, writhing frantically between the metal tips.

He holds it up, inspecting it with a grimace before tossing it into the sink. The clang of its body hitting the porcelain echoes in the silence.

"One down," he mutters, his voice tight.

He goes back in. Each tug is worse than the last, the pain mounting, blood pooling in my eye socket, thick and warm as it trickles down my face. The worms keep coming, each one a grotesque reminder of my own desperation, my own stupidity.

By the time he stops, the sink is gore and horror, speckled with blood and the pale, writhing bodies of the worms. My body is trembling, my breaths shallow and uneven. Nathan tosses the tweezers onto the counter with a clatter, wiping his hands on a towel.

"That's the best I can do for now," he says, his voice flat, devoid of sympathy. "I can't get them all. God knows how many of those things are still crawling through you." He pauses, his eyes scanning me like I'm a puzzle he doesn't want to solve. "I'll get you a dewormer."

I nod weakly, unable to bark, unable to think. The room

spins around me, the air thick with the scent of blood and disinfectant. Nathan steps back, shaking his head as though he's disgusted with me, with the mess I've made of myself.

I close my eyes, the pain ebbing slightly but the horror still sharp. I can feel them inside me still, crawling, alive. The worms. The fetus. Both of them, consuming me from the inside out. My vision swims, the world around me blurring into smudges of pink and white and red.

TWENTY-NINE

When Master Nathan isn't looking, I eat things I shouldn't. It's ritual now—a secret rebellion that's more desperation than defiance. Each forbidden bite is an offering to the impossible, to the hope that I can rid myself of the thing growing inside me. A thumbtack, small and cold against my tongue, its point pressing sharply before I swallowed it down in one agonizing gulp. An injured fly, its weak, buzzing body crushed between my teeth, wings dissolving into pulp. Anything, everything that might disrupt the fragile life forming inside me.

But the pregnancy hasn't stopped. Even the worms didn't stop it. I waited, patient and hopeful, for the sharp relief of a miscarriage, but nothing came. It's been months since the parasites, and still I feel it inside me—a stubborn, silent growth. Most mornings, I throw up, bile rising hot and acidic in my throat. Master Nathan doesn't connect it to pregnancy, just treats it like another nuisance he doesn't want to deal with. My stomach isn't flat anymore; the slight swell is a warning, a countdown. I can't let it get further. I can't let myself start showing.

One evening, Master Nathan is drunk again. His steps are slow and heavy, his words slurred as he stumbles through the kitchen, a bottle hanging limply from his hand. He drops a glass, the sound of shattering cutting through the air.

"Damn it," he mutters, crouching down unsteadily to collect the larger shards. His movements are clumsy, indifferent. He doesn't notice the smaller fragments, the ones too fine to see unless you're looking.

I am always looking.

The shards catch the dim light, tiny edges glittering like stars against the floor. My pulse quickens. I crawl closer, careful, slow. He's still at the counter, his back to me, muttering something about work, about money. His tone is distracted, detached, a rare crack in his vigilance.

My hand darts out quickly, scooping up a small shard. It's cool in my fingers, the edge biting into my skin as I clutch it tightly. I glance at him again—still turned away, still muttering to himself. I bring the shard to my mouth.

The first bite is electric. The glass slices into my tongue, the taste of blood blooming immediately. I chew slowly, carefully, each crunch vibrating through my jaw. The pain is bright, searing, but I welcome it. The glass grinds into smaller pieces, each swallow a calculated agony. It scrapes my throat raw, leaving behind tiny cuts, but I force it down. This pain is a gift, a sacrifice for a greater goal.

The rat comes back to me in flashes—the wild frenzy of its death, the hot burst of blood, the crack of tiny bones between my teeth. It wasn't just sustenance; it was power, raw and visceral. I need that again. I need to destroy something wild, to feel its life slip away in my hands. I crave the rush of it, the primal satisfaction of devouring.

But the sickness has become my constant companion. The nausea twists through me in relentless waves, but even that isn't enough. Nothing I've done has been enough. The fetus remains, defiant and unwelcome, and my time is slipping away. The slight swell of my belly feels like a clock ticking down, each passing moment narrowing my chances.

I wait for the next shard, the next rat, the next moment where I can claw back even a sliver of control. The taste of blood lingers on my tongue, and I swallow hard, letting it settle deep in my stomach. For now, it's the only thing that feels real.

THIRTY

Finally, one morning, it happens like a knife slipping between my ribs. The pain starts sharp, then blooms outward, radiating through my body in waves that steal my breath. I'm lying on the bed when it hits, my pink nightgown crumpled around me, sticky against my thighs. My hands fly to my stomach, pressing against the source of the agony, as if I could hold it in, as if I could stop it.

I scream, the sound raw and guttural, ripping through the still air of the Pink Room. And then, without warning, I start laughing. It's a manic, deep and demonic sound, tumbling out of me in bursts I can't control. The laughter feels wrong in my throat, foreign, but it's unstoppable. I laugh until I'm choking, until I can taste bile rising.

I reach between my legs, my fingers trembling as they search for confirmation, and when I pull them back, they're slick with blood. Dark, wet, undeniable. I stare at it, my breath catching, my pulse hammering in my ears. *This is it*, I think, the realization cutting through the chaos. *It worked.*

The laughter fizzles out, replaced by another wave of pain that grips me, sharp and merciless. I curl into myself, clutching my stomach as the blood begins to soak through the fabric of my nightgown, staining the pastel pink a deep, violent red. It pools beneath me, spreading out like an accusation, like evidence.

And then the nausea hits. It is violent, immediate. My stomach twists hard, and I barely manage to lean over the edge of the bed before I'm vomiting blood. It spills from my mouth in heavy bursts, thick and dark, splattering onto the pristine rug and trailing down my chin. The taste is overwhelming, thick and cloying, and the smell—the iron tang of blood mingled with bile—fills the room, suffocating and nauseating.

I wipe my mouth with a shaking hand, smearing blood across my face. My stomach lurches again, and I gag, spitting more blood onto the floor, watching it soak into the pink fibers of the rug. It's everywhere now—the blood, the smell, the suffocating reality of it. My body is a battleground, my insides tearing themselves apart, but I can feel it. I can feel it happening.

Another cramp rips through me, sharper than the last, and I feel something heavy, unnatural, shifting inside me. My body knows what to do, even if I don't. I slide off the bed onto the floor, the blood warm and sticky beneath my knees, pooling around me as I spread my legs. The instinct to push takes over, ancient and undeniable.

I glance up at the camera, its red light blinking steadily. If there's people watching, I'll make sure they see everything. If they think I'm boring, I'll really give them a show, change how they view their own lives forever.

I brace my hands against the floor, my fingers slipping in the blood, and I bear down. The pain is white-hot, blinding, carving through me in sharp, relentless waves. My breaths come in ragged gasps, my body trembling violently as I push, the weight inside me slowly shifting downward.

It feels endless, time stretching out and bending under the strain. The room blurs around me, the pink walls and white trim dissolving into a haze of color and light. My entire world narrows to the searing, tearing pressure in my abdomen, the overwhelming sensation of something being forced out of me.

And then, with one final, desperate push and the help of my hand pulling it out, it's over.

The thing lying on the blood-soaked floor is small but malformed, its body pale and hairless, its limbs too long and spindly, ending in tiny, clawed paws. The head is canine, unmistakably so—its snout too pronounced, its mouth hanging open to reveal sharp, needle-like teeth. The skin is thin, almost translucent, veins spidering beneath its surface. Its closed eyelids bulge, too large for its head.

I'm too tired to care. I collapse onto my side, shaking, my body spent, my mind teetering on the edge of consciousness. My breaths are shallow, uneven, but they keep coming, each one a small defiance.

It's there in front of me, surrounded by blood and tissue, a grotesque, fibrous thing that doesn't look human, but still carries the weight of what it is. What it was. I can't look away.

The room is silent now, save for my labored breaths and the faint, distant hum of the house. Master Nathan isn't home. I've done this alone. For the first time in years, I feel something like triumph, tangled and bloody, raw and unrecognizable.

The blood doesn't stop. It seeps from me in steady streams, soaking into the rug, pooling around my legs. My nightgown clings to me, ruined, sticky, and damp. The smell of blood and vomit is thick in the air, pressing down on me, making me gag as I try to sit up, to orient myself.

I close my eyes, my head heavy, my body trembling with exhaustion. The pain is still there, dull and insistent, but the worst of it is over. For the first time in months, I feel like I've won, even as I lie here in the wreckage of my body, the weight of what I've done pressing down on me.

His fetus is gone.

THIRTY-ONE

When Master Nathan finally comes back home and opens the door to the Pink Room, his face goes slack. It's a rare, unguarded expression, stripped of calculation or control. Fear, confusion, disgust—they all collide, layering his features like a smudge he can't wipe away. He doesn't step inside. He stays framed in the doorway, his knuckles white around the doorknob, as if anchoring himself to the only clean thing in reach.

The room is a crime scene. Blood streaks the floor in erratic, looping patterns, smears climbing the walls like something feral was let loose. I had taken great pleasure in smearing every surface with my blood, knowing he is the one who must clean it up. Vomit mixed with blood pools by the bed, its acidic stench mingling with an iron tang, the air so thick with it that even I feel dizzy. The pink of the room is almost gone, swallowed by red.

"What . . ." His voice is a rasp, barely audible. "What the fuck happened?"

He doesn't move. His eyes dart around the room, frantic, searching for something solid to hold on to, but there's nothing.

This is my masterpiece, and I've taken care to leave no corner untouched.

I'm on the floor, crouched in the middle of the mess, my hands sticky and stained, my dress clinging to me in wet patches. I crawl toward him, slow and menacing, the sound of my knees dragging through the blood making him flinch. His body stiffens, and I see it—the hesitation, the tremor in his hands. It's in his eyes, too, the way they dart back to the hallway, weighing his escape.

I smile, letting it stretch wide across my face, my teeth streaked red. "Woof," I say, low and steady, my voice dragging the word out, daring him to come closer.

"No," he snaps, finally stepping into the room. The movement feels forced, like he's trying to prove something—to himself or to me, I can't tell. "No, tell me what happened. Right fucking now."

I tilt my head, slow and exaggerated, mocking the same gesture he's drilled into me for years. The corner of my mouth twitches, my smile edging toward something feral, and I repeat, "Woof."

His face twists, the fear bleeding into fury, and he strides toward me. The slap comes fast, his hand cracking against my cheek, sending my head snapping to the side. Pain blooms, bright and hot, but I don't flinch. I turn back to him, slow and deliberate, my cheek hot with the sting, and I smile again.

"Speak!" he shouts, his voice splintering under the weight of his anger. "Speak right fucking now! This isn't funny, Gia!"

I freeze. It feels like a knife slipped between my ribs, sharp and foreign, the sound of it cutting through me. *Gia.* It's been so long since I've heard it that it takes a moment to register. It doesn't belong to me anymore, not really.

I blink slowly, tilting my head again, and then I crawl to the bed. My movements are slow, the blood-soaked floor slick beneath my hands. His eyes track me, wary and wide, his breath shallow as I reach under the bed. My fingers close around it—the bloody mass I'd hidden there hours ago, waiting for this moment.

When I pull it out, the weight of it feels solid, grotesque in my hands. The blood drips down my arms, thick and viscous, pooling at my elbows before splattering onto the floor. I hold it up, letting him see it in all its horror—the shape of it barely human, its limbs twisted and malformed, its head wrong, more snout than face.

His reaction is instant. He stumbles backward, his eyes bulging, his hand flying to his mouth as if to keep from retching. "Is that . . ." His voice is a whisper, trembling. "Is that supposed to be a baby?"

I nod, slow and steady, holding his gaze. The blood seeps into the carpet, the dark stains spreading outward like ink. He's staring at the thing in my hands, his chest heaving, his breath coming in short, uneven bursts.

And then, without breaking eye contact, I lower the mass to my mouth. My teeth sink into its gelatinous flesh, the texture soft and wet, the taste acrid and overwhelming. Blood gushes into my mouth, warm and salty, running down my chin in thick streams.

I chew it slowly, savor the delicious morsel.

Nathan pales, his face turning a sickly shade of white. His body jerks as if he's been struck, his feet stumbling backward until he hits the doorframe.

"What the fuck," he chokes, his voice barely audible. "What the fuck is wrong with you?"

I stare at him unblinking, letting the blood drip down onto my dress, my hands, and the floor. I swallow, the taste lingering on my tongue, and I tilt my head at him one last time, baring my bloodied teeth in a grin.

"Woof," I say softly, and the sound sends him running.

THIRTY-TWO

The next morning, the door swings open with a sharp crack, and Nathan steps in like he's holding the room itself accountable. His face is slack, exhausted, with shadows sinking into the hollows of his eyes and the sharpness of his jaw. He looks as if he hasn't slept, the stubble on his face darker than I've ever seen it, and his movements are sharp, staccato, as if he doesn't trust himself to stay still.

I'm on all fours on the bed, the blood-stiff nightgown clinging to my skin, the fabric rustling faintly as I shift my weight. My stomach is full—heavy and satisfied. I finished the fetus hours ago, and the taste still lingers at the edges of my memory, warm and gushy, giving me energy, giving me strength.

He stops in the doorway, his gaze flicking over me, scanning the room as if he's trying to take inventory. His face twists in something I can't name—anger or exhaustion, maybe disgust. But there's hesitation, too. A crack in the façade that makes my chest tighten.

"Stand up," he says, his voice low but sharp, cutting through the heavy air.

I tilt my head, confused. *Stand up?*

"Stand up," he repeats, louder now, the edge of his patience showing.

I stay frozen, my hands sinking into the mattress, my body stiff. The words don't make sense. My body doesn't know how to answer them. Then I notice what he's holding—my clothes. The ones I came here in. A black t-shirt and yoga pants, balled up in his hands.

My chest tightens. Is this it? Is this the end? Did I finally push him too far?

The clothes land on the bed with a dull thud, the bundle unraveling slightly to reveal the worn fabric. "Dress," he says, his voice flat, almost bored. "Meet me out there in five minutes."

Then he's gone, the door shutting softly behind him, not with the force of his entrance but with the finality of an afterthought. I sit there, staring at the pile of clothes. The black fabric is dull with age, worn thin in places. It looks too normal, too clean, too real.

My thoughts spiral in endless loops. Is this a trick? A test? Or is he finally done with me?

I take a deep breath, the air heavy in my lungs, and shift my weight slowly, pulling my knees out from under me. My legs crack as I straighten them, my body swaying slightly as I stand upright for the first time in years. The floor feels unsteady beneath me, foreign, as if I've landed on a planet where gravity works differently.

I peel the nightgown off, the bloodstained fabric stiff and

clinging as I pull it over my head. The cold air bites at my skin, and I shiver, the movement awkward and unsteady. I reach for the t-shirt, pulling it over my head. The fabric smells faintly of something old and clean, a scent that doesn't belong here. It hangs loose over my frame, slipping over my hipbones, which jut sharply beneath the waistband of the yoga pants as I pull them on. They sag, too big now for my tiny frame.

I take a step toward the door, my legs trembling, my knees threatening to buckle with the effort. My feet feel too light against the floor, as if they've forgotten how to press firmly into it. Another step. And another. My balance wavers, each movement unfamiliar, unsteady, the floor tilting slightly with every shift of weight.

The doorknob is cold in my hand, and I press my palm against it, grounding myself before twisting it open. The hallway beyond is dim, the shadows stretching long and narrow. Each step echoes softly, the sound foreign to my ears after years of crawling.

When I get to the living room, he's leaning against the counter, hands shoved deep in his pockets, all casual, as if he's just another man in his kitchen. But it's all wrong—his posture too still, his eyes too flat. There's nothing to grab on to in his face, no way to read the silence in which he's wrapped himself. And that silence feels heavier than any of his tantrums, louder than his fists.

My eyes flick to the counter behind him, and that's when I see it. My purse. My jacket. My shoes. They're piled there like trash he's been meaning to throw out, the leather worn, the fabric dulled. But they're mine. My life from seven years ago sits right there, inert, untouched, as if it's been waiting for me to come back to it.

Something sharp and mean blooms in my chest. I swallow it down.

"Woof?" The sound slips out before I can stop it, instinctive, ridiculous. It feels too small for this moment, a sound that belongs to someone else.

"You're free to go," he says, the words so flat, so devoid of anything, they feel as if they might fall and shatter between us. *Free. To go.*

I stand there, my knees locking, my heart slamming into my ribs, waiting for the hook, the twist, the knife to land. My head swims with the possibilities, the cruel scenarios he might be playing out.

But he just stands there, watching me with that same blank stare, his face carved out of nothing.

I look back at the counter. The sight of my belongings hits like a fist, the memories rushing in too fast, too vivid. They look wrong now, foreign, like props from a movie in which I barely remember acting. My throat tightens.

"Free?" I whisper, the word catching in my mouth. It doesn't feel real. It feels like a test, a cruel little game he's thought up to see if I'll fail one last time.

He doesn't answer, just watches me with his unreadable face, his silence stretching out into something massive and unbearable.

I take a step toward the counter, my legs shaking, my whole body trembling under the weight of what this could mean. The floor feels unsteady beneath me, like it might open up if I get too close. Each step feels impossibly long, as if I'm wading through a dream.

When I reach the counter, I pick up the jacket first. It feels stiff in my hands, the fabric rough and strange. I struggle to get my arms in the sleeves, my hands clumsy and shaking. The shoes are next, heavier than I remember, their weight foreign against my feet. I glance up at him, watching him watch me, his eyes tracking every move as if he's cataloging it.

Then he moves. Walks to the hallway closet, casual, like this is nothing, like this is just a normal day. My breath catches. I know what's in there. The safe. I've seen him open it a dozen times, his back always blocking the keypad.

He punches in the code, and the faint beeping echoes through the room, each tone landing too loud. I stand there frozen, my hands gripping the edge of the counter, watching as he pulls out stack after stack of cash. Neat bundles, the edges crisp, as if they've never been touched. He doesn't even glance at me as he shoves them into a pillowcase, the fabric sagging with the weight.

He walks back to the counter and drops the bag beside my purse with a thud. "There you go," he says, his voice so casual it makes my stomach turn. "Two hundred thousand dollars. For your time."

The numbers hit me like a slap. I stare at the bag, my mind

spinning, trying to make sense of it, trying to figure out what this is. A bribe? A payment? A joke? Whatever it is, it's not even close to what he promised me.

"What?" My voice is hoarse, cracked, the word barely there.

He shrugs. "I told you that you'd be compensated. I'm a man of my word."

The room tilts. The cash. My purse. The open door. None of it feels real. I glance back at him, waiting for the punchline, the trap, the thing that will make this all fall apart.

But there's nothing. Just his empty face, his hands shoved back into his pockets, his posture still too casual, too loose.

"Take it," he says, his voice firmer now.

I stare at him, waiting for the catch. But he doesn't move, doesn't say anything else, just watches me with that same blank expression.

I want to ask him why. I want to demand answers, to scream, to cry, but I stay silent. The rules still feel too heavy, too ingrained, holding me back even now.

He steps closer, the air between us charged and sour, his tone tightening like a noose. "Let me explain something to you," he says, his words clipped, cold, steady as a scalpel. He's rehearsed this. It's in the careful way he delivers each sentence, the calculation in his eyes, as if he's been waiting for this moment, sharpening it into a weapon. "If you go to the police, they won't believe you. I'll tell them you took the payment I gave you seven years ago. I'll show them the messages. The ones where you agreed to do this. You came here *willingly*."

The words land heavy, stacking up in my chest like stones. My breath catches, my face burning cold as the weight of it presses down on me. He's not wrong. I can already see the flickering courtroom fluorescent lights, the slow shake of heads, the disbelieving looks. The lawyer's sneer as he holds up the messages like damning evidence.

"It won't look good for you, Gia," he says, and the sound of my name feels like a hook sinking into my skin. He's using it now, softening his tone, trying to make it land just right. "You can take the money and live a great life, or you can spend years in court trying to convince people you were kidnapped and held against your will. Even then, you might lose. You'll be worse off than you were when you got here."

His voice is calm, rational, almost kind, as if he's offering me a way out, as if he's doing me a favor. But it's the tone that scares me the most—the casual assurance that he's won, that I've already folded. He steps back, his posture loose, his hand resting near the bag of money on the counter as if to say, *Your choice.*

I stand there, frozen, my body heavy and trembling, my mind swooping in tight, endless loops. He's right. Of course he's right. No one would believe me. I know how they treat women like me. They'll see me for what he's turned me into. I agreed to this.

I'm in, I wrote.

The messages—he has all of them. I know what they say. The careful narrative he's constructed, the story he's been curating for years, each piece designed to paint me as complicit.

Am I allowed to leave whenever I want?

Yes.

A woman who agreed to act like a dog for cash. They'll eat it up. They'll see his clean-cut face, his steady demeanor, the messages, and they'll believe him. They always do.

But then something cuts through the panic, a thought sharp and clear, slamming into me like a freight train.

No.

There's another option.

The idea is sudden, jarring, and it grips me hard, refusing to let go. My eyes dart to the bag of cash on the counter. Then to him, standing there, so confident, so assured in his control, his victory. The open door behind him, sunlight streaming in like it's taunting me.

I look at him—at his blank expression, his steady stance—and for the first time, I feel something shift. My breath steadies, my muscles coil. The thought solidifies, and I don't let myself question it.

I *could* take the money. I *could* leave. Or I could make sure he never does this to anyone else again.

I nod slowly, lowering my gaze as I whisper, "Woof."

He smirks, satisfied, and turns away, giving me just enough time to look around the room, to calculate my next move.

"I'm sorry I had to keep you for so long. But that was always the plan," Nathan says, his tone casual, almost conversational, as if he's explaining a minor inconvenience. His hands are still in his pockets, his posture relaxed, his expression unreadable. "Not a lot of women would agree to this if they knew I like to keep my Girl Pets for years until I'm done playing with them, and that little stunt of yours yesterday did it for me. My clients are not happy with what you did last night. I'm done. You're free to go now," he says, gesturing vaguely toward the door, his voice light and dismissive. "Thank you for your time, Gia. Your car is out front. I made sure to keep up with the maintenance. Even gassed it up for you this morning. You're good to go." He smiles.

My mind races, spiraling into an uncontrollable loop of thoughts, each one bigger, louder, more intrusive than the last. The room feels too bright, too loud, too close. My vision begins to blur, not with relief but with something darker, hotter.

Rage.

The sound of his voice, the sight of his face, the casual ease with which he dismisses everything he's done—it fuels the fire inside me until it consumes everything else. I was thirty years old when I first entered this house. Now I am thirty-seven. Valuable years of my life gone. Because of him.

For the last time, I get down on all fours, and lunge.

My body moves on instinct, driven by a force that feels primal. My hands reach for his throat, my fingers digging into his skin with a ferocity that surprises even me. His eyes widen, the calm, detached mask slipping as he stumbles backward, trying to pry my hands away, only to fall, his leg bending the wrong way with a sickening crack, the sound of his leg bone popping out of its socket. He screams—a high, raw sound that echoes through the room—but it only fuels me further. I drive him to the ground, my knees pinning his chest, and I slam his head against the floor with a sickening thud.

The first bite is clumsy, my teeth sinking into the soft flesh of his neck. Blood spurts out in hot bursts, coating my lips, my tongue, my chin. The taste is intoxicating, the warmth of it filling my mouth.

I bite again, harder this time, tearing away a chunk of skin and muscle. Nathan screams again, his voice hoarse, desperate, but I don't stop. I rip into his throat with my teeth, eating his vocal cords, the blood pouring out in thick, viscous streams that pool around his head.

His hands claw at me weakly, his strength fading, his movements slowing. I grab his shirt and tear it open, exposing his chest. I tear a hole through his stomach with my claws and then my hands dig into it, my fingers slipping in the blood as I tear through the flesh, the muscle, through sinew.

I pull his intestines out, the slick, coiled mass warm and heavy in my hands. The smell is overwhelming, a mix of copper and bile and something earthy. I raise them to my mouth and slurp them up like spaghetti, the texture rubbery, the taste salty.

His screams turn into gurgles, his body twitching beneath me as I work. I sink my teeth into his liver, tearing it free from its cavity, the organ heavy and wet in my hands. I bite into it, the taste rich and iron-filled, the blood dripping down my chin and onto my clothes.

I keep going, driven by an insatiable hunger, a need to consume, to destroy, to *erase* him completely. I rip through his chest cavity, my hands slick with blood as I pull out his heart. It is still faintly beating, the rhythm weak and erratic, and I sink my teeth into it, tearing it apart with a savage growl.

By the time I stop, the room is silent except for the sound of my ragged breathing. Nathan's body is unrecognizable, a mangled, bloody mess of flesh and bone. I sit back on my heels, my hands coated in blood, my face slick with it, my stomach full and heavy.

The rage leaves slowly, like the last embers of a fire. What remains is something hollow, a calm so thin it feels like the edge of a blade. I look down at what's left of Nathan, his body slack, blood soaking into the floor in broad, blooming circles. The room smells of copper and ruin, the kind of smell that burrows into your skin and stays there. This will stay with me forever.

Suddenly, the door swings open, and her voice cuts through the silence.

"Hey, how'd it go? Did she take the money?"

Her words are casual, light, as though she's arriving at the aftermath of a business meeting. She steps inside, and her heels click against the floor. I hear the sound before I see her, and then there she is, framed in the doorway like a ghost from my past.

It's *her*.

Cupcake.

I know her immediately. I've burned her face into my mind over the years, etched it into memory. She's here, alive, wearing a tan trench coat that clings to her waist, blonde hair perfectly straightened, her heels unmistakably Louboutin. She looks every inch the woman I imagined her to be—elegant, untouchable.

And now she's staring at me. Her eyes widen as they take in the scene: Nathan's body, lifeless and open like a dissected animal. My hands, my face, my clothes—all dripping in gore, evidence of what I've done.

Her scream cuts through the room, jagged and raw.

"*No, no, no!*" she cries, stumbling backward, her hand flying to her mouth. The sound is high-pitched and guttural, like something breaking in her chest. Tears pour down her face, tracing paths down her carefully powdered cheeks.

She looks at Nathan, then at me, her expression flipping between disbelief and devastation.

"Why'd you do that?" she wails, her voice cracking. "I loved him!"

The words hit me like a slap. Loved him? *Loved him?*

"He was letting you go!" she screams, her body shaking with the force of her grief. "*He was letting you go!*"

I straighten slowly, my joints stiff, my muscles trembling from the exertion. Blood drips from my fingers onto the floor, each drop marking time, and still her words echo in my head.

"He didn't deserve to live," I say, my voice low and steady, though my own chest feels as if it might cave in.

She takes a step forward, unsteady on her heels, and kneels beside Nathan's body. She doesn't touch him—her hands hover, trembling, wanting to touch but afraid to make contact with the carnage.

"He changed my life," she says through her sobs, her voice splintered. "He gave me everything! Oh God . . ."

I stare at her, my mind reeling. "But . . . he held you captive," I say. My voice quivers despite my attempt at control. "He kidnapped you."

She shakes her head, tears falling faster. "*He let me go!*" she screams, her throat raw with grief.

I step closer, feeling the distance between us tighten like a noose. "How many years did he take from you?" I ask, my voice rising. "How many?"

Her lips tremble, and her shoulders collapse inward. She whispers, "Ten. Ten years." Her knees buckle, and she sinks to the floor, her head hanging low. Her voice drops to a whisper. "But I loved him."

The words linger in the air, and I feel the weight of them press against my ribs. Ten years. Ten years of this.

I stare at her as she cradles his arm, the only part of him not bloody; she grips it as if it is still alive, her tears pooling on his body. "We were going to get married," she says softly, her voice distant. "After he let you go. He told me he was going to stop all this."

I shake my head slowly, my throat tightening. "He didn't mean it," I whisper. "It was just another way to control you. To keep you quiet. I'm sure he tried to bribe you to not go to the police."

Her sobs hiccup into silence, but her body keeps shaking. She doesn't respond. "Please, just go," she says finally, her voice breaking.

I swallow hard, the lump in my throat almost unbearable. "Come with me," I whisper.

She lifts her head, her face streaked with tears and contempt. Her voice tightens into fury. "Why would I go with you? You killed the love of my life," she growls.

I hold her gaze, my chest tight with something I can't name. "I killed your captor," I say, my voice trembling. "I killed your predator. Your *rapist*."

She shakes her head slowly, her hands still gripping Nathan's arm as if it's a lifeline. "No," she whispers again, quieter this time.

I stare at her for a long moment, the silence between us heavy with all the things we cannot say. She is too far gone. I stand, wiping my bloody hands on my ruined clothes. My purse, the bag of money—all of it waits on the counter. I gather them. I pull my car keys out of my purse, the metal cool against my palm.

Before I leave, I look back at the woman one last time. She's still there, crouched beside his body, her shoulders shaking with quiet sobs. "Are you going to call the cops and tell them I killed him?" I ask, my voice steady.

She doesn't meet my eyes. "Just go," she says, her voice hollow. "I'll call in ten minutes. Enough time for you to get away."

I nod slowly. "You came in and found him like this," I say.

She looks up at me, mascara smeared across her face. After a moment she repeats the phrase, her voice quivering. "I came in and found him like this."

I linger for a moment longer, searching her face for something—hope, understanding, anything. But she's lost in the wreckage. She won't tell the cops about what I did, I know for certain, I know it deep within me. She sees me.

Maybe she isn't too far gone. Maybe one day, she'll come back to herself.

Hopefully.

I turn and walk out the door, the freezing air hitting me like a slap. I climb into my car, the leather seats cold against my legs. My hands shake as I start the engine, my breath coming in short, shallow bursts. The car smells like blood and sweat and freedom, and for a moment, I don't know where one ends and the others begin.

My hands grip the wheel, but they're not hands anymore—they're claws, thick and dark, the tips sharp enough to leave faint scratches in the leather as I back out of Nathan's driveway. The transformation has been slow and inevitable, like the way sunlight fades color from fabric. A part of me knew this was coming, even as I fought to pretend I was still human.

But now, as the fur spreads across my chest, my face, my legs, I feel no fear. I feel no grief for the girl I once was. She's already gone, worn away by years of crawling, of barking, of bending to survive. What's left is something raw, something honest. Something real.

I press the gas harder, the engine roaring beneath me, the wind rushing through the cracked window, carrying scents I never noticed before. Grass, rain, roadkill—a symphony of life and death that feels so bright it's almost unbearable. My nose twitches, catching every nuance, every shift in the air.

The sky stretches wide and bruised above me, the storm clouds low and heavy, pregnant with the promise of rain. It feels alive, pressing down on the earth, and I want to meet it, to throw myself into its embrace. My claws tighten on the wheel, and I laugh, sharp and guttural, the sound strange in this half-formed throat.

I glance over at the money. It's sitting in the passenger seat, crisp bills stuffed into a bag, but it feels absurd now, a relic from a life I don't recognize anymore.

The headlights catch the curve of the road too late, and I don't try to stop. I let the car slide, the tires skidding, the world tilting as metal crunches and glass explodes around me. The sound is deafening, a symphony of destruction, but it feels distant, unimportant.

When the car finally stops, tilted and broken in the middle of a field, I crawl out, my body moving with a fluidity that feels new, instinctive. My legs are longer now, stronger. My paws press into the soft earth, the grass cool and damp against my pads.

The air is alive, crackling with energy, every scent sharper, every sound clearer. The car doesn't matter. The money doesn't matter. I think about Turtle, the man at the park, the man who grinned with crooked teeth and made poetry out of nothing. I think about the way he could balance a hacky sack on the curve of his foot as if he was built for it, as if he didn't need a house or walls or anything but the feel of the earth under his toes. How content he seemed, even with nothing. Maybe especially with nothing. His freedom looked like madness at the time, but now I wonder if I envied him all along.

The wind shifts, and it's as if the whole world shifts with it. I feel it press against me, insistent, wrapping me up and pulling me forward. I don't need the car, don't need the leather seats or the steel or the hum of the engine. My feet are the engine now, my legs pulling me faster as I break into a sprint, my body slicing through the air like I belong to it. Everything I need, I've got on me. Everything I need is here.

I run faster.

I don't think about Nathan, or the house, or the years I spent folded into that small, pink room. I don't think about Cupcake's grief, or the blood on my teeth, or the life I took on my way here. On my way to becoming this version of myself. I think only of the wind rushing past me, the ground firm beneath my paws, the sky vast and open above.

The fur ripples along my back, the muscles in my legs stretching, pulling me forward faster and faster until the field blurs around me, the horizon swallowing me whole. My heart pounds, steady and relentless; a rhythm that feels ancient, older than language, older than fear.

I am free. I am finally free.

BEFORE

BEVERLY'S STORY

I don't have friends. No boyfriend either. Never had them. At nineteen, it sits different than when I was a girl. Lonelier. More humiliating. A roll call of nevers: never driven a car, never sipped liquor, never kissed with the weight of it, never pressed against another body without guilt roaring after, black and hot.

My parents are Mormon. Devout doesn't cover it—they wear devotion like skin. The church is the air they breathe, the rhythm their blood keeps. Scripture and sacrament, rinse and repeat, and I am snagged inside it, caught like a fly pinned in glass.

I try. I fold my hands. I bow my head. I pray until my throat is raw, and Ma tells me patience, patience, always patience. But my patience has spoiled to something bitter. Nothing changes. The walls don't split. The door doesn't open. I am still here.

The house thrums with its own warmth. Gwendolyn singing nonsense, Elias giggling from the floor. Ma stirring, Pa grumbling. It's a hive, and I hover outside of it, buzzing but unwelcome. Their life, not mine.

I gather scraps of courage like bones in my pocket. Today I

will ask. It feels heretical. A phone. A chance to belong. Friends. A boy, maybe. Work. Something with teeth. I've been good. They know it. Scripture each night, obedience each morning. If only I can force the words out.

The hall mirror throws me back—chewed nails, plain face, dull eyes. Not beautiful. Never beautiful. Beverly Woods is beautiful, still talked about for that one country song she sang at seventeen, the one hit that bought her a lifetime of glow. She steps into church and people look like they've seen God. I dream of being her.

But I am not Beverly. I am Patricia. Average. Trembling.

"Ma, Pa," I start, my voice cracked from disuse. "I've been thinking . . . could I get a phone?"

The silence is iron. Ma's eyes narrow. Pa stills, a plate frozen in his hand. I rush to patch the hole my question has torn. "I've been good. I read every night. I take care of the kids. It would help me—help me meet people, get a job maybe—"

I'm spilling over, frantic. "I feel like I'm missing so much."

The truth escapes, feral, and I can't catch it.

"No," Ma says. Plain as a slap.

Pa doesn't lift his eyes as the knife scrapes his plate. "Stupid of you to even ask, Patricia."

"Ridiculous," Ma says, like I've asked for a needle in my arm.

Heat floods my face. My hands shake. I stay standing. A child in their eyes, still.

"I'm not a fucking child," I say. The words rise from some pit inside me, ugly and whole.

Gasps. A fork drops. Pa's voice cracks like a whip. "What did you just say?"

I meet him. I let the fury keep me steady. "I said I'm not a fucking child. I'm nineteen years old. And I want a phone."

The kitchen pulses with silence. Pa's mouth curves, ugly, amused. "With what money?" he sneers. "You don't have a dime. If anyone buys you a phone, it'll be me. And it's not happening. Young lady."

The words choke me. They're true. I am broke. I am trapped.

I sit. I chew. I swallow. My anger gutters down into the smallest flame. Small, but stubborn. The kind that keeps burning, even in the dark.

The punishment for my outburst is the Closet. The Praying Closet, that's what they call it. It's a pantry-sized box with the water heater hissing in the corner. Bible open. Thirty minutes. But thirty minutes in there is a lifetime. Sweat sticks to my skin. God watches, silent.

I come out. Do the dishes. Try to fold myself back into their evening. They read scripture, start on a puzzle. I am excused from joining. Too tainted. Too disobedient.

I tend to Elias, my little brother, only four years of age. Blond hair, soft brown eyes. He splashes in the tub, ignorant of anything ugly. To him, I am just big sister. He doesn't know what I know. That I had given birth to him. I still remember those nine months, where I was forced to stay locked in my room. Forced to not see anyone until I gave birth. And then after he was pulled from me I was told he is my brother and he would live as my brother. Letting people know I had a child out of wedlock would be shameful.

I dry him, wrap him, tuck him into bed. Whisper stories of Noah and his ark. He sleeps, perfect.

Then I tend to Gwendolyn. My real sister, who is six. For an hour we braid hair, play with dollies. "I'm tired," she finally says, eyelids heavy. I kiss her forehead and tuck her into bed. "Goodnight, Gwen."

The house quiets.

I change. Not into pajamas. Into the pink bra and panties. He left the note in my Bible, slipped between Psalms and Proverbs. Careful, clever. So Ma wouldn't see.

Pink bra and panties. Midnight.

I lie down under the covers, feigning sleep, my heart breaking itself against my ribs. I wait, just like he told me to.

The floor creaks in the hall. It's him.

Just another night. The same.

Morning is thick with silence. Pa doesn't look at me as he buttons his shirt. His jaw locked, his eyes sliding past me. He acts as if the night didn't exist. As if it weren't folded into me, sour and heavy, impossible to wash away.

I dress Gwendolyn, smooth her curls, tell her she is pretty. I tame Elias's cowlick with spit, tie shoes tight. My hands are steady only on the outside. Inside, everything shakes.

At church, the carpet smells like mildew and perfume. We slide into the pew, Ma gripping her Bible like a weapon. The hymnals crack as they open.

And then I see her.

Beverly.

Her hair spills gold, heavy and sleek, like it was spun from light itself. I want to sit behind her, close enough to breathe her in. To touch that brightness, as if some part of it might cling to me.

We sit behind her, and it feels ordained. My hands sweat against the Bible's cracked leather.

Pa watches her too. His eyes fix, his throat works. He always stares, like he can't help himself. His gaze is worship. Mine is hunger. He looks at her like the sun. I look at her like the sky. I want to peel off my skin and step into hers.

She turns, smiling, polite, her lips glossed pink. "Good morning."

My heart kicks wildly, my pulse scraping my throat. She is the most beautiful thing I have ever seen.

Pa glances at me. Quick, sharp. The look lands heavy, sinks through me like a stone in a well.

My chest rattles. I know. Something terrible is already curling on the horizon.

And I can't tell if it will arrive tonight. Or if it's been here all along.

Dinner is quiet, knives dragging against plates, the air heavy with boiled potatoes and steam. Then Pa says it, easy as a cough, like it isn't going to tear my chest apart.

"Beverly is coming for dinner tomorrow night."

My fork clatters. My body goes stiff. Beverly Woods. Here. At our table.

I look at Ma. Does she know? But her face is the same as always—drained, slack, sagging into resignation. She is furniture now. Furniture that stirs pots, folds clothes, bends under weight.

"I'll make a roast," she murmurs, her voice dragged from the depths, flat as stone.

"Beverly Woods? She's beautiful, Papa!" Gwendolyn chirps, curls bouncing. She says what I have always thought. Beautiful. Untouchable. A holy figure.

I can't believe it. The woman I have worshipped from afar, who glows even when the light in the room is nothing but yellow bulbs—tomorrow she will sit in our house, eat from our chipped plates. My heart beats fast, wild. "I need to find a good outfit," I whisper, desperate. "May I be excused?"

Pa shakes his head, a smile cutting across his mouth. "Now, I know you're excited, Patricia, but you gotta eat your dinner."

"Why's Beverly coming over, Pa?" Elias asks, small voice round with innocence.

Pa leans back, eyes shining, and lets his grin stretch. "Well," he says, "sometimes, in the Mormon church, men can have more than one wife. Tomorrow, we're going to see if Beverly is a good fit for the family."

The air thins. My skin crawls. I look at Ma again—her face pale, her lips pressed. Not happy. Not at all.

"She's gonna be our mom? Yay!" Elias claps, giddy.

Pa laughs, deep and pleased, like a man at the head of a feast. "Possibly. We have to see if it's a good fit first."

My fork trembles. My stomach twists. Whose idea was this? Did Beverly know? Or is it only Pa's design, his hunger dressed up as scripture?

Tomorrow she'll be here. And I don't know whether to pray for it or to run.

Beverly Woods sits at our table as if she belongs, as if her golden hair and polished nails don't clash with the linoleum curling up at the corners. She wears a cream blouse that shimmers when it catches the light, tucked into a midnight skirt. Her lipstick is ripe and red, a strawberry split open. She looks older and more mature than she does at church, but softer, her beauty turned quiet, confident.

I can't stop staring. I wish I could shed my boring, unattractive, unappealing skin and become her. Become someone shiny and bright.

Pa looks at her the way he looked at me last night—his smile too wide, his eyes too sharp. My stomach knots tight.

She laughs at something he says, smoke in her throat, and lets her hand fall onto his lap. It lingers.

"So you really want to be part of the family?" I blurt. I didn't believe it. I needed to hear her say it, not Pa.

Beverly smiles, glossy and sweet. "Well, me and your pa talked over coffee plenty before and we really clicked." She says it like it's nothing, like it isn't a knife in the dark. Then she turns to Ma. "I love how open you are to bringing in another wife, Mrs Jennings."

The words slap me cold. Coffee? Talking? How many times? My eyes fly to Ma—her face drains to stone, all blood gone. She didn't know either.

Dinner grinds on. Food turns to sawdust in my mouth. Beverly smiles when Pa jokes, nods at his words. She never looks at me. Not once. And I ache for it. Burn for it.

When it's over, I linger, heavy in my chair. I can't move, can't leave her with him.

"Bedtime, Patricia." Pa's voice slices the air.

I don't move.

"Now." Hard, final.

My throat closes. I gather Elias and Gwendolyn, their warmth pressed against me, and usher them into the dark. I braid Gwen's hair. Brush Elias's teeth. Lay them down, their lashes closing, soft, unknowing.

Back in my room, I slide under the blanket. The house creaks and groans like an old ship, holding its secrets. I wait. For the sound of her heels on the floor, for the door to open, close. For her voice, one last time.

But the door never opens.

And the silence is worse than any sound could be.

Morning drags itself gray across the windows, light already tired before it's begun. I dress quickly, plain clothes, nothing worth remembering. Gwendolyn wriggles under my hands as I braid her hair. Elias blinks, eyes gummy with sleep, slow to button, slow to tie. I rush them along, polish them neat. Mrs Ren will be here soon, with her stiff spine and her hymn book in her purse, letters and scripture tucked into the dry lines of her mouth.

We go down the stairs, the three of us. I brace myself for the smell of eggs, bacon, Ma's soft hum at the stove, Pa's knife scraping toast. But the kitchen is hollow. No breakfast. No Ma. No Pa.

I freeze.

"Where's Ma and Pa?" My voice breaks too high, too bright. I set the kids at the table, paste on a smile that tastes like salt. "Don't worry. I'll fix you cereal."

They nod, unblinking. They never question. I pour flakes, drown them in milk, set spoons clinking like everything is normal. But inside my gut turns. Ma never misses breakfast. Even fevered, trembling, she cooked. Always.

When they bend over their bowls, I leave. My worry spills ahead of me in quick steps. The living room: empty. The yard: wet with dew, still as bone.

Upstairs, the air thickens. Pa and Ma's door is cracked, a thin slit. From inside, sobbing. Low, torn open.

"Ma?"

I push the door. She's curled on the bed, her back a fragile ridge, her shoulders shaking.

"What's wrong?" My voice is small; I already know.

She turns, slow, and her eyes are raw, the skin bruised with sleeplessness. "Your daddy . . ." Her voice a rasp. "He's sick."

The words rot in the air. Heavy. Final.

I back away. Of course I knew. I had always known. But hearing it in her mouth—Ma naming it—makes the walls lean in closer.

Downstairs again, the kids sit stiff at the table, cereal soggy, spoons dangling. Their eyes fixed on the basement door.

"What is it?" I whisper. My voice cracks. Cold runs down my spine.

Elias's face is pale, his mouth trembling. "We heard a dog barking in the basement."

The house sinks quiet again. But not the same quiet. A listening quiet. A breathing quiet.

Their eyes don't move from the basement door. I feel mine dragged too, as if pulled by string. My body shifts without permission. Step by step. My palms wet, my breath thin.

I press my ear to the wood. Nothing.

The knob chills my hand. I twist. Hinges groan. The door yawns open, just a sliver.

The basement is not a place I know. Boxes. Tools. Damp cement. That's all it should hold.

But Pa is there. His back hunched, wide, a shadow.

And there—Beverly.

She is bound to a narrow bed, wrists tied, a strap circling her throat. A gag presses her mouth. Sounds leak out, muffled, breaking. Her body small, folded, caged.

My blood drains fast. The doorframe holds me upright.

Pa leans close, his voice low, words smudged out by distance. His hand moves. Beverly shakes her head, trembling. And then—her eyes.

They rise. Lock on to me.

One second. We are bound. Her eyes widen, full of terror, full of fury.

I stumble back, my heart pounding so loud I expect Pa to hear it. I pull the door inch by inch, begging the hinges for silence. My hand shakes on the knob until it shuts, the latch clicking soft.

Then I run. My feet slap the tile. I lurch to the sink, grip the edges, and vomit until acid burns my throat raw.

The clock ticks on, loud as a fist as my mind whirls, trying to make sense of what I just saw. I sit in silence, stunned. And in that silence, something old stirs up in me, a memory I'd buried. I was four, maybe five years old. The day a woman knocked on our door. She was beautiful in a way that felt startling. Pale skin, hair the color of blood. She said her car had broken down, her phone had died, she asked if she could use ours.

I remember standing in the hallway, peeking around Ma's skirt while Pa and Ma talked to her. Pa's eyes wouldn't leave her face. Hungry, fixed.

The next week she came back. Pa introduced her as my new babysitter. She bent low, smiled at me like she'd never seen me before, though I remembered her from that day at the door.

The same pale skin. The same hair like fire. Emily, she said. Her name was Emily.

I liked her. I liked her more than anyone. She wasn't too proud to sit cross-legged on the rug with me, to play dolls or silly games. She made the house feel lighter, like it wasn't only rules and silence.

I can't recall how long she stayed. Maybe it was months, maybe only weeks. Time is slippery in memory. All I know is one day she was gone.

"Pa, what happened to Emily?" I asked once, my small voice lifting into the air.

He never answered. Ma wouldn't hear it, either. She looked almost glad, as if Emily's leaving had been a relief.

There was no explanation. Just absence.

But I remember the nights after. The sounds that kept me awake. Barking. Low, scary, strange.

"Ma, what's that sound?" I whispered once.

"Just the pipes, sweetie. Just the pipes," she told me, tucking me back under the blanket.

I believed her. I was a child. I didn't know better.

But I know better now.

That beautiful red-haired girl—Emily—was locked in our basement.

An hour oozes by, thick as tar. We sit stranded in the living room, the four of us locked in a silence that feels nailed down. Elias curls heavy in my lap, his small body an anchor dragging me under. Gwendolyn wriggles against Ma, who strokes her curls without looking, without humming. Her face is a knot—swollen eyes, tight mouth, no air in her. The clock ticks loud as gunfire, every second cracking the room open.

Then the door opens.

Pa fills the frame, sweat slick at his temples, shirt wrinkled, collar bent like it's been yanked. His chest heaves as if he's run a mile. He doesn't fix himself, doesn't bother pretending.

We all stare. Still. Afraid.

His eyes pin me.

"What did you see?"

My throat shuts. I glance at Ma, lashes still wet, gaze nailed to the floor. She won't save me.

"I said—what did you see?" Louder now, the sound splitting

the air. Gwendolyn jerks, fists clenching at Ma's dress, and then she cries, small and sharp.

"Please," I whisper. My voice trembles. "Not in front of the kids, Pa."

His jaw ticks. He drags a wet hand through his hair, pacing, restless. Flustered. A man caged inside his own house.

"Don't go down there again." His voice drops low, dark as tar. His eyes slice across each of us, cutting. "None of you. Or you'll regret it."

Elias whimpers. I press him close, my heart pounding into his back.

"And if anyone comes asking about Beverly," Pa says, words sharpened thin, "she lives here now. But she doesn't want to see anybody."

The silence that follows is suffocating, thick enough to choke on.

Ma rises then, slow, heavy, as if every bone resists her. "Nathaniel," she says. Her voice shakes, but it still carries. "What are you doing?"

The whole house goes still. Pa stares at her, long and flat, chest heaving. He says nothing.

Finally, he jerks his chin. "Call the kids' teacher. Tell her not to come today." Then he turns, fast, and takes the basement steps two at a time. The door slams shut, the thud rattling through the floorboards.

We sit frozen. The children crying softly. Ma staring at the rug as though she can see the dirt below, the beams, the locked room underneath. My chest splits open with the truth I can't put into words: Beverly Woods is in our basement. And she isn't leaving.

The next week drags like a fever dream. Pa stops pretending. He lives in the basement now. Work at the rig becomes an afterthought—half-days, then hours, then nothing. By noon, he's home again, sweat-stained, jaw locked, descending those stairs like the house itself belongs to him and the thing he keeps caged.

The rest of us drift like ghosts, afraid to touch the walls.

At night, Beverly's sounds rise. Not words. Not cries. Barking. Splintered, sharp noises, stripped of human shape. They travel through the vents, seep into the hallways, scratch at our ears while we try to sleep.

The children wake slick with sweat, nightmares staining their small faces. "The barking," they whisper. "It's scary." So they climb into my bed, two small bodies pressed into me. Some nights Ma folds in too, and the four of us pile together in her bed, one sad heap of flesh and blankets, clutching pillows over our ears. But the sounds still get through. Always.

Sometimes I wonder if he feeds her. I never see food for her. Only once—last Thursday—when he hauled a giant bag of dog food down the steps. The smiling Labrador on the front grinning back at me.

Later that night, he carried a bucket out to the yard, muttering under his breath. By morning, a sour wet patch stained the grass. The stink clung. That's when I knew what the bucket was for.

Beverly Woods. The most beautiful woman I had ever seen. The girl I had worshipped, memorized, wanted to become. Her song still stuck in my head: 'Your Heart is My Home'. A one-hit wonder, but I still thought the world of her.

Now she's chained underground, collared, gagged, eating food meant for dogs.

The house doesn't breathe like a house anymore. It feels dug up. Hollow.

It feels like a grave.

When Pa brought Beverly up from the basement, everything changed.

She stayed mostly in the living room, always low to the floor, the leash trailing, the blue collar snug at her throat. The gag never left her mouth.

We all interacted with her in small, broken ways. Elias tried to give her a toy car once, rolling it across the rug toward her, his laugh nervous, fragile. Gwendolyn braided a strand of her tangled hair with a pink ribbon, whispering nonsense, as if Beverly were another doll to play with. Even Ma—one night—sat close enough to smooth Beverly's hair back, her hands shaking, tears streaking down her face. She said nothing. Just touched her like she was remembering something soft and far away.

And me—I couldn't stop looking at her. The woman I'd worshipped, envied, wanted to become, now gagged and collared, her eyes glassy, her body moving only when Pa gave her permission. Beautiful, even ruined.

I knew I had to save her. Ask for help. Scream if I had to. But Pa's shadow hung over all of us. If I told, if I even tried—he'd kill me. Kill Ma. And worse, the kids.

So I stayed quiet. And the silence rotted in me like spoiled fruit.

Morning. Pa's voice slams through the house like a hammer. "Everyone in the living room. Now. Got something important to say."

The air goes brittle. Ma moves slow, dragging her feet like she already knows. I follow her in, my hands shaking. Beverly is already there, crouched low on the rug, the leash looped slack in Pa's fist. The blue collar gleams in the gray light, the charm swinging whenever she shifts.

"Where are the kids?" Pa asks, his voice sharp, expectant.

"They don't need to hear this," I say. My words come steady, surprising even me. "Whatever you have to say, those kids don't need to hear."

Pa's face twists, anger first, quick and hot. Then it changes. Smooths out. A slow, smug contentment spreads across his mouth like rot.

He stands. The leash snaps tight. Beverly's head jerks up, hair falling back from her hollow face.

"Me and Cupcake are going away for a bit."

The words drop heavy, sinking into the floorboards, into my chest.

Ma covers her face, her shoulders shaking. When she lowers

her hands, her skin is streaked, her eyes raw and empty. "What do you mean?"

Pa doesn't answer right away. He just stands there, grinning wide, proud and awful. Then finally: "Started a new business. Need to be away for a while. Get it off the ground."

He tugs the leash. Beverly crawls forward, hands and knees on the carpet. The little charm clinks with each move. *Cupcake. Cupcake. Cupcake.*

I want to scream. To run at him. To pull her away. But I don't move. My body stays nailed to the floor. My chest trembles with dread.

"Tell the kids I said goodbye." His voice slices the air, flat and final.

The door opens. Light floods in, bright and merciless. He steps through it. And then he's gone. Beverly follows, crawling behind him into the glare until both are swallowed whole.

The silence that follows is unbearable. Worse than the barking. Worse than the muffled sobbing that filled the nights.

Ma folds in on herself, collapsing to the floor like paper. I stay frozen, staring at the door until my vision blurs.

Beverly Woods—golden-haired, beautiful Beverly, the woman I wanted to be—is gone.

And the only sound left is the clock, ticking steady, merciless. Each second widening the crack inside me, until I don't know if anything is left to break.

AUTHOR'S NOTE

I wrote *Shy Girl* because I wanted to explore the tangled intersection of power, control, and the resilience of women navigating impossible circumstances. It's a visceral dive into the claustrophobic grip of captivity and the psychological toll of manipulation—a situation far too many women around the world have faced in one form or another.

At its core, this is a story about reclaiming agency. About revenge, not as an act of malice, but as an assertion of autonomy in a world that often strips women of choice, dignity, and freedom. It is about confronting systems—be they societal, relational, or internal—that silence and oppress, and dismantling them piece by piece, no matter how messy or unpalatable the process might be.

Women have always been cast as caretakers, peacekeepers, and forgivers. We're told to endure, to adapt, to rise above. But sometimes the only way to heal is to rage. Sometimes, justice isn't quiet or clean; it's feral and bloody and unapologetic.

Shy Girl holds a mirror to the darkest parts of control and trauma while also asking questions about survival and resistance. What does it mean to escape a cage, whether physical or metaphorical? How do you reconcile the parts of yourself shaped by those cages? And what does freedom truly cost?

More importantly, it's a reminder: Women deserve to own their stories, their bodies, their futures—on their terms. And when that autonomy is stripped away, revenge becomes less about vengeance and more about rewriting a narrative in which women refuse to remain victims.

Read on for an additional spine-tingling
short story

HAROLD

HAROLD

For Shirley Jackson,
who taught me that horror doesn't have to come from the outside—
sometimes, it's already sitting at the dinner table,
smiling.

The kitchen smells like onions and butter collapsing into each other, the kind of smell that carries even when the windows are closed, like something living is in the house. The woman, Marian, wipes her hands on her apron, careful not to smear grease into the yellow flowers stitched at the hem. The light above the stove flickers and hums, and she stares into it, as if by willpower alone she can make it steady. The children are somewhere behind her, their small voices muffled by the walls. She thinks about how her mother used to tell her that silence meant trouble, but she doesn't go check. Her hands are wet. Her hands are wet because she is rinsing greens in the sink and because she is nervous. Her husband is late.

He left two hours ago for milk. Just milk. And he is not a man to dawdle. He is a man of angles and straight lines and errands executed with precision. She tries not to imagine his car wrapped around a tree. She tries not to think about him deciding he is done with this life, or that there is a woman somewhere else who doesn't have two kids and an apron with yellow flowers and a voice that pitches high and sharp when she's tired. A woman who listens and does what he says without question.

When she hears the car in the driveway, she exhales. She doesn't run to the door—that would be unbecoming—but she listens for the sound of his boots on the steps. The door opens, and the man steps inside. She turns, her lips already forming the beginning of a rebuke for his lateness. But when she sees him, the words die. The man standing in her kitchen looks like her husband, like Harold. Same hat, same dark overcoat. But it isn't him. The tilt of his head is off. The eyes are too steady, too knowing. He smells different, too, like something metallic and faintly sweet.

"Where's Harold?" she asks, her voice tight. She wants to scream but doesn't. She doesn't know why she doesn't.

He smiles, setting the milk down on the counter. "I'm right here," he says, and there's an ease in his voice, as if he's laughing at her, as if she's forgotten some essential detail about her own life.

The kids come skidding into the kitchen. "Daddy! Daddy!" they cry, throwing their arms around his legs. And that's the part that makes her knees weaken. They don't hesitate. They don't notice. They don't stop to ask where their father is because this man, this stranger in her husband's skin, looks their father.

She sits at the dinner table because she doesn't know what else to do. The food is already on the plates, steaming, ready, as if nothing has changed. The man cuts into his meatloaf with perfect precision, holding his fork the way Harold always did, shoveling green beans into his mouth like he hasn't eaten in days. The children chatter about school, about the neighbor's dog, about whatever passes for important in their tiny, elastic brains. He nods in all the right places. He smiles. He laughs.

She does not eat. She watches him, her stomach a hard knot, her hands trembling in her lap.

"What did you do to him?" she whispers, trying her best not to let the children hear her, to see her in distress.

The man looks at her, his mouth full of mashed potatoes, and swallows with a strange deliberation. "What are you talking about?" he asks, his voice thick with innocence, his smile too wide, stretching his face too far.

Her youngest, a boy, spills his glass of water, and she stands abruptly, grabbing a rag to clean it up, anything to put space between her and that man at the table. She glances at the window above the sink, the glass warping her reflection into something monstrous. The backyard is empty, but she feels watched. She feels something closing in, like the edges of the room are curling inward.

The children finish their dinner. They kiss him goodnight. He tucks them in. She watches from the doorway, her breath shallow, her hands clutching the frame as if it might be enough to hold her upright. He brushes the hair from their foreheads, and they giggle like they always have.

When he comes back downstairs, the lights flicker again. He sits on the couch and opens the newspaper, perfectly at ease, perfectly like Harold. She wants to ask him again—*Where is my husband?*—but she is afraid of what he might say. Or worse, of what he won't.

The milk sits on the counter, untouched. She stares at it, at the way it sweats under the dim light, a bead of white running down the carton like a tear. Somewhere in the house, a floorboard creaks. She doesn't know if it's the kids, or if it's something else.

The man wearing Harold's skin sits in the armchair, the one Harold always liked, the one that still smells like him—woodsmoke, sweat, that soap he uses that comes in the blue tin. He crosses his legs, his pants riding up just slightly to reveal the curve of his ankle, the soft browned flesh beneath his sock. The newspaper is still in his lap, folded neatly, as though he isn't reading it but pretending to.

He's been waiting for me to go upstairs, I think. *Waiting for me to make this mistake.*

"Aren't you forgetting something?" he says. His voice hooks into me like barbed wire, slow and deliberate, a pull that leaves me bleeding beneath my ribs.

I stop halfway up the stairs, my fingers curling around the banister. His voice is Harold's. But it isn't Harold. It's too smooth, like a record that's been wiped clean of scratches, too polished to be real.

I turn, and I smile the way Harold likes. The way I think *this thing* will like. I smooth my apron, even though I took it off hours ago and it's just me in my sweater and house skirt, bare feet on the stairs.

"Oh, of course," I say, my voice high and bright. "How could I forget?"

The smile stretches my face so much it hurts.

The man uncrosses his legs, leaning back in the chair as if he's waiting to be served. I descend the stairs slowly, the wooden steps groaning under my weight. I have to force my knees to bend, my body to move. My mouth is dry. My stomach feels hollowed out.

Of course, I know what he's talking about. Harold likes his nightly foot rub, and I don't mind doing it—didn't mind, at least. Harold worked hard all day, and he liked the way I pressed my thumbs into the arches of his feet, how I rolled the tension out of him. It was one of those private, intimate things between a husband and a wife. Something no one else could know.

So how does *he* know? How does this man, this stranger, know?

I sink to my knees in front of him. I can hear the children upstairs, the hum of their bedtime music through the thin walls. I glance at the stairs, wondering how fast I could run. Wondering if I could scoop up the kids and make it out the back door before he caught us.

But his eyes are on me. They are Harold's eyes. But they are also not. They are too focused, too still, like glass pressed over a dark, dark void.

"Long day?" I ask, forcing a laugh as I reach for his foot. I

HAROLD

lift it carefully, cradling it as if it might shatter, or worse, as if it might move of its own accord. Strike me in the face. I press my thumbs into the ball of his foot, and it is warm. Real. But somehow that only makes it worse.

"You could say that," he says, leaning his head back, closing his eyes.

I rub his foot the way I always have, pretending this is normal. Pretending this is my life. The faint smell of something lingers on his skin. Not Harold's soap, not Harold's aftershave, but something faintly sour. This man emits a strange smell.

"How's work been?" I ask, because this is what Harold and I do. We talk about his job as a claims adjuster, the same anecdotes I've heard a thousand times, the way his boss is a prick, the way the new guy can't seem to keep up.

The man opens one eye, his lips curling slightly, like he knows what I'm doing. "It's fine," he says.

His voice is too calm, too level. Harold used to complain when he talked about work. Harold used to grit his teeth and wave his hands in the air like the act of speaking wasn't enough to contain his anger.

"Good," I say, digging my thumbs deeper into his heel, trying to make my hands steady.

"*Good*," he repeats, mocking me in a sassy tone, smiling.

I glance at the clock. It's past nine. He should be getting tired by now. Harold always went to bed early. But this man doesn't seem tired. He seems as if he could sit here forever, waiting for me to slip, waiting for me to say something wrong.

I finish with one foot and reach for the other, but he stops me, his hand darting out, quick and cold. He grabs my wrist, and the smile drops off my face before I can catch it.

"That's enough," he says. His grip lingers just a moment too long, the pressure of his fingers bruising into my skin. And then he lets go.

I stand, my legs unsteady, my heart beating too fast.

"Goodnight," I say, my voice barely above a whisper.

"Goodnight, Marian," he says, his mouth curling around my name like a blade.

I climb the stairs, and his eyes follow me the whole way. I feel them pressing into my back, crawling up my spine, even after I close the bedroom door and lock it behind me.

Even though I locked the door, or thought I did, I hear it creak open behind me. The sound slides into the room like something alive, like it's waiting for me to turn around and see what I already know. My back is to the door, my body pressed tight to the edge of the bed. I try to breathe quietly, my hands clutching the sheets, my face wet. I think if I don't move, maybe he'll go away. Maybe he'll think I'm asleep. Maybe I can disappear into the dark.

But he doesn't leave. I hear the rustle of fabric, the belt sliding out of its loops, the whisper of a zipper. He's undressing. He's taking his time. He's humming something I almost recognize, something that might've been on the radio earlier, but now it's wrong—off-key and drawn out, as if he's mocking the tune.

I bite my lip to keep from whimpering, but the sound slips out anyway, small and sharp, like a splinter working its way out of my skin. His humming stops.

It isn't but a few seconds later that I feel the bed dip. My heart jumps to my throat, and I squeeze my eyes shut. The mattress shifts as he crawls in, the springs creaking, the sheets tugging against my body as he pulls them over himself.

He's close. So close I can smell him, that sour-milk smell mingling with something sharp and metallic, like blood, like rust. He slides an arm around my waist, his hand heavy and too warm, fingers spreading across my stomach as if they're claiming me. His breath fans against the back of my neck, damp and rhythmic, like the ocean sucking sand.

And then he nuzzles his head into my hair. That's when I know for sure. This is not Harold. Harold never did this. Harold ran hot—sweated through the sheets in the summer, kept to his side of the bed, complained if I got too close. He hated the feeling of being tangled up in the night.

But this man doesn't care about space. He doesn't care about anything but the weight of his arm on my body, the press of his chest against my back, as if he's trying to burrow inside me.

I feel his lips brush the shell of my ear, and I start to shake. His voice, when it comes, is low and wrong, as if it's traveling through him from somewhere else. Somewhere deep and dark.

"Marian," he says, my name stretching and splitting as if it's a new shape he's trying out. "I'm your husband now."

I feel it, the truth of it, like something wet sliding down my spine. I'm paralyzed for a moment, my body frozen under the weight of his words. But then something inside me snaps. I scream. I scream so loud my throat feels as if it's tearing. I twist out of his grip, his arm falling away too easily, as if he let me go on purpose, as if he wanted me to run. My feet hit the floor

HAROLD

before I realize what I'm doing, my legs moving on instinct, blind and frantic.

I don't look back. I can't. If I do, I know I'll see something I can't unsee. Something worse than what's already in my head.

But I hear him. I hear the way the mattress shifts as he sits up, the way the sheets slide off him, the way his bare feet hit the floor. He doesn't rush. He doesn't have to.

"Where are you going, Marian?" he calls after me, his voice trailing me down the hall. It's calm. Patient. As if he's already won.

I grab the phone from its cradle, my fingers shaking so badly I have to dial twice. The buttons feel wrong under my fingers, sticky with something that wasn't there before. The dial tone hums in my ear like a heartbeat. When the dispatcher answers, I don't wait for her to finish her greeting.

"There's an intruder," I say, my voice cracked and raw. "In my house. He's pretending to be my husband. My children are here and I'm afraid."

The dispatcher's voice is calm, steady in a way that feels wrong against the chaos in my chest. "Ma'am, are you safe right now? Can you get to your children?"

I nod, then realize she can't see me. "Yes. I—I think so. I'll go to them now."

"Lock yourself in a room with them. Stay there until officers arrive."

I quickly rattle off my address and hang up without saying goodbye. I set the receiver down gently, so quietly it doesn't make a sound, and I move through the dark house, every step careful, every shadow alive. The children's door is open, a pale stripe of moonlight cutting through the gloom. I slip inside, closing the door behind me as softly as I can.

They are asleep, their small bodies tangled in the sheets, and I almost cry with relief. I crouch in the space between their beds, pressing myself against the wall, my knees pulled up to my chest, listening to the sound of their sweet lullaby music coming from the music box I got them for Christmas, the soft twinkling of it. I close my eyes. I don't hear him anymore. The man in my husband's skin. But I know he's still there.

I see his shadow first, sliding like oil beneath the door. It stays there, perfectly still, as if it knows I'm watching. My breath catches, loud enough that I clap a hand over my mouth. I don't blink. I don't dare.

The doorbell rings, sharp and sudden, cutting through the silence. I scramble up, my hands gripping the doorknob before I think better of it. I hesitate, my ear pressed to the wood, listening. I hear the click of the lock, the slow creak of the front door swinging open.

"Good evening, gentlemen," he says, and his voice is so smooth, so easy, it almost sounds like Harold's. Almost.

I don't move. I should stay with the children. That's what they told me to do. But I can't. I have to see. I have to know.

I open the door just enough to slip out. The hallway feels longer now, stretched and warped, the walls bending inward like the house is trying to swallow me. I press myself against the banister, peering down into the entryway.

The police are standing in the doorway, their hats in their hands. They look tired, bored even, as if they've already decided this is nothing. And then there he is, standing between them and me, wearing Harold's face like a mask.

"My wife," he says, his voice warm, almost indulgent, "hasn't been herself lately. She's been on a new medication, and it's been . . . well, it's been hard on all of us."

The officers nod, their faces softening. One of them leans slightly toward him, lowering his voice as if he's offering condolences. "We see this kind of thing all the time. It can be tough for families. Is there anyone else who she can stay with for a while? Maybe a friend or relative?"

The man smiles, just a small tug at the corners of his mouth. "I'll take care of her. She just needs rest."

I want to scream, but I feel it boiling in my throat, choking me. I try to make a sound, any sound, but nothing comes.

One of the officers looks up and sees me standing there, half hidden in the shadows. "Ma'am," he says gently, "may we talk to your children?"

I hesitate, and the man—*the thing*—tilts his head slightly, just enough for me to see the glint in his eye, the silent warning there.

I don't want to let them because I know my children don't notice anything wrong, but the word tumbles out anyway. "Yes," I whisper.

They climb the stairs, their boots heavy on the creaking wood. The man stays where he is, watching me. He doesn't blink, just smiles.

HAROLD

When the officers come back down, their faces are set, unreadable. One of them looks at me, then back at him. "The kids say that's their father."

I feel something in me break, sharp and hot.

"Because they don't *know*!" I shout, the words spilling out before I can stop them. My voice sounds strange, high and thin, like it's coming from somewhere else. "They don't know! He's not my husband! He's not—"

"Ma'am," the officer interrupts, his voice firmer now. "I think you should rest. Let your husband take care of things tonight."

I try to protest, but they're already backing away, already putting their hats back on. The door closes behind them, the sound echoing through the house like a final word.

And then it's just us.

The man turns to me, his smile growing wider, stretching his face until it barely looks human. "Now," he says, his voice soft, almost amused. "Where were we?"

The light in the kitchen is different in the morning. Harsh, yellow, all edges, as if it's trying to show me something I don't want to see. My legs feel brittle as I step into it, my bare feet sticking to the linoleum. The smell of coffee curls through the room, bitter and heavy, and for a second, I think I'm still dreaming.

The chair creaks, and I see him. Sitting at the table. The man wearing Harold's skin. His body is slouched in a way Harold never would allow himself to slouch, too relaxed, his hands spread wide around the coffee mug as if he's been here forever, like this is his house, his life. The newspaper is open in front of him, pages trembling slightly in the draft from the window.

I stop. My hand is on the fridge handle, and I stop, because I can't look at him too long. I'm afraid of what I might see if I do. The angles of his face are wrong. His cheekbones too sharp, his eyes too flat, the way his smile lingers even though his lips aren't moving.

"Morning," he says, his voice soft, honeyed. He flicks his

eyes up from the paper, and they stick to me, dragging over my skin as if I'm something new he's still figuring out how to touch.

I don't answer. I can't. My voice is trapped somewhere in the tight space between my ribs, and all I can think about is how I woke up in my daughter's princess bed, my knees pressed into a plastic toy, my hand resting on her tiny chest just to make sure it was still moving. I didn't sleep; I kept the door locked, the lamp on, and waited for the sound of his footsteps in the hall.

But he didn't come upstairs. He stayed here, in this room, waiting for me.

I open the fridge and grab the milk, the chill bleeding into my fingers. I reach for the cereal box on top of the fridge, my arm trembling as I stretch. I don't want to turn my back on him, but I have to.

The kids come padding into the kitchen, still soft and sticky from sleep, their hair wild, their pajamas twisted around their small bodies. They don't hesitate when they see him. They run to him.

"Daddy!" my daughter says, climbing into his lap. His hands, those hands that aren't Harold's, settle on her back, patting her softly, rhythmically.

I almost drop the cereal.

I pour the milk into their bowls, my hands shaking so badly the milk splashes out. They don't notice. They don't notice anything. My son sits at the table, happily slurping down his cereal, while my daughter curls into the man's chest, her face pressed against his shirt.

I stand at the counter, my back to him, not able to look at my daughter in a strange man's arms. My hands grip the edge so hard my knuckles go white.

"How'd you sleep?" he asks, his voice light, as if we're in some sitcom where the mother wakes early to kiss her husband on the cheek and scramble eggs.

"Fine," I say, the word slipping out before I can stop it. It feels like a betrayal, like I've just handed him a piece of myself, but I can't stop now. I have to keep going. "You?"

"Like a rock," he says, and I hear the scrape of the chair as he leans back, hear the rustle of the paper as he folds it.

I risk a glance over my shoulder, and he's looking at me. Smiling. His teeth are too perfect, too even, like a line of fence posts.

"Did you dream?" he asks, and his voice dips, just slightly, enough to make the hairs on my arms stand on end.

I turn back to the counter, gripping the edge tighter. "No," I lie.

Because the truth is, I *did* dream. I dreamed of Harold, the *real* Harold, standing in the doorway of our bedroom, his face pale and slack, his eyes wide with something between pain and surprise. I dreamed of his hands reaching for me, his fingers curling as if he wanted to touch me but couldn't quite remember how. The man behind me chuckles softly, as if he can see it. As if he knows.

I feel his eyes on my back, feel them crawling up my spine, resting on the nape of my neck. I turn slowly.

HAROLD

"Kids," I say suddenly, my voice sharper than I mean it to be. "Go get dressed for school." They groan but obey, sliding off their chairs, the man's hands lingering on my daughter's shoulders as she skips away.

When they're gone, I turn back around. The room feels smaller. Hotter.

The man stands, the chair groaning at the release of his weight, and I hear his footsteps moving toward me. I don't turn around. I can't.

He stops just behind me, so close I can feel his breath on the back of my neck. He doesn't touch me, but his presence presses into me like a hand.

"You'll get used to it soon," he says softly, his voice curling around my ear like smoke. "You'll get used to me."

I grip the counter so hard I think it might splinter. The milk from my son's bowl drips from the edge of the cereal bowl, pooling onto the floor, and I don't move to clean it up. I just stare at it, watch the white spread like something alive, like it's trying to crawl away.

I see Debra Jacobsen before she sees me, her hair wrapped up tight in a scarf the color of butter, her heels clicking against the pavement. She's standing by the drop-off lane at the kids' school, half turned toward her car, yelling something at her son, who's dragging a backpack twice his size. She looks frazzled, which is normal, but there's still that Debra ease, the kind of woman who can scream at a child and wave at a neighbor in the same breath.

When her eyes catch mine, she grins and starts toward me, her arms wide. She's all perfume and jangling bracelets, and when she hugs me, she smells like home—like tea leaves and talcum powder. For a moment, I feel like I can breathe again, like I'm not a woman slowly dissolving in her own home.

"Marian!" she says, pulling back, her hands still on my shoulders. "You look . . . tired."

"I am," I say, and it's the closest to the truth I can get.

She tilts her head, narrowing her eyes, trying to get a read on me. Debra has always been good at seeing through the cracks, but she's polite about it, careful not to press.

HAROLD

"How's Harold?" she asks. "Haven't seen him around lately."

And it's that question, that simple question, that makes my throat go tight. I glance around the lot, at the cars crawling through the lane, at the kids yelling and stomping their way into the building.

"He's... good," I say, forcing a smile. "You should come by soon. Bring your boy. Bring Steve. Bring Steve's friends. Bring anyone you'd like." The words rush out of me too fast, and I can feel her hesitation before she speaks again.

"Dinner?" she asks, one eyebrow arched.

"Yes," I say quickly. "Dinner. Just something casual. It's been too long. I'll cook a fabulous meal."

Debra laughs, that rich, throaty laugh I've always envied, and shakes her head. "You're up to something. What's going on?"

I laugh, too, because it's easier than explaining. Easier than saying, *I need you to see. I need you to look at this man in my house and tell me I'm not crazy, that this is not my husband.*

"It's nothing," I say, waving a hand as if it's all so trivial. "Just miss having you around, that's all."

She squints at me for a moment, and I know she doesn't buy it, not completely, but she nods anyway.

"Okay," she says. "We'll come. Steve is coaching the kids' soccer practice until six, but after that we're free."

"Perfect," I say, my smile stretched too tight. "Perfect."

She hugs me again before leaving, and I stand there for a moment, watching her car pull away, feeling that brief weightlessness slip through my fingers.

The kids are already inside. The bell has rung. I climb back into the driver's seat, gripping the steering wheel so hard my knuckles go white. I sit there for a long time, staring at the school, the parking lot emptying around me, and think about what happens if she doesn't believe me. If no one does.

When I get home, the man wearing my husband's skin is in the living room, sprawled out on the couch like a king, like he belongs there.

"Where were you?" he asks, his voice lazy, too casual.

"Dropping the kids off," I say, keeping my voice light, easy, as I set my purse down.

"Took you awfully long."

He watches me with that too-wide smile, the one that makes my stomach churn. I don't look at him for too long. "Debra and Steve are coming for dinner," I say, trying to keep my voice from shaking.

His smile grows, spreading slowly across his face as if it's about to split open. "Lovely," he says, his voice dripping with something I can't name. "I can't wait to see them."

I don't respond. I just trudge upstairs, each step heavier than the last, the weight of his smile pressing into my back. I don't bother asking him why he didn't go to work, why he's still here, stretched out on my couch like a predator pretending to sleep. I know this man does not sleep.

I reach my bedroom, close the door quietly, lock it and then drag our lounge chair that I sat in to nurse both of the kids in front of the door. The sound of it shoved flush against the door

HAROLD

is small but final, a faint thud that doesn't feel strong enough to hold him out. The air inside feels thick, as if it's already been breathed too many times. I sit on the edge of the bed, staring at the door, waiting for his shadow to slide beneath it, for his knuckles to rap softly against the wood, for his voice to slither through the cracks, coaxing me out.

But it doesn't come. The silence feels louder.

I press my palms into my lap to keep them steady, my breath shallow. The house groans faintly, shifting under the weight of his presence, under the weight of something I can't name.

I tell myself I'm just tired. That it's okay to sit here for a while, to let the door stay locked, to pretend I'm somewhere else. But even as I think it, I know it's a lie. Because I can hear him downstairs. His humming. Low and soft, curling up the stairs like smoke, as if it's coming from inside me.

Debra and Steve with their young son in tow arrive just after six, and Harold—the man wearing Harold—stands beside me at the door, his hand on the small of my back, pressing lightly, a reminder that he's there, that he's always there. The porch light catches his smile, wide and gleaming, and I glance at Debra, at Steve, at their son, waiting for something—anything—to flicker across their faces.

Debra kisses my cheek, her perfume cloying and familiar, and Steve shakes Harold's hand, grinning as if nothing is wrong, as if he isn't gripping the hand of a stranger.

The man in Harold's skin says all the right things. He compliments Debra's scarf, claps Steve on the back like an old friend, and tousles their son's hair with the easy charm of a man who knows the boy well. I stand beside him, frozen, my nails digging into my palms, waiting for Debra to see it, for her to recoil, for her to ask me quietly in the kitchen, *Who is that?* But she doesn't.

The night grinds forward. I bring out the roast, the green beans, the potatoes, and Harold—*not Harold*—carves the meat as if he's done it a hundred times before. He laughs at Steve's stories, pours wine into Debra's glass without asking. I watch them laugh, watch Debra wipe her mouth with the corner of her napkin and lean toward him, her body loose, unguarded, *comfortable*.

I barely eat. The food is tasteless, dry in my mouth, sitting heavy in my stomach. My eyes dart to the clock, and each tick feels like the narrowing of a noose. The later it gets, the closer I am to being alone with him again, to the door closing behind the Jacobsens, to the silence pressing down on me like a second skin.

Debra stretches, her arms overhead, her bracelets clinking together. "Well, Marian," she says, "this was lovely. But I'm afraid I'm—"

"No!" I blurt out, louder than I mean to. The room goes still.

Debra stares at me, her eyebrows raised. "Sorry," I say quickly, my voice too high, brittle. "I just—stay a little longer. I made pie. Coffee. You can't leave yet."

She looks at Steve, and he shrugs, reaching for his wine glass. "Sure," he says slowly. "Coffee sounds nice."

I scramble to the kitchen, my hands shaking so badly the cups rattle on the tray. I pour the coffee, dark and steaming, trying to ignore the sound of his voice in the dining room, rich and smooth, pulling Debra and Steve into him, weaving himself into their lives with every laugh, every easy nod.

When I return, he's leaning back in his chair, his arm draped casually over the backrest, his face lit with the kind of warmth that should feel familiar. But it doesn't.

The pie and coffee keeps them another half-hour, but not longer. Debra pushes her chair back, her napkin falling to the floor. "We really need to go. It's been a long day, Marian."

"No," I whisper, but it's lost under the sound of chairs scraping against the floor, of Steve thanking Harold for the meal, of their son yawning loudly as Debra pulls on his coat, of the kids chattering and saying goodbye to each other.

They're moving toward the door, and I feel the panic rising in my throat, thick and sour. I grab Debra's arm as she steps onto the porch, pulling her aside, the cool night air cutting sharply against my skin.

"Debra," I say, my voice urgent, cracking. "That's not Harold."

She blinks at me, frowning. "What are you talking about?"

"It's not *him*," I hiss. "It looks like him, but it's not. It's something else. He's—he's wearing him."

Her face shifts, a flicker of something like pity softening her features. "Marian," she says slowly, carefully, as if I'm fragile, like I might shatter if she speaks too loudly. "You've been through a lot. It's just stress, or—"

"It's not stress!" I say, my grip tightening on her arm. "You know Harold. You *know* him. *That's not him!*"

She pulls away, her bracelets jangling. "I think you need to get some rest. You're scaring me, Marian."

"I'm scared, too," I whisper, tears welling in my eyes. "Debra, please. Please don't leave me here with him."

But she's already stepping back, already shaking her head. "We have to go. I'll call you tomorrow, okay? Get some rest."

HAROLD

I watch them walk down the driveway, their voices trailing behind them, the headlights of their car cutting through the dark.

When I turn back, he's standing in the doorway, his silhouette sharp against the warm light spilling out behind him. He's smiling, his teeth white and perfect, his eyes glinting with something vicious.

"Everything okay, sweetheart?" he asks, his voice rich with amusement.

I nod slowly, stepping inside, the door closing behind me with a final, echoing click.

That night, he comes to me. I hear the door open and close with a softness that feels calculated, as if he's practiced the exact pressure of the latch to make it sound tender. I'm lying in bed, stiff and still, staring at the ceiling and counting the cracks I've already memorized. My chest is tight, as if there's something sitting on it, something heavy and invisible.

He slides under the sheets, the mattress groaning under his weight, and I turn to stone. His body is warm, too warm, radiating heat like a thing that shouldn't be alive.

"Marian," he says softly, his voice dipping low, intimate.

I don't answer. I can't.

His hand finds my shoulder, his fingers brushing over my skin, and I flinch, but he doesn't stop. He slides closer, his breath warm against my neck, and I squeeze my eyes shut. I think about Harold—his hands, his weight, his smell. I try to summon the memory of him, of the way he used to love me, but the details are slipping away, like trying to hold water in my palms.

HAROLD

"I've missed this," he whispers, and the words wrap around me like barbed wire, sharp and pulling.

His hands are too steady, his touch too knowing. I want to scream, to push him away, but I don't. Because what if I do, and he doesn't stop? What if I do, and it makes him angry?

So I let him. I let him kiss me, his lips pressing against mine with a familiarity that feels stolen. I let him press me into the mattress and make love to me, his weight settling over me like a shroud.

I cry the entire time. Silent tears that slip down my temples, pooling in my hair. He doesn't notice. Or maybe he does, and he just doesn't care. My guess is the latter.

It doesn't feel right. None of it feels right. His movements are practiced, smooth, as if he's mimicking something he's seen but doesn't quite understand. He's too close, his breath too even, his body too warm. I think of Harold again, of how he used to pause sometimes, his breath hitching, his weight shifting just slightly—small, human imperfections.

This isn't Harold. This isn't even human. This is something else.

When it's over, he stays close, his arm draped over my waist, his fingers tracing patterns on my skin. "I love you," he says, and the words sink into me like stones.

I don't respond. I keep my eyes closed, my body still, waiting for his breathing to slow, waiting for him to slip into sleep.

When I'm sure he's asleep, I slide out of bed and stand in the corner of the room, watching him. His chest rises and falls in steady rhythms, but even that feels wrong—too smooth, too controlled, as if he's performing it for me.

    I press my back against the wall, my hands gripping my arms so tightly I feel my nails digging into my skin. I don't sleep. I just stand there, staring at the thing wearing my husband's skin, and wonder how much longer I can survive this.

It's been weeks now, and the world has tilted into something unrecognizable. Every morning he's there, the man in Harold's skin, sitting at the table with his coffee and his paper, his smile spreading across the room like a shadow. Every night, he crawls into bed beside me, his heat suffocating, his breath damp on my neck, his body heavy and too present, as if he's trying to sink into my skin.

I've tried to tell people. I told Debra, again and again, until she stopped answering my calls. I told the pastor of our local church, gripping his arm so tightly I left half-moon indents in his skin, whispering the truth into his ear as the congregation hummed around us. He patted my hand and gave me that same look Debra did—pity, concern, a faint sheen of discomfort. I tried to tell the school secretary, the woman at the grocery store, the mailman. The police won't help. I've tried them more times than I can count.

"No one will believe you," he said once, his voice light and amused, as if he was talking about the weather. And he was right. They don't. Worse than that, they think I'm crazy. People have started avoiding me, their smiles too tight, their conversations trailing off when I walk by.

And Harold—*not Harold*—seems to know. He watches me with that too-perfect smile, his eyes lingering on me like he's cataloging every desperate thing I've done, every word I've wasted trying to warn people.

Every time I see him, it's as if the edges of the world blur, as if the air gets thicker, heavier. Like always, I walk into the kitchen, and there he is, sitting at the table, his hands folded neatly around his coffee cup, his paper spread out in front of him. The way he sits, so still, makes my skin itch.

"Morning," he says, his voice syrupy, too smooth.

The smell of coffee fills the room, but it's bitter, almost metallic, the smell of something rotting beneath the surface. I can't eat anymore when he's around. His stench is overwhelming. I can barely swallow my food.

Sometimes I find him standing in the living room or the hallway, watching me. He doesn't move, doesn't say anything. He just stands there frozen, his hands at his sides, his eyes following me as I pass. I don't look at him for too long. I'm afraid of what I'll see if I do.

The kids still don't notice. They laugh with him, sit on his lap, cling to him the way they used to cling to Harold. I watch them with a tightness in my chest, wondering if they're already forgetting. If this version of him is starting to overwrite the real one, slipping into their memories like a stain they can't scrub out.

HAROLD

They are children; they don't know that something is off. He is kind to them. He doesn't harm a hair on their body. Not like me.

One night, I watch him tuck them into bed. He presses a kiss to each of their foreheads, his lips lingering just a moment too long.

"That's enough," I whisper as he keeps his lips on my daughter's forehead for far too long. When he turns to leave the room, his eyes catch mine and I freeze. His smile spreads, slow and deliberate, and he nods at me as if he knew it would bother me.

I can't breathe when he looks at me like that.

I've started dreaming of Harold again—*the real Harold*. In my dreams, he's always standing just outside the house, his face pale and drawn, his hand pressed against the window as if he's trying to get in. His mouth moves, but I can't hear him. I wake up gasping, my hands clawing at the sheets, and the man in his skin is always there, his body too close, his breath steady and warm.

"You're tired," he says sometimes, his voice dripping with false concern. "You've been through a lot. You should rest."

But I can't rest. I can't close my eyes without seeing the man wearing Harold's face, without hearing that too-smooth voice whispering my name.

One night, as I sit at the edge of the bed, my hands clenched tightly in my lap, he leans over and presses a kiss to my temple.

"You'll get used to it, my love," he says, his voice low, almost gentle.

I want to scream, but the sound stays trapped in my throat, stuck there like a stone, heavy and unyielding.

The house is silent, the kind of silence that feels alive, pressing against the walls like a breath held too long. I told myself I'd be ready for tonight, that I'd keep watch, that I wouldn't let him surprise me. But lying here now, the bed too big, the sheets cold, I realize I've already lost. He's somewhere in the house—he could be in the kitchen, the living room, standing just outside this door. I'll only know where he is when he wants me to.

I've stopped trying to sleep most nights, but tonight my body betrays me. I drift off to sleep, into small, fragmented moments of darkness punctuated by the sound of the house settling, the faint hum of the refrigerator. Every creak, every shift in the air, feels like him, slipping closer.

When I wake, the room is heavy with something I can't name, and I know he's here before I open my eyes. The door is open now—it wasn't before. He's standing there, his frame backlit by the dim light of the hallway.

"Harold?" I whisper, my voice breaking, but I know better.

HAROLD

He's smiling, his teeth too white, his eyes bright and wide, and he doesn't move. He just stands there, watching me, his head tilted slightly, like he's admiring something fragile.

"Please," I say, my voice shaking as I pull the blankets up to my chest. "Please leave me alone."

His smile doesn't falter. It spreads, slow and deliberate.

Finally, after what feels like forever, he speaks. "But I love you, Marian."

The words make my skin crawl, not because of what he says, but because of how he says it—like Harold, but smoother, richer, like the voice of a man who's never felt doubt or fear or pain.

"You're not my husband!" I scream, the words ripping out of me before I can stop them.

The smile twitches. His head tilts further, his eyes narrowing slightly, and I think for a second he might step closer. But he doesn't. He just stares at me, letting the words hang in the air between us, thick and oppressive.

I close my eyes, just for a second, just long enough to gather myself, but the second I do, I hear it—his breath, close, too close, soft and warm against my ear.

"You're right," he whispers, his voice low, almost reverent. "I'm not Harold."

I jolt upright, my heart pounding, and he's in the corner of the room, standing there like he never moved even though I just heard his voice, his breath, in my ear. His smile is too wide now, splitting his face in two.

He takes a step back, his body sinking into shadow, but his

eyes stay locked on mine, glinting as if they're reflecting something I can't see.

And then, slowly, he begins to change.

At first, it's subtle—the way his shoulders hunch, the way his neck elongates just slightly, the way his hands, hanging at his sides, seem to grow longer, the fingers stretching unnaturally. His skin ripples, the texture shifting as if something underneath is trying to break through.

The smile stays, even as his mouth widens, the corners splitting, his teeth sharper now, glinting faintly in the dim light. His eyes go black, the whites swallowed whole, and I can't breathe, can't move, can't scream.

He tilts his head again, a slow, deliberate motion, like he's waiting for me to say something, to do something. But I can't.

And then he steps back, further into the hallway, his body folding into itself, his limbs twitching as if he's still figuring out how they work.

"Goodnight, Marian," he says, his voice no longer smooth but guttural, a low rumble that makes my teeth ache.

And then he's gone, leaving the door open, leaving me shaking, the sound of his voice echoing in the hollow of my chest.

I have decided I've had enough. There's a kind of quiet that comes with that knowing, the final click of a door you won't open again. I sold my wedding ring yesterday, the one Harold gave me in a velvet box with shaking hands and too much hope. I sold the necklace from our first Christmas, the earrings from our anniversary dinner eight years ago where he spilled wine on my blouse and couldn't stop laughing. I sold the whole glossy story, piece by piece, until it fit in a plain white envelope with a bank's return address.

I took a loan out, too. A stupid, desperate loan with interest that eats itself. But it should be enough. Enough for me and the kids to start over. A nest egg. A motel for a while. Maybe a studio apartment with carpets that smell like old toast. It doesn't matter. As long as it's away from that man.

But I know—God, I *know*—he's not going to let us leave.

The man in Harold's skin doesn't sleep. He doesn't rest. He's always watching. Not always with his eyes, but with *something*.

Something inside him that stretches through the walls, through my chest, like wire.

I must do it in secret. I don't tell Debra. I don't tell anyone.

I drive to her house after dusk. The sky is bruised and low. Her porch light is shaped like a tiny lantern, flickering as if it's struggling to stay lit.

The kids have been with her for two nights. Two nights of peace, if you can call it that. Two nights where I imagined him pacing the house, folding the same shirt again and again, cutting his meat too perfectly, smiling at a mirror.

Debra opens the door in slippers, her hair up in a claw clip, her face soft with wine and warmth. "Marian," she says. "Everything okay?"

"Just wanted to bring them home," I say. "Like I told you, we are working through a little marital spat. Things have resolved."

She nods, slowly. "I'm glad. You two—well, you're strong. You've always seemed strong."

I smile. I lie with my teeth. "Thank you for keeping them."

She pulls me into a quick hug, and I let her, even though lately I do not want to be touched.

The kids tumble out of the living room, mid-giggle, smelling like popcorn. My son wraps himself around my waist. "I miss Daddy," he says into my stomach. "I can't wait to see him."

My heart stutters. I smooth his hair down, kiss the top of his head. "You'll see him soon," I whisper.

But I don't mean it.

I don't tell Debra I'm leaving. I don't tell her I'll never be back. I don't tell her she might see us on a milk carton in a month, or in a newspaper, or not at all.

We load into the car. The night stretches out in front of us, thin and endless. I drive slowly, as if the tires can feel my fear.

When we pull into the driveway, I see the lights on. The curtains are drawn perfectly, each one hemmed to match. The house looks posed, like a dollhouse.

Inside, he's waiting.

Of course he is.

He's standing in the living room in a suit. Always a suit. As if this makes him a better man. As if this moment needed dressing up. The jacket is navy, the tie red, the pocket square white. Patriotic. Picture perfect.

"Hello, my precious family," he says.

The kids scream with joy. They run to him, arms outstretched.

I stand in the doorway, the night still clinging to my back, and I watch. Watch the man who is not my husband kneel and kiss their cheeks, hold them tight, stroke their hair like he remembers how.

My heart is thudding so loud I think he must hear it.

They love their father so much. They're going to hate me. Maybe forever.

But I'm doing this for them.

They cannot grow up watching their mother be afraid.

I make dinner like I always do. Like I haven't sold everything that ever sparkled on me. Like I didn't sign my name at the bottom of a loan agreement with hands that wouldn't stop shaking.

Lasagna. Thick and hot and layered. The recipe Harold's mother gave me after we got engaged, her handwriting soft and looping as if she never expected it to end like this. I boil the noodles. I mix the ricotta with a little lemon, because Harold likes it that way even though I don't. I do everything *right*, because if I move like a woman planning to leave, he'll know. He always knows.

After dinner he heads to the living room, his legs crossed just so, one hand draped over the arm of the couch. The television glows blue against his face, and he laughs at all the right times. He laughs when nothing's funny at all.

"I'm going to tuck them in," I say, drying my hands on a dishtowel. My voice is sugar, breathy, small.

"Of course, sweetheart," he says robotically, without looking away from the screen.

HAROLD

Upstairs, the air feels lighter, but only just. I move fast. I open drawers and roll up pajamas, stuff socks into the corners of backpacks. Toothbrushes. The book my daughter sleeps with pressed to her cheek. The bear with one eye missing.

"Mama?" my son says behind me. His voice is so quiet it splits me. "Where are you putting our stuff?"

I turn. His arms are crossed over his chest, his face small and furrowed, that squint he makes when he's trying to be brave.

"Shhh," I say, crouching beside him. "I'm just . . . getting things ready. A little surprise. Don't wake your sister."

But it's too late.

There's a shadow in the hallway before he says a word.

"Yeah," the man says. His voice is still sweet, still soft, but it lingers. "Why are you packing their stuff, Marian?"

He's leaning against the doorframe as if he owns it, one arm resting high above his head, blue suit wrinkling.

My spine straightens on instinct. I look up at him with the kind of smile women have been perfecting for centuries.

"Oh," I laugh, like I've forgotten. Like I'm silly. "I was going to do laundry earlier, but I never started. I thought I'd do a load before bed."

He steps into the room. His shoes make no sound on the carpet.

"You just did all the laundry two days ago," he says.

"I did?"

He smiles. Not wide. Not menacing. Just a twitch of the mouth, a dimple that doesn't reach his eyes.

"Yes. But maybe you forgot."

My son shifts closer to me. I feel his small hand slip into mine, and I squeeze it, gently, once, the way I used to when he was learning to cross the street. The man looks at the bags. He looks at me. "Everything okay?" he asks. His voice isn't kind anymore. It's too on edge. As if he's already planned what he'll do if I lie again.

I nod.

"Everything's fine," I say.

And I pray to every god I don't believe in that he believes me.

The next morning, I dress with hands that won't stop shaking. My earrings are small pearls—nothing fancy, nothing that says *I'm leaving you today and never coming back*. I latch one on, then the other, staring at myself in the mirror with a face I no longer recognize. I didn't pack anything for myself. Not a shirt, not a pair of shoes. I don't care. If the kids had their things, their coats and toothpaste and pajamas, I could live in ash and ruin and wear the same clothes forever as long as they were good.

Downstairs, I hear the hiss of the coffee percolating, the unmistakable crackle of bacon in a pan. The house smells like morning, as if someone has taken care. But he never makes breakfast. Not even when it was *really* Harold.

He's suspicious. He knows.

I move fast. Not too fast. Just enough to stay ahead of the shaking.

I slip into the kids' room like a shadow, the light still watery and grey through the curtains. The bags are where I left them, under the bed, packed tight with small shoes and storybooks and socks that don't match.

I slide the bedroom window open as quietly as I can, the wood moaning like it doesn't want to let us go. The air outside is damp, cool, forgiving. I toss the first bag out, then the second, and then I pause.

I freeze.

Footsteps.

Maybe. Or maybe just the house settling, the creak of old bones, the weight of what I'm about to do pressing through the floorboards. I pull the curtain across the window, swallowing the sound of my own breath, the beat of my heart wild and too loud in my ears. I listen.

Nothing.

So I shut the window. Soft. Final.

Behind me, my daughter stirs.

"Mommy?" she says, rubbing her eyes, her voice sticky with sleep.

"Shh," I whisper, smoothing her hair down. "It's okay, sweetie. Just get up and get ready for school."

I wake my son next. He's limp, heavy with dreams, and I kiss his forehead to coax him back to the world.

"Time to go, baby," I say. "Get dressed. We're running a little late."

I button their shirts, tie laces, press cowlicks down with damp fingers, and I tell myself over and over that I just have to get through *this* moment. Just the stairs. Just the door.

HAROLD

We come down together, the three of us, like a normal family. Like we aren't about to disappear.

And there he is.

Standing by the dining table in that same perfect suit from last night. His hair neatly parted. A plate of bacon, eggs, and toast arranged like a magazine ad. He looks like a husband. Like a father. Like a lie drawn in perfect pencil lines.

"Good morning, my loves," he says, smiling with all his teeth.

The kids beam. They run to the table, their laughter soft and real.

And I stand there, stomach knotted, heart trembling in its cage, smiling back like I'm not about to steal them away. Like I don't have escape in my pocket and goodbye under my tongue.

"Morning," I say.

The keys are already in the ignition.

The kids buckle into the back seat, my daughter humming the song Harold always sang when he brushed her hair. My son rubs sleep from his eyes, yawns big. I force myself to smile at them in the rearview, to make them believe this is just another school run, not the start of a jailbreak. The bags are in the trunk. The window toss worked. Everything is in motion.

I reverse out slow, careful not to peel away too fast. I don't want to wake suspicion, don't want him to hear the grind of tires.

But then I see it—*him*.

He steps out of the house. Still in that suit. No jacket now. Just the crisp white shirt, the red tie loosened just enough to make him seem human again. His arms hang loose at his sides, like he's not surprised. Like he's been waiting.

How did he know?

I press the gas. Not hard. Just steady.

He watches the car move. His head tilts. His smile doesn't fade.

HAROLD

And then—he breaks into a run full speed.

I scream. The kids flinch. My daughter starts to cry.

He's fast. Faster than any man should be. His hands slap the side of the car just as I hit the street. I swerve. The tires screech. My heart tries to claw out of my chest.

"Hold on!" I shout, and I punch the gas.

We fly. Past the school. Past the bakery. Past the church with the broken bell. I don't know where I'm going. Only that I can't let him catch us.

I look in the rearview and watch as he finally slows down to a stop.

My daughter is sobbing now. "What's happening, Mommy? Why was Daddy chasing us?"

"He's not your daddy," I whisper. "He's *not your daddy*."

I sit at a red light, my finger tap-tapping on the steering wheel.

"Come on, come on," I whisper, my heart pounding hard like a drum.

But I see the headlights behind us, the flash of Harold's bright blue Thunderbird. He's in his car now. I press on the pedal hard, run the red light and manage to swerve just as a car comes right at us. I ignore the angry honks from the cars and look out at the rearview mirror.

He's chasing us. And he's *gaining*.

I drive fast with no destination, and eventually swerve onto a back road, tires spinning gravel, the trees whipping past in a blur. My son is shaking in the back seat, whispering prayers he only half remembers from Sunday school.

And then the engine hiccups.

A cough. A stutter. A *stop*. I forgot to fill up the car with gas.

"No, no, no, no—" I slam my fists on the wheel.

We coast to the shoulder.

And then—silence.

The engine dies on a back road with no name. It sputters once, twice, then rolls into silence, the trees thick and tall around us, their shadows like reaching arms.

I hit the wheel, once, twice, panic rising in my throat like bile. In the backseat, my daughter is crying again, her little body curled like a question mark. My son is quiet, his fingers clenched around the straps of his backpack. They know. Even if they don't have words for it, they *know*.

I see headlights behind us. A slow, steady crawl. No rush. No panic. He knows we've lost.

I throw open the door. "Out!" I hiss. "Now. Into the trees. Run. Don't stop."

They hesitate. My daughter whimpers, "Mommy—"

I grab their hands, shove them toward the woods. "I love you. Now *run*."

I don't wait to see if they do. I turn. He's already out of the car. Standing in the road. Calm. Beautiful in that sick, Sunday-best way, like a painting of a father that would hang above a fireplace.

He walks toward me slowly, his hands in his pockets. I back away. Gravel shifts under my feet. My legs tremble.

"Please," I say, my voice cracking. "Please, Harold—"

HAROLD

His smile twitches. "Don't call me that. You said I wasn't him."

"I was scared," I say. My voice is high and brittle. "I didn't mean it. I was confused. We were all just—confused."

He tilts his head. "You tried to take them from me."

"They're *not safe* with you." My voice breaks like glass. "You're not real. You're not right."

He stops just a few feet away. The day hangs between us like a noose.

"Please," I say, and I fall to my knees. The gravel bites into my skin. "Think of the kids. They love you. They still love you. Don't do this. Don't take me from them."

For a moment, he looks down at me, and his smile is gone. His face is slack. Almost human. And I think—maybe. Maybe there's a piece of Harold in there. Maybe something left.

"You begged them, too," he says. "The pastor. Your friend. The cops. *Help me*. You said it with your whole mouth. And what did they do, Marian?"

Tears fill my eyes. "They . . . they didn't believe me."

"No," he says, crouching down to meet me eye to eye. "They never do."

I reach for him—not to fight. Just to touch. Just to remind him I'm real. That I loved the man he stole. That I tried.

But he moves like smoke. One hand wraps around my neck, gentle at first, then tighter.

"I could've been good to you," he says. "I was *trying*."

I gasp for breath. "You're *not* Harold. You haven't been him in a long time."

He smiles again. That awful, beautiful smile.

I feel myself fading. Slowly, so slowly. My vision darkening. I think about my children. How they'll never know the truth of it. How this cruel, cruel world took their mother from them. I cry harder. I cry not only for them, but for myself. I cry for the life I once had. That beautiful glimmering life with a beautiful husband who loved me so.

And then—darkness.

Days later on a lonely country road, they find the car. But no body. No Marian.

Just two children, barefoot and shaking, wandering out of the woods with wild eyes and tears streaming down their faces.

When asked what happened, the daughter says, "Daddy said Mommy didn't love us enough to stay."

And no one questions it.

They tell each other she ran. That she broke down, abandoned her children on the side of the road. That she couldn't handle it. That she was crazy.

They say he's still looking for their mother.

And at night, in a quiet town that doesn't ask questions, a man in a crisp white shirt tucks them in and kisses them both goodnight. No one makes an effort to find out what really happened to Marian because then they'd have to admit they didn't believe her when she warned them about her husband. Because then they wouldn't be able to fucking sleep at night.

Mia Ballard is an American poet and fiction writer. She loves all things horror and is passionate about writing stories about feminine rage. She lives with her partner and dog in Northern California.

Other works by the author include

Sugar
We All Rot Eventually: A Horror Novella

Keep in contact with the author
@galaxygrlmia on Instagram